S0-BNU-402

MARIE-CLAUDE BOURQUE

ANCIENT WHISPERS

LOVE SPELL   NEW YORK CITY

LOVE SPELL®

June 2010

Published by

Dorchester Publishing Co., Inc.
200 Madison Avenue
New York, NY 10016

ISBN 10: 0-505-52833-9
ISBN 13: 978-0-505-52833-9
E-ISBN: 978-1-4285-0885-9

In memory of my father
Pierre-André Bourque
1940-2006

To Logan and Finlay,
Imagination rules!

ACKNOWLEDGMENTS

My deepest thanks go first to Leah Hultenschmidt, who, in the summer of 2007, changed my life by requesting the whole manuscript of *Ancient Whispers* for the American Title V, and who then worked her own magic to make this story true to my dream. *Ancient Whispers* would also not exist if not for the amazing feedback, hard work and support from my best friends and writing partners: Jennifer Bray Weber, John Roundtree and Candi Wall. I am forever grateful to those three very talented writers. Thanks also to the members of the Charlotte Dillon Romance Writers' Community who ruthlessly critiqued this first attempt at writing.

To Steve Bellemare for believing in me, to Chadwick Ayers for keeping me sane and to Adam Stronge for keeping me grounded with his friendship and music.

To the staff at *RT Book Reviews* for this incredible opportunity and the thrill of a lifetime, and to all the romance readers who voted to see this story published. For their tremendous support, thanks to authors Gerri Russell, Terry Spear, Monica Burns, Emily Bryan and Jeanne C. Stein. To my writer friends at GSRWA, FF&P-RWA, CHRWA, HHRW, RWA-Online and Backspace. To the Bourque and Paul-Hus families in Québec, the McNeil clan in Scotland, the Wedgwood crowd in Seattle, the friends in RI and B.C., the Oceanographers, Harold Gagné, the Cinq sisters and the *gang du local*. To Joshua Garcia, Michael Yeager, Rodney Larck, Velda Arsenault Stanley and all my Pagan and Acadian friends on MySpace and Facebook.

And to the one person who stayed behind me every step of the way, who didn't bat an eye when she learned that her scientist daughter wanted to write a romance novel, and who provided me with the best example of strength, compassion and dignity a person can have. To my mother, Nicole Bourque, *merci*.

ANCIENT WHISPERS

Wives were torn from their husbands, and mothers,
* too late, saw their children*
Left on the land, extending their arms, with wildest
* entreaties.*
So unto separate ships were Basil and Gabriel
* carried,*
While in despair on the shore Evangeline stood with
* her father.*
—Henry Wadsworth Longfellow, 1847

Le Grand Derangement

Grand Pré, Acadie
October 1755

Gabriel LaJeunesse sat stunned, staring at the shore. He could smell the fear around him, the dread, the sorrow.

His mother sobbed nearby, clutching a bundle packed with family belongings. Françoise-Marie, his sister, gripped the plain wooden cross hanging from her neck while in a low voice she prayed.

Gabriel's shirt was no longer white after days spent in captivity. Thick with smoke, the maritime air stung his eyes, shortened his breath.

Echoes carried from the beach, soldiers barking orders in clean crisp English, children screaming in French for their mothers. Woman wept and called the children's names in panicked voices. The elders sang gently, as if resigned to their doom.

The boat carrying Gabriel and the villagers sharing his fate headed for a tall ship moored offshore. His father and older brothers, Baptiste and Pierre-Octave, lay silent beside him. All strong and solid Acadians, they had survived many harsh winters—and those who wished to destroy their way of life. The redcoats had not yet crushed their spirits, not by burning their homes and fields, not by forcing them on ships sailing to faraway lands.

Frantic, Gabriel searched the crowds waiting on the beach. Today would have been the most important day of his life. Today he would have married Evangéline Bellefontaine, his childhood sweetheart.

The day should have been filled with love, laughter and fulfilled promises, the church packed, a large feast from this year's harvest. The *ancêtres* would have told stories; the *violoneux* would have played gigues and reels, making old and young dance well into the night.

Warmth rose within Gabriel at the thought of how he would have lain with her, his sweet and gentle Evangéline. In the dark of the night, tasting her skin for the first time, he would have shared the warmth she hid under her thick homespun skirts. He would have known her passion, finally.

There she is. Gabriel's heart suddenly overflowed with hope. He pointed toward shore, where villagers carried trunks and bags of their cherished possessions, packed in haste. Then he turned to the blond soldier standing above him.

"I see her. Let me go." Gabriel struggled with his broken English. "*C'est ma fiancée.* She was left on the shore."

She wore a light-colored sturdy dress, her white cap and apron. Her dark curly hair had been undone during the confusion and tumbled down to the middle of her back. She stood beside her father, Benoit Bellefontaine, the richest farmer of Grand Pré.

Monsieur Bellefontaine's farm burned now, along with the rest of the village, along with the modest house Gabriel had built for their new life.

Ignoring the sorrow of his loss, Gabriel shouted and waved at Evangéline as she looked around, likely searching for him. He was too far. So many people swarmed around her. She could neither hear nor see him.

Gabriel repeated his plea to the soldier, forcefully this time. "Please let me go. I'll swim back to shore."

But the redcoat paid him no heed.

The villagers on the boat quieted and watched Gabriel, their silence broken by a few muffled sobs. The waves splashed against the small boat. The women's caps flapped in the autumn wind. A seagull cried in the distance.

Gabriel got up. Strong from years spent in his father's forge, he towered over the soldier.

"Gabriel," his mother said through her tears.

As the soldier drew a hand to the hilt of his sword, Gabriel showed him the shore again.

"I just want to get back to my fiancée. I'll get on the next boat."

The Englishman shot him a dead stare, spat at Gabriel's feet, then turned his back to the Acadian.

Gabriel could no longer contain his rage.

The last days of his humiliations as a prisoner of the English rushed fast at him. His family had been at the mercy of soldiers who didn't even speak their language. They had burned and destroyed everything they could, tearing the villagers from their land because the king thought them a threat to his rule.

He lunged at the soldier and knocked him hard on the back.

The man staggered, Gabriel clenching his enemy by the throat before he could draw his blade.

His mother shrieked, begging him to stop. *"Ils vont le pendre.* They will hang him."

The Acadian farmers yelled at Gabriel, telling him to let go of the soldier.

"Maudits Anglais. You have no right to take our land, ship us all away." He shook the blond soldier with violence, his hands squeezing the man's throat. "Lock us up in the church for days, burn our village. You took my life, my future."

The villagers gasped.

"Mon Dieu, priez pour nous." Françoise-Marie prayed louder, crossing herself over and over again.

Gabriel's father attempted to restrain him with all his strength, his hands digging painfully into Gabriel's arm. Baptiste and Pierre-Octave pulled at their younger brother from behind. The boat rocked in the crashing waves.

"Mon fils, stop." His father's voice was calm. "Don't get yourself killed."

Gabriel's arm had become numb from his father's powerful grip. His brothers knocked the wind out of his lungs as they clutched at him. Yet he kept his grip tight, his hands still crushing the man's throat.

The soldier could barely breathe.

Another redcoat suddenly reached them and slammed Gabriel's head with the butt of his musket. Sharp pain radiated through his skull, his thoughts becoming a blur of fury.

The soldier pounded hard, hitting his head and neck while his father tried to protect him without much success. Repeated musket blows hammered him. Hands gripped his dirty shirt. A knee found internal organs and banged, again and again.

Gabriel was blind with pain.

At his father's urging, he finally let go. He sank to the flat bottom of the boat, his brothers supporting him.

"How sad." The redcoat returned the musket to his side. "These French people, no dignity." He wiped sweat from his forehead, readjusted his coat and moved to the bow.

The blond soldier caught his breath, coughing a few times, then crouched down to Gabriel. He took the Acadian's head into his hands, their faces almost touching. Gabriel winced, a dark curl obscuring his vision.

"Remain seated, Frenchman."

Hatred overriding all emotions, Gabriel silently narrowed his eyes at him.

The soldier spoke in a hoarse voice. "I was at Beauséjour last summer. They hanged quite a few traitors. Many were much younger than you." He stood up. "Take care of your mother."

Gabriel's mother rushed to him, then gently patted his hair away from his forehead while Baptiste and Pierre-Octave still restrained him. They knew their little brother well; his fiery temper needed more than threats and a beating to be controlled.

Gabriel struggled to shake them away. He wanted to retaliate, beat the man to death or just take the chance to swim to shore. Then he controlled himself, not wanting to put his family at risk.

He remembered Evangéline's words as she'd joined him in the church where the English had kept the villagers prisoners. *Courage*, mon amour. *Our true love will keep us from harm.* She had been so brave, so patient, so trusting in their future despite their unjust fate, convinced they could start a new life in the colonies of Louisiana.

Gabriel's gaze returned to the shore, his spirit sagging as the boat glided at a steady pace farther from their home. On shore Evangéline was talking to her father, who hunched over an old travel trunk. Père Félicien, the village priest, comforted them. Monsieur Bellefontaine collapsed in the sand, and Evangéline rushed down to him. He saw the panic of the villagers surrounding them. Then, as their shapes became smaller, he saw nothing. Just smoke rising from what had been the village of Grand Pré on the rugged coast of Acadie.

And he lay there, his brain entirely numb. What had happened to them all?

His brothers relaxed their grip. His mother was calm now, singing a song from the old country. A song she would sing when they were children, about a French sailor who drowned while fetching the lost ring of a beautiful maiden.

Confused, Gabriel looked at his hands, at the calluses earned from a lifetime of hard work. How could he be sailing without her? Evangéline was everything to him. He needed her to breathe, needed her serenity to control his bold nature. She was his entire life.

He sat paralyzed with grief, lulled by the slow rocking of the boat now approaching the tall ships.

"Gabriel LaJeunesse," someone said to him.

Puzzled, he turned toward the voice calling his name and looked into the stormy gray eyes of an old man sitting in front of him, his long silver hair tied back, matched by a shimmering gray beard. Strange symbols were faintly drawn at his temple—Micmac body paints, perhaps. In homespun breeches and a white shirt, he was dressed like any other Acadian.

The old man took Gabriel's hand, and everything went black.

He panicked. The Atlantic coast was gone.

Lying in a barren land, he was suddenly surrounded by a thick mist and grayish standing stones covered with moss, unable to recognize the strange scents rising from the damp soil. Where was he?

Tearing his hand away from the old man's grip, he was back on the boat again.

Le Diable, Gabriel thought, horrified the devil was among them.

"Do not fear me." The old man smiled softly. "*Ton destin*, Gabriel. I am your destiny." His French had an odd accent.

Gabriel recoiled. They said the dark beast seduced his prey before taking their souls.

"She will come back to you, Gabriel." The old man's spoke in a melodious tone. "I promise you," he added. "You will see Evangéline again."

One

Providence, Rhode Island
September, Present day

When Gabriel Callan woke up, a sharp pain seared his left bicep.

Ignoring the sting, he untangled the sheets twisted around his naked thighs and stretched, taking a look outside.

The sun hung low, its faint rays dreary through the long, sheer drapes. It did nothing to entice him to get up.

Coffee, I need coffee. Morag could wait.

He left his bed and, still naked, made his way to the kitchen. As he crossed the living room, he stopped at his MP3 player docked on the antique wooden table where he'd left it. After pressing a few buttons, loud guitar riffs and fast drums filled the room, numbing his thoughts.

Faint city noises filtered in through the kitchen window. Another bleak day, but it would soon be over. A few more hours and the sun would set. Darkness was peaceful.

Gabriel grabbed a bag of coffee from the bare counter and got busy with the machine, the sound of grinding beans making him wince.

He wondered what Morag wanted. The High Priestess didn't often call upon them. When she did, they had no option but report to her. The last time she'd used the mark was a year ago, requesting that Gabriel move to Providence.

Cities held no appeal to him, and he didn't enjoy the nearby beach scene either. But at least he could escape to the wilderness alone with a few minutes' drive.

The flat was soon full of the aroma of strong coffee. After filling his mug, he returned to the bedroom and sat on his bed, covering himself loosely with the sheets. Then he reached for the laptop lying near a thick pile of ancient textbooks on the hardwood floor. While sipping his black coffee, he logged on to his e-mail account.

Good, Roan had returned his earlier message. They'd worked all night, e-mailing back and forth.

> Gabe. Checked the Prophetissa again. Solution should be 2:1 sulfur and antimony. Give the mix time to crystallize. I was right. We're close. I'll e-mail when I have fired the distiller up.

Gabriel started typing.

> The Alchemyst will be pleased. I'll inform him ASAP.

Roan was probably the best among their group. Too bad he lived so far away. They could not be called friends but were as close as two Priory sorcerers who lived on opposite coasts would ever be.

A flash of anger rose in him at the increasing burn on his upper arm where intricate Celtic symbols had been tattooed in a brace. All thirteen members of the Priory of Callan had the mark.

And Morag Callan used it to control them. Only one member of the Priory was not affected by her power: Iain, their leader, and consort to Morag.

She claimed she was there to help, that the mark was practical. But to Gabriel, her help was only another name for control.

Grunting, he reached down for his cell phone to dial Morag's number, the crisp sheet shifting over his bare body.

She answered at once. "Gabriel, what took you so long?" Her diction was impeccable, with a lilt typical of the Highlanders.

"I was making coffee. I just got up. What do you want?"

"You are waking up now? At five o'clock. Isn't it a tad late to start the day?" Her slight mocking tone made him cringe.

"Roan and I were working all night. We're busy with your Reality elixir."

"The elixir, yes. But listen. This is important. Our wait is over. I read the signs last night." Gabriel heard the excitement in her voice. "She is close. She is coming back to you."

His heartbeat quickened. Was it possible? Would he finally see her? Centuries had passed, centuries of waiting, thinking of nothing but her. "Are you sure?"

"I have never been so certain. The Days of Beltz are now upon us. New beginnings, Gabriel, do believe me."

He wanted to believe, but he hated to be in Morag's debt.

"Your soul mate is returning to you, Gabriel the Voyager. I was told last night."

Even if he didn't want to know how she learned these things, he had to admit she was never wrong.

"You have to come to the lake."

"Why?"

"I need your presence to get a few more answers." She paused. "And bring the ring."

Gabriel got up, letting the sheet slide off his body, and started to pace the bedroom. It would be only a half-hour drive to reach the shingled cape near Langdon

Village, where she and Iain lived, but Gabriel hated Morag's rituals. They always made him uneasy. "Is it necessary?"

"Yes. I am afraid Theuron may be close."

Theuron, the dark mage. In all these centuries, Gabriel had never been near him. But whenever Morag spoke his name, a hint of fear pierced her voice.

"Will he be after her?" Foreboding loomed in his heart.

"I do not know, but I sensed a shadow. It may represent a test for you. I cannot be sure without further information. Falconer and Monk are on their way. And Tara is here."

Tara, the Warrior. Of course, she would be good protection for Morag.

"But I talked to the Highwayman, and he won't leave Seattle. Quite the rebel, that one."

Gabriel sighed, knowing Roan had his own reasons not to come, and they were none of Morag's business.

"I'll be there." He stopped his pacing and stood at the window, looking down at the WaterFire structures along the river. People were hurrying home to their families. Soon downtown Providence would be empty, dead in the bleak evening.

"Come right away, will you?" It was more an order than a question.

He told her he would and snapped the cell phone shut, his mind lost in the past.

The familiar despair haunting him became shaded with hope. Evangéline would be different now, of course. But the reborn woman would have his love's soul, her essence.

All these years, he'd been faithful to her memory. Deep in his heart, he'd never loved another woman.

Shaking his thoughts away, he grabbed a pair of faded fatigues from a pile on the floor and hiked them on, the black leather belt hanging low on his hips. After sliding a black thermal shirt over his chest, he went to the living room, where he turned the music even louder, letting the pounding of the heavy base throb in his blood. He should get going.

He sat down to put on his leather boots and gazed at the dark clouds now hiding the sun.

He had thought that becoming a member of the Priory would help him find his lost love. But only after the rituals had Gabriel learned the truth. Iain and Morag never had any intention of helping him find Evangéline. The sorcerers had told him she would be reborn centuries later. They had to wait.

Uisge Beatha. Gabriel had been given the water of life, made immortal. There was no turning back. And now he was just another of Morag's pawns.

Evangéline. He could still feel her silky hair between his fingers. The taste of her full lips still lingered on him. His body hardened at the memory of her sweet scent, mixed with all that was his Acadie, his lost homeland.

He would learn to love the new woman she had become. He would.

Burying his feelings, Gabriel fetched his laptop and cell phone from the bedroom. After turning off the music, he headed for the hall, where he grabbed his long black coat and the keys to his motorcycle. Labor Day traffic would slow him down, but he should be at the lake within the hour.

Soon he was out of the door, careful not to let himself become too excited at the prospect of Evangéline's return. Repeated deceptions had taught him not to expect too much out of life.

* * *

As Lily Bellefontaine got out of the car to stretch, the air felt thicker, slightly foggy. She stepped upon a patch of sand covering the pavement. The saline scent of the nearby ocean overtook her.

Music blasted from an open Jeep parked behind her car at the gas pump. Two bare-chested young guys in baseball caps sat at the back. Their gaze lingered a little too long in Lily's direction.

She walked briskly past them. The drive from Providence was only a half hour, but her body ached from a day spent on her feet. Nursing staff had been short again all week.

Lily went straight for the coffee machine at the back of the convenience store and poured herself a cup. She added lots of creamer and three packs of sugar, and stirred the whole thing. Cradling the cup with both hands, she welcomed the warmth on her frigid fingers.

She took a sip out of the small hole of the plastic lid. The coffee taste remained on her tongue, hot, sweet and comforting. Her headache receded, her body relaxed. Maybe this weekend getaway at the Davenports' beach house would be good after all. She hadn't had a holiday in so long and couldn't wait to unwind in peace with a glass of Chardonnay.

Lily paid for her drink, then headed toward the door, where a display of local greeting cards caught her attention. She stopped to admire them, their soft colors soothing. The cards were watercolor paintings of the area, beach scenes mostly. A few depicted the local wildlife—a deer in the woods, plovers on the dunes. She picked one up that showed a dreamy lake surrounded by pine trees. She read the name of the painter on the back: Morag Callan.

"Miss, you dropped this."

She jumped at the rich masculine voice behind her.

After hurrying to replace the card in the stand, Lily turned to the man who'd spoken.

She swallowed.

He was tall and broad shouldered, wearing low-slung dark pants exposing a sliver of dark skin. His fitted black T-shirt revealed well-defined and powerful muscles. Dark curls brushed his shoulders and a twinkle lightened his smoky green eyes. What had he just said to her?

"Miss Lily Bellefontaine?" He showed her the hospital name tag, an amused smile on his lips. "RN?"

Rooted to the spot, she remembered putting the tag in her cardigan's pocket after her shift today. "Thank you, sir."

He handed her the piece of plastic, and as she took it from his hand, their fingers touched for a second.

She caught her breath.

At his contact, a wave of raw energy crashed through her and rose along her arms to end in the middle of her chest. She looked at him, stunned.

Bending closer, he surrounded her with his dangerous scent.

"Not *sir*," he whispered in her ear. "Gabriel." His voice had a faint French accent. "I'm Gabriel."

The words pronounced so sensually sent shivers through her body. A tingle spread deep within her. She found herself wanting to bury her head in his muscular chest. What was happening? He was a complete stranger.

A hint of sadness crept in when Gabriel straightened up, gave her one last look, then stepped out into the hazy late afternoon. Still fascinated, she stared at him through the window, above the card display. With both hands she hugged her cup and rested her lips on the plastic lid.

She watched him stride off to a black motorcycle, then open one of his saddlebags. After retrieving a long black coat, he slid it over his shoulders. Even in the distance, she detected danger radiating from him.

The enticing stranger straddled his bike, revved the engine and rode off.

A strange sense of loss swept through her. Why did she feel as if she'd known him forever?

She shook her head slowly, and with a hint of sorrow in her heart she whispered, "Nice to meet you, Gabriel."

Two

Eight thirty. Exhausted, Lily checked her watch. Dusk made it harder and harder for her to see as she hiked back down toward the Davenports' house. The woods would soon be pitch-black.

She had needed a break from her friends' household, now full of relatives and friends. But her hike had taken her a bit farther than she'd planned. Her stomach grumbled. Sure, the sunset from atop the hill had been pretty, but now all she wanted was the big bowl of chowder waiting for her at the beach house.

She'd been walking for a good hour. Where could she have ended up? As she climbed over a large fallen tree, a faint sound caught her attention . . . there, very close. Three animal shapes cut through the shadows, right in front of her.

Her heart nearly stopped. *What now? Dogs?*

She stood completely still, her palms moist despite the cold air. She drew in a deep, slow breath. As the animals got closer, she realized they weren't mere dogs. It was three wolves. *Don't panic,* she commanded herself.

The beasts turned her way. Fear shot through her body. Would they attack?

The predators stared at her for what seemed liked hours, not making a single move, while Lily didn't dare breathe.

Then they turned and melted into the darkness.

As soon as they disappeared, she bolted. She ran as fast as possible into the woods, away from the wolves, jumping over branches and small bushes.

She tripped and fell, her face seared by the scratches of stiff brush and prickly thorns. A big branch hit her forehead hard, and pain crushed her, black spots splattering her sight. As she flipped over on the ground, wetness crept up her left leg and along her back.

Stunned and hurt, she lay immobile for a few seconds. She'd fallen into a small stream.

She sat up, becoming aware of the cold water plastering her sweater to her skin. The rear of her jeans had been completely soaked through. Freezing and dizzy, she shivered. Her head hurt. She was an absolute mess.

She blinked, tears stinging her eyes. She breathed long and slow, refusing to succumb to panic, then wiped her tears on the sleeve of her muddy sweater. She couldn't deny the fact that she was utterly lost. The question now was, what would she do about it? She knew she couldn't be too far from civilization, but she couldn't even hear the ocean anymore to get her bearings. She'd always heard the best thing to do when lost was to stay put so it would be easier for a rescue party to find you. But the thought of spending all night in the woods filled her with horror. Surely lots of people lived nearby. She could find a road or a house. Suddenly frantic with worry, she shouted for help. Maybe someone was close. If only she hadn't left her cell phone at the house.

No answering call came, only the wind's howls as it blew through the branches surrounding her.

Follow the stream, she thought. It would lead her to a lake. She'd find houses by a lake.

As she sank her hand in the cold water, she studied the way the stream flowed. Then she wiped her fingers on her jeans and got up, a bit wobbly, hoping she hadn't sustained a concussion.

Shaking off her dizziness, she started walking. The walk became strenuous, and near darkness surrounded her.

Tall and bare trees looked like bleak skeletons in the gloomy evening as they creaked slowly with the wind.

While tripping over dead branches, Lily kept her mind on the creek. Thorns scratched her face, caught her hair. Her watch said ten o'clock, but time no longer mattered. The night was fully dark, without a single moonbeam to brighten the way. Her vision had adjusted to the lack of light, but she could only distinguish shadows. She tripped more and more, then finally resorted to kneeling on the ground, her ears focused on the sounds of the stream.

Tears filled her eyes as she went down, and she found herself unable to stop crying. Sobbing and crawling, she proceeded through the dark, her knees digging in mud. Her hands patted brittle dead leaves and rough snapping branches.

How much longer could she keep going? She was lost, lost in hell.

She would not think of the wolves, not think of how scared she was. She just crawled on, tears and sobs shaking her entire body.

Just keep going.

Then she entered what seemed a larger clear space near a lake. As she crawled along, smooth grass brushed her hands. Shaking in surprise, her palms met a very tall stone that seemed to tower over her. The boulder was polished, and it felt as though there were strange symbols carved in it.

She rested on the erect stone to catch her breath but felt dizzy, black spots dancing in front of her. There was no sound of civilization anywhere, no light in the distance.

She could just curl up right here. Fall asleep. Just hang in there until morning.

Still on her knees, clutching herself, she heard a branch crack.

Wolves. Her heart stopped.

She looked into the dark and saw nothing.

Eventually, she distinguished a large shadow striding toward her.

A man. He was tall and broad, and getting closer. Leaves crunched under his feet. He seemed to have no trouble seeing her. Would he help her? Or be worse than the wolves?

Her breath thinned, her body tensed. She lifted her chin to gaze at his shadowed features, ignoring the cold.

It was too dark.

"Are you okay?" His voice was rich, entrancing, a caress on her beaten spirit. He bent down to her level so that their faces were really close, and she distinguished long, dark curls.

She bit her lip hard. "Not really."

He pushed her hair away from her face, in a slow movement, as if not to frighten her. "Everything will be all right, Lily Bellefontaine." He knew her. He could see her.

Yet she still couldn't distinguish his face. "How—?"

"Come. I'll take you home." He stroked her arm as if to encourage her, the back of his hand warm through the damp wool of her sweater. He helped her up, his strong hands wrapping around her cold fingers. "I'm Gabriel," he said. "Remember, the gas station?"

Relief swept over her. She didn't know him, but it didn't matter. At this moment, he was her salvation. He would take her to safety. To warmth.

"I was lost." Her voice sounded very small as she leaned on him. Shaky again, she would have fallen if he hadn't held her in his solid arms.

"You're in no shape to walk." He swept her in a powerful embrace, lifting her from the ground, surrounding her with his warmth, with his power, while she fell into churning blackness.

Three

"Hello, dear, how are you?" An old man in a wrinkled tweed jacket sat in front of her. His shoulder-length silver hair was tied back and strange geometrical lines had been tattooed along his temples.

Lily blinked with caution, taking in the unfamiliar surroundings. She found herself resting on a firm couch, her head buried in a velvet pillow, a plaid blanket covering her. The large room where she lay was lovely, lace curtains adorning tall windows, stripes of faded pinks and yellows papering the walls.

Where was she? Lily tried to push herself up and, slightly dizzy, leaned back on the armrest, tucking her knees to her chest.

"I'm Iain." The man smiled. "Professor Iain Callan. This is my house. Gabriel brought you in."

"Hi." She searched around her. "Gabriel?" Had he gone? Her numbed brain clung to the shadowy image of him as he'd bent over her in the woods.

"He'll be right back." Iain smiled softly at her. "You gave us quite a fright, lass. How are you feeling?"

"I don't know. Okay I think." The heat from the fireplace seeped warmly into her body, the scent of burning wood comforting her. "How long have I been out?"

"I'd say a few hours or so. Do you live around here?" Iain's gray eyes sparkled with kindness.

"No, I just came for the weekend to visit some friends." She tried to sit upright again and felt a little better.

"They'll be wondering where I am." They were probably searching for her now.

"Shall I call them for you?"

Grateful, she nodded. "That would be nice." Then she frowned. "Wait, I don't have anyone's number. I don't have my phone with me."

"Maybe I can find out for you. What is your friend's name?"

"Davenport, John Davenport."

"My wife knows everyone in the village. I'll ask her."

Lily slid a hand through her hair; it was clean and smooth. Someone must have brushed it. "I'm Lily, by the way."

"I know. Gabriel told us. You must be hungry. Let me get you something to eat." He stood. "I'll be right back."

Lily relaxed as she looked around. The old professor seemed nice enough. His house was beautiful, the room filled with antiques. Lily wondered how far she was from John's house. She shivered at the memory of the cold and fear she'd suffered in the woods, grateful to be warm and cozy under the thick blanket.

"Hi there." A distinctive masculine voice startled her as it echoed in the room. "Glad to see you awake."

She glanced up and a rush of euphoria mixed with nervousness rose in her. Gabriel.

Leaning on the doorway, his arms folded in his chest, he stared at her, his gaze of smoky green touching her very soul. He wore the same dark clothes she remembered, the faded thermal shirt revealing every muscle of his powerful upper body. His presence seemed to fill the room.

"Hi." She was surprised by the strength of her own voice.

"My aunt is making you something to eat."

Her sense returned. Even if he was incredibly handsome, she needed to leave, return to her friends' beach house. "No need to bother anyone. I should go." Her voice was firm and decided.

"Your clothes are in the dryer." Gabriel lips curled into an amused smile and she became aware that she only wore a thick white bathrobe on top of her bra and panties. Someone had removed her clothes, socks and sneakers. Blushing slightly, she felt even more determined. She had to go.

"Let me get up." She tried to stand, but her legs gave out.

He lunged toward her. "Easy, babe." He caught her arm and helped her back onto the couch, his touch strangely comforting.

Babe? Who was this guy? Curiosity suddenly replaced her eagerness to leave.

"You're not going anywhere. You need something to eat." Letting go of her arm, he smiled at her again, kindly this time. "And I like having you here."

Gabriel kept his gaze on her as she wondered what to say. She noticed how silky Gabriel's hair appeared. She wanted to reach and touch the dark curls falling into his eyes, then pushed the thought to the back of her mind.

Iain returned, carrying a tray loaded with food. "Here, a wee snack." He set the tray on a drop-leaf table in front of her.

"Thank you so much. That's very nice of you." Lily's hunger returned in force at the sight of a bowl of heavy soup accompanied by thick slices of homemade bread.

"My wife is making some calls to find your friend John." Iain took an ornate carved chair and sat beside Gabriel. "Lucky Gabriel found you," he said as she dug into the food.

"What were you doing in the woods all by yourself?" Gabriel's voice sounded full of concern.

She put the bowl back on the tray. "I wanted to see the sunset and got lost."

"Could be dangerous," Gabriel said.

"I know." She shot him a dark look.

Lily was spared from having to give any further explanation by a woman walking in. She carried a large steaming cup between her slender fingers. "I managed to find her friends. Rhonda knew the Davenports' landscaper."

Small built, with a tumble of thick fiery hair, and wearing a long black dress belted by a loose multicolored braid, she seemed ageless—thirty, or even fifty, perhaps?

Something about the woman put Lily on edge.

"It is all set. Lily will stay with us tonight," the woman said.

"Good," Gabriel said.

Uneasiness caused Lily to shudder slightly as they discussed her without a glance in her direction. She became even more uncomfortable to see the woman stride toward her.

"Here, Lily." The woman handed her the cup. "Drink this."

Lily looked up at her, confused.

The woman laughed. "I'm forgetting my manners. I'm Morag Callan, Gabriel's aunt. I'm so glad he brought you here." Her voice had an unusual musical lilt to it. She pushed the cup into Lily's hand again. "You must drink this."

Lily took the tea, her nose wrinkling at the strong smell. The tea was pungent but not totally bad. She sensed her muscles relax, then quickly finished her tea before leaning on the pillow. Her eyelids closed.

She became enfolded by a comforting masculine scent. As a hand stroked her hair, she found herself pleasantly falling out of consciousness. The horror of the previous hours made her even more appreciative of the warmth around her and the softness of the touch on her skin.

Just before sleep overtook her, a faint voice whispered, "Evangéline, *mon amour*. You're back."

It was her; it had to be.

The same silky skin on his fingers, the similar strong and graceful body, the full mouth. Only her eyes were different. Where Evangéline's eyes had been dark brown, Lily's were hazel, catlike. They could have been sisters.

Glad Morag had left the room for a minute, Gabriel played with Lily's hair, twirling the dark strands one at a time, mesmerized. "She's just like her."

Iain nodded. "You didn't expect that, did you?"

"I didn't know what to expect." Gabriel sighed. The woman stirred a series of conflicted emotions in him, filled him with a primal need to possess her, an urge he'd never felt for a woman other than Evangéline.

She shifted in her sleep and the white bathrobe opened to reveal a touch of lavender lace at her cleavage. He had to force himself not to bring his hand down under the soft satin and cup the breast offered to him.

"She's so modern."

"Living for so long is not easy. We see all sorts."

"You've lived forever, haven't you, Alchemyst?"

Iain laughed. "The roles of men and women keep changing, back and forth over the centuries." He raised one eyebrow. "And I have lived many, many centuries."

Gabriel sensed a heavy burden weighing on the old man. How could one live so long and stay sane?

Morag strode back from the kitchen, disturbing the

peace of the room. "Well, Gabriel, you have what you seek."

Gabriel stopped playing with Lily's hair to caress her cheek again, so soft. "What did you do to her? Did you force her to come here, alone in the woods?"

Lily seemed so vulnerable. How shocked he'd been at the sight of her, bloody, dirty and nearly unconscious beside the Cerrwiden stone. His hand shook. He was ready to cut down anyone who'd done this to her.

"Calm yourself, Voyager. I did nothing to her. She is the one foolish enough to wander by herself in the woods." Morag put the blanket over Lily's chest, taking care not to wake her. "She is very pretty. She will learn our ways eventually."

Gabriel raked a hand through his hair. "She won't be your recruit, Morag. Our bargain ends here. She came back to me. We don't need you anymore."

Morag straightened, her expression blank. "You want to leave the Priory?"

"Of course I want to leave. Why wouldn't I?"

"You agreed to the covenant," she said. "Bound with your own blood. You can no longer leave." Her lips curled into a half smile. "You are tied to us, forever."

Her precise, lilting voice made Gabriel's blood run cold. There was no rest, no freedom. Ever since the English soldiers came to his peaceful village, someone else had been in control of his destiny.

They faced each other, fury consuming him. Gabriel's muscles tightened. He forced himself to breathe.

"Carry her upstairs, now. Take her to your bed. I made sure she will not wake for a while." Morag clasped her hands together. "She is all yours. Join with her tonight. It will speed things up."

"Morag, you're a monster."

The priestess suddenly drew herself to her full height. She seemed to fill the whole room, soaring over Gabriel, casting her shadow far beyond them. Her eyes sparkled like crystal, her hair wildly crowned her harsh features.

He knew she was using an illusion spell. It didn't frighten him, no. But her feral persona reminded him of the power she held over them all.

"I am the High Priestess of the Callanish Coven." Morag's voice echoed far in Gabriel's mind. "You will do as I say."

Lily opened her eyes and surveyed the dark around her.

A faint light shone through a partly open door, revealing the setting of a bedroom.

A hint of panic rose in her. What was this?

Then she remembered. Gabriel, Morag . . . She'd fallen asleep on the couch. They'd probably brought her to a guest room.

Her body ached, stiff from the ordeal in the woods. Drawing the robe tighter, she buried herself deeper in bed and tried to fall asleep again.

Gabriel. He filled her mind. She couldn't stop thinking about him—his body, the gaze of his green eyes burning into her, the thick dark curls. She imagined him naked, imagined his golden skin, the flexing of his muscles.

Suddenly filled with unusual longing, she craved his weight on her, to be surrounded by his strength, his heat. She wanted him kissing her body, his hands exploring her, making her his. The images warmed her, and she loosened the robe again. Her heartbeat pulsed harder.

What was wrong with her? She didn't know this man. Yet she thought about him in the most intimate detail.

She shifted a few times, trying to go back to sleep, but found she couldn't. She pushed the quilt away and sat up in bed. The warm light by the door beckoned to her.

Unable to resist, she got up. She wrapped herself in the bathrobe and tiptoed barefoot across the room, then pushed the door open. The hall glowed in a soft light. She couldn't hear a sound.

Where could he be? Why was she so obsessed with him?

A door next to hers was ajar. Was this where he slept? For some reason it felt vital to make sure he was near.

She pushed the door open and glowing light flooded into the dark room. There he was, sleeping on his back, his powerful body barely covered by a white sheet, looking like a large predator at rest.

She listened to his breath, imagining its warmth over her sensitive flesh. Her whole body flushed, her breasts tingled and heat flowed in waves between her thighs.

Uncontrollable desire overtook her. She had to have him.

She walked to his bed, shaking at the thought that he would wake and discover her.

What was she doing? She didn't know him. Yet she couldn't stop herself.

She sat next to him and held her breath, listening. He hadn't woken.

He was stunning.

In her imagination, she slid her hand slowly along his naked chest, traced the lines of his muscles, down to the ripples of his exposed navel. Lower even, under the white sheet exposing his every contour. In her mind, she saw herself caress the solid fullness of him. He would be too big for her hands, too big inside her, sliding in and out.

"Lily?"

She gasped.

He gazed at her now, the faint glow in the room showing the concern on his face. Had he been waiting for her?

He hiked the thin sheet over his chest. "Lily, what are

you doing here?" His voice was deep, sensuous, filled with sleep.

She wanted him. All rational thought had disappeared.

He reached out to her. "Are you all right?"

She took his hand in hers, wished its warm roughness were all over her skin. "I couldn't sleep."

"You had a terrible fright tonight. Come here with me, if you want."

She hesitated, biting her bottom lip, unable to understand the force that had drawn her to come to his room. In her whole life, she had never, ever, been so bold.

"I'll just sleep right here." She settled at the edge of the bed, aroused by his tempting scent, still lingering on the sheet. He took the comforter, which had fallen on the floor, and pulled it over both of them as she nestled in his bed, satisfied to be near him.

But it wasn't enough.

They were so close, almost touching.

Gabriel wondered what could have brought Lily to his bed. *Morag*, he suddenly realized. A simple love spell. His jaw tight, he silently cursed the High Priestess. She should have let him deal with this at his own pace, stayed well away from his life.

His mind swirled with confusion. It was too soon. He needed to control his body. Drawing the cotton sheet tighter around him, he got up to close the bedroom door, then returned to sit on the bed. She appeared to be asleep.

"*Solas*," his voice echoed in a whisper. A fat candle on the night table lit as he spoke, bathing the room in a faint radiance.

He settled next to her and listened to her gentle breath, admired her long hair spilled on the pillow. She was too close to him, too similar to Evangéline.

He had to restrain himself from taking her here and now. All he wanted was to grab her, remove the heavy robe.

He wanted to see her naked, cup her breasts, feel her taut nipples under his palms, taste them on his tongue.

Overtaken with yearning for her, he wanted to claim her soft body, get into her wet warmth, find the release he needed. He longed to hear her moan for him.

His body hardened as he cursed his frustration.

Morag had brought Lily to his bed with her spells. Trapped again. The temptation would be hard to resist. Morag knew it too well. Fate had become his master, again.

He rolled on his side and put a gentle hand on Lily's hip.

She edged closer to him.

He wrapped his arm around her. "You're so beautiful," he whispered in her ear. He kissed the top of her head as she buried herself in his chest. "Don't worry, baby, just sleep here. I'll watch over you." He meant that. She would fall asleep, warm in his arms. He wouldn't touch her further.

She felt so supple crushed to him though, her sweet scent rose to him, called him. He knew then that he wouldn't be able to restrain his powerful urge to possess. And he suddenly realized that Morag had worked her spells against him as well.

In despair, he clenched his teeth. *Damn you, Morag. I don't want it like that*.

Lily slid the tips of her fingers along Gabriel's back, contouring his well-defined muscles.

She delighted to hear him groan at her gesture, and let him push his strong leg against her, part her bathrobe.

She knew he wore nothing under the thin sheet wrapped around his waist. Trembling with expectation, she also wanted to be naked for him.

He slid his hand to the middle of her back, taking her lips, tender at first, but soon more forceful, commanding.

She responded eagerly to his powerful demands, opening to his nibbling. Her tongue intertwined with his, tasting his intoxicating male essence, while his passion made her yearn for more.

Her mind tried to reason. She should go now, pull away before it was too late. She couldn't just sleep with him tonight and then leave. No, she couldn't do that.

As if he could sense her hesitation, his kisses stopped, and he just lay there, embracing her.

But it was already too late.

Craving overtook reason. She wanted him—now.

She wrapped her legs around him, pushing the cotton sheet away, and soon felt his erection heavy on her bare thigh, demanding more of her.

He found the hook at her back and undid the tiny fastener of her bra. Sliding the satin straps over her arms, he peeled the lacy fabric away from her, exposing her breasts to him.

"*Tellement belle*," he whispered. "You're so beautiful."

His lips gentle and wet, he kissed one beading nipple. Oh, how good this felt, his tongue darting to the sensitive tip. Then he flicked it, sending waves of need between her thighs.

She took in a deep breath, closed her eyes. She needed him closer. Her legs wrapped around his back, opening herself to the soft skin of his navel as dampness clung to the thin cotton at her crotch.

He cupped her other breast in his large rough hand. His thumb brushed over her nipple; he rolled it between his fingers.

As he deliciously pinned her to the bed with his weight, his fingers touched her cheek, traced her lower lip with his thumb.

She kissed it, her sensitive lips quivering at his slow

touch. Her tongue licked the callous pad; then she took his whole thumb in her mouth and sucked hard.

"Babe, you're too much."

She melted at his groan, which he followed with another brisk flick at her nipple.

Her mind was no longer her own. She was completely taken into his world, his reality. Nothing mattered more right now than her need to melt with him, to meet his desires.

She pressed her pelvis toward him, wishing the thin fabric of her panties gone.

He inched himself above her, his arms on the bed at each side of her head. Then he pushed her legs together and straddled her hips with his muscular thighs.

She felt the loss as he held his weight away from her, and she looked up to meet his gaze.

She saw his lust, was mesmerized by his power. He wanted her completely. The intensity of his need made her sigh with delight. He would be all she wanted.

He took possession of her mouth and grabbed the thin fabric around her hips. In one quick motion, he got rid of it, raking her buttocks.

He bore his full weight back down on her, pushing his knees between her legs.

She welcomed his heat, his strength, his mouth filling hers, and parted her legs wide to meet him. His erection pressed on her moist opening and she cupped his buttocks, drawing him tight against her. How wonderfully hard.

Gabriel ached to possess the spellbound woman under him, his desire tricked by Morag. He was getting lost in it.

His body screamed with the need to claim her. Yet he sensed more—peace, finally, fresh and cleansing. His tortured soul was relieved by his lover's existence. Elation took over his heart. She would save him, cure his obsession.

He held his weight on one elbow and his fingers covered her wet center. In a gentle stroke, he parted moist curls.

She pushed herself against his hand, trailed her nails on his lower back down to the rear of his legs, sending tingling over his entire body. She grabbed his buttocks, pressed him hard against her wet slit.

He resisted her slightly. He only wanted her pleasure. *"Mon amour."* She was his true love. He had waited so long, and there she was, as wonderful as he had imagined.

His fingers found her most sensitive spot. He drew circles around it with a gentle touch. She moaned in response. He delighted in her surrender and continued to stroke her, first in sweet circles, then more firmly as she bucked against him.

"More." Her voice was raspy, pleading. "I want more of you."

"Sweetheart, I want all of you." His ache for her almost pained him. When he finally slid his hard tip along her, he found warmth, slickness and a slight release to his throbbing need that sent shivering tremors through his whole pelvis. He edged inside her a little at first, sliding in and out, summoning all his self-control to keep it slow.

She reached one hand between them to touch him. How silky his skin felt on her fingertips, hard and pulsing for her.

Her grip on his buttocks urged him closer. She wanted all of him, his boldness bringing her alive.

In one powerful thrust, he plunged fully into her.

Together at last. Her body recognized his; she knew him. He filled her again and again, his finger stroking her in time with each thrust. She welcomed him with a low moan as the motion brought searing waves of pleasure deep inside her.

"You feel so good, babe," he whispered, his voice a gentle breath in her ear.

Desire overwhelmed her. Tides of need and pleasure radiated from her center, spreading over her whole body. *Just a few more strokes. Keep the rhythm. Yes, almost there.*

"Let yourself go." Gabriel's tone was commanding. "Come for me."

Release suddenly crashed into her, shattering her very core. Time was suspended. Her moan became louder.

She gazed at him and saw that she was not alone lost in surrender. Together they rode the most primal pleasure.

He slid and stroked until she was completely spent with satisfaction. She wrapped her limbs around him, held with all her strength. He embraced her tight. Every inch of their damp and hot skins touched, their bodies solidly clasped together.

Their breathing finally slowed. Gabriel remained silent, his head buried in her neck.

Her senses recovered slowly, and she became aware of her surroundings. Something caught her eyes on the ceiling above her, a faint shimmering symbol. Probably an effect of the candle.

She blinked.

The symbol was still there, a five-pointed star within a circle, a clear white light glowing in darkness.

A chill shivered down her spine. *The symbol of witchcraft.*

"Baby, you taste so good." Gabriel shifted on his side, kissed the cradle of her neck, sending little shivers along her shoulders.

She hugged him closer and kissed his temple. When she glanced up again, the mark had gone. Shaking her head, she gave a soft laugh, then buried her cheek in Gabriel's dark curls.

The symbol remained branded in her mind.

Crazy. She was really crazy, wasn't she?

Four

What happened? Lily opened her eyes carefully, Gabriel's heavy arm pinning her against his body.

They lay tangled in the sheets, facing each other on the lacy pillow, their limbs wrapped together. The sun poured into the bedroom, spilling on them both.

"Good morning." His thick voice drove tendrils of pleasure within her.

Her cheeks flushed. "Hi."

"You were cold last night."

"I was." She remembered the intensity of their passion. What had she gotten herself into? Now she ought to leave his warm bed, get back to her friends.

Silently she traced the bicep holding her, drawn to the series of intertwined black lines curling around it, the dark ink a sharp contrast to his flawless skin.

"Any special meaning for this?"

"No." His eyes darkened. "It's from a long time ago. I was a foolish kid."

"It suits you." She fell into an uncomfortable silence.

He flashed her a charming smile. "Are you always so serious in the morning?"

"I should get up. Call my friends at the beach house."

"Oh."

"Yes, they'll come pick me up." Lily needed to get away from this awkward situation.

"So soon? You're not thinking about leaving right now, are you?"

With tenderness, he pushed her hair back. "You have such pretty eyes." His fingers traced her eyelids. "Stay a little longer, will you? Stay with me."

Stay here with him. There was nothing else she'd rather do. Yet a little voice in her head told her to run away. He was too handsome, too wild.

She gazed into his smoky green eyes and got lost in them.

"Lily." His rich voice lingered on each syllable. "I love your name." He took a strand of her hair and wrapped it around his finger. "Like a beautiful flower, pure and delicate."

"Oh, really?" She forced a laugh.

"Please don't leave. Stay with me today." He brushed her lips with his. "I promised you breakfast, remember?"

At once, her body responded to his kiss, to his musky scent so near. Hot tides of desire flowed through her. Yet, still sleepy, she was ready for him again. Her friends wouldn't really miss her; their beach house was packed with kids and relatives for the holiday. He drew her close, his arm around her waist, and pushed one knee between her legs. The muscles of his thigh pressed against her skin, parted her.

Then in one swift motion, he found her wet center. He slid inside her, filling her with a solid erection.

She gasped, wanting to protest. But a sense of belonging overtook her. Why did this feel so natural?

"Please stay with me." He rocked slowly in her and she quivered at the intense sensations vibrating through her pelvis. "I need you close."

She stroked the soft skin at the curve of his back. He was too much. She absolutely couldn't resist him.

"I guess I can stay for a little longer. It seems you're very persuasive."

Holding on to her hips, he shifted onto his back, then

pulled her on top of him. Overtaken by the sweet invasion, she took him deeper inside her.

"Please stay the whole day with me. You can leave tomorrow."

His body was just perfect, large and muscular. The sight of him under her and the feel of his luscious skin on her palms drew a passionate yearning again.

Her naked breasts brushed over him, her arms supporting her weight at each side of his shoulders. The cool air pricked her skin as the blanket swept down along her back, the heat from his body radiating up to her chest.

"You *are* awfully hard to resist." Her lips curled into a seductive smile. She had lost all judgment, but it did feel so good right here with him.

"The whole day . . . what am I saying? Stay the whole weekend." He trailed soft lines to her belly, lifted his palms up and cupped her breasts. He rolled her nipples between his thumbs and forefingers.

The darting pulse of pleasure made her inhale deeply. "You're pushing your luck."

She suddenly drew herself upright, her knees digging into the mattress, straddling him. She gasped at the intense pressure inside her. He was so hard, almost too large.

She rocked back and forth, taking him further and further, getting her fill of him with each thrust. His hands grasped her hips, his fingers dug firmly into her flesh, full of restraining power.

"Come on, stay. I'll drive you to the city on Monday." He parted her slit with both hands as he admired her. He found her tight little nub and his thumb flicked it upward while his other fingers held her wide open.

She yelped at the touch, then moaned as his finger kept at his strokes, up and up. Pleasure swirled around her and she felt playful. This was unlike her. What was it with him? He made everything so light and fun.

Filled with blissful warmth, she noticed how different her desire was today in the sunlit room. Last night had felt unnatural, almost scary. But now, this morning, she controlled it and wanted to take him with her, give him all she could.

She bent to whisper in his ear. "I really, really want you to drive me to the beach today." Her teasing voice was raspy with desire. Then she straightened back up to ride him again.

"I'll take you everywhere you want." His hips pushed against her inner thighs. He plunged inside her, meeting each of her rocking motions, still flicking her with his thumb, hard and fast, yet smooth from all the moisture of her arousal.

She was so close to release, waiting for him to join her in ecstasy.

She then drew herself farther back, anchoring her hands on his thighs, offering her body, taking even more of him inside, riding the sweet ache of his deep penetration.

He gazed at her, his eyes filled with intensity. "Everywhere you want, babe. I'll take you everywhere you want."

Settled in an Adirondack chair next to Gabriel on the back deck, Lily admired the view spread before her. The sparkling lake was peaceful, surrounded by tall pine trees.

Her freshly laundered tank top exposed her shoulders to a soft breeze and to the warmth of the late-August sun.

She sipped her coffee. Good, strong and very sweet, as she always liked. "This is all yours?" she asked Gabriel.

"No, not all. The land around Callan Lake used to belong to the family, but not anymore." He stretched, exposing a sliver of golden skin above his black fatigues, below the tight plain white T-shirt he'd put on this morning. "Iain donated a big part of the land to make a park."

She noticed half a dozen large birds paddling on the lake. "What are those? Snow geese?"

"Yes, on their way south. They always stop in the fall."

"It's nice and peaceful here." The fresh scent of pine trees hovered in the air.

"A little piece of paradise." Gabriel's smile added to the serenity of the surroundings.

Lily pulled her legs under her and nestled deeper in the cedar chair.

"I'll take you for a walk later if you want, or we could go for a swim."

"I don't have my bathing suit."

"You don't need it. I won't mind." He grinned.

She felt herself blush.

"Don't worry. We'll go get your stuff after breakfast. A swim, then?"

"Sure, I love swimming. But isn't the lake cold at this time of year?"

"Not really. It's perfect. I used to swim in much colder lakes when I was young."

"And where was that?"

"Oh, all over." His eyes went dark.

"Where are you from, Gabriel?"

"I've lived everywhere. I was in Seattle before I moved to Providence a year ago."

"Where were you born? France?"

"Let's not talk about me. It's boring. What about you? Born and bred in Rhode Island?"

His reluctance puzzled her. Why was he being so guarded about himself? "Yes. Always lived in Providence."

"Never wanted to travel, see the world?"

"Maybe, but I have my great-aunt to look after." She raised her chin a little.

"Hope she wasn't too worried about you."

"No, she had planned to have some of her quilting friends over last night, Mrs. Desmarais and the gang. She was fine, didn't even try to reach me. You live in the city, right?"

"Yes, downtown. I'll take you over sometime."

She froze, surprised he expected to see her after this weekend, not sure how she felt about that.

A loud honking disturbed her thoughts. The geese had gotten out of the water and wobbled on the lawn in front of them.

"They seem to want something."

Gabriel laughed. "They want to be fed. Better not give them anything. They won't leave and they'll die over the winter."

The geese waited for a moment, then went back to the lake.

"You like animals, don't you?"

He fixed on the view in front of him. "Better than some people." He turned to her. "I'm not really a city guy. I need this—the water, the trees, the stones. I go crazy after a while if I don't hear the birds. I grew up in this, no noise and fast cars, surrounded by nature.

"Don't get me wrong. The city is okay," he added. "I don't need to cook, with so many takeout options and coffee shops."

"I don't go out much. I'm pretty quiet."

"I like quiet. But maybe I can take you out one night. You might find it fun. Some of my cousins are coming to Providence. I want you to meet them."

"We'll see." Was she thrilled he wanted more than a weekend? She'd scared herself by sharing his bed so soon.

It struck her that she really didn't know anything about him.

What strange twist of fate had put them together?

As they picked up their breakfast dishes and headed to the kitchen to clean up before Morag and Iain returned from a trip to town, she reflected that their morning together felt strangely normal. Part of her wanted to stay with him forever. But her more practical side intervened. What about Angèle? What about her work at the hospital? She liked her life's routine—helping patients, swimming workouts, dinner with her great-aunt, a good book in bed at night.

Until she met Gabriel she hadn't realized anything was missing.

But she did enjoy the intimacy of this morning, the companionship, the constant sensual tension crackling when Gabriel came near her.

Beneath his playful nature, she sensed an incredible power and determination. He was solid, strong. She could get lost in his arms and know she would be safe forever.

His eyes often filled with amusement, but she had caught more in them, a glimpse of an ancient soul, as if tragedy had hit him, left him scarred. What had happened to him?

She watched Gabriel walk in front of her and longed to touch him, trace his muscular back and round buttocks. He moved as smoothly as a large cat on a lazy day.

She'd agreed to stay for the weekend, knowing she would pay later. He'd break her heart. But she didn't have the strength to deny him just yet.

The kitchen they entered was slightly old-fashioned, like the rest of the house. A thick wood refectory table sat in the middle of the room. A Rayburn oil stove stood next to a more modern gas unit. Copper pots hung from the ceiling, along with large bunches of dried flowers and herbs.

Lily opened the dishwasher to load it up.

"So you've never left Rhode Island?" Gabriel got busy at the sink.

"No, I went to nursing school here, and then the hospital offered me a job. No reason to go elsewhere."

"I bet you're a good nurse." He scrubbed hard, his muscles flexing under the tight white T-shirt.

"It's not the most glamorous job."

"I don't know. I think it is wonderful. You work at saving lives. I mean, what do I do? Spend my days at the laptop, getting stuff shipped around. Who really cares?"

"Shipping?" Finally he'd given her a hint of himself.

"My friend Roan and I got this little shipping business going, for hard-to-find chemicals mostly. He handles the West Coast and I'm East. Kind of a hobby that got out of hand. But you, you make people get better."

"It can be hard, though. I mostly work in pediatrics, and some of the children are so sick, we know they won't make it, yet they're so brave." She closed the dishwasher door. "It breaks my heart sometimes. The ends of my days can be sad. I don't know if I'll see them again when I come back in the morning." She'd never expressed these feelings before. How easy it was to confide in him.

"You're very calm. They must be less scared having you around." He dried his hands on a linen towel.

He was right. She had her gift.

The only power she allowed herself, the power of stillness. She didn't know how, but she would hold their hands and breathe, center herself. Peace would flood all over her body.

Then she'd look into their fearful eyes and wish really hard for a similar peace for them. Every time, without fail, she would transfer it like a physical wave surging from her heart, down her arm and fingers, then to the child. And the child would relax, his fear and suffering ebbing, until he'd smile back at her. She always felt an incredible power at the sight.

She'd spend her morning rounds greeting each child that way, calming them. She was always exhausted afterward, but in comparison to what the kids were going through, it was the least she could do.

When she was younger, she used to see how far she could push her limits. But after one disaster, she'd pushed it all down, blocked it all out and just allowed herself this one small gift. Her secret.

"Yes," she finally said to Gabriel. "I probably make them feel a bit better."

They had finished the dishes when Iain and Morag walked in.

Iain was in the same tweed jacket as the previous night. Morag looked different, her trim body in tight black jeans and a corseted black top trimmed with lace. Her copper hair was tied back in a thick, long braid. Lily still couldn't guess her age.

"Hello, you two. Had a good night?" Morag set a paper bag on the counter.

Lily shivered at the question. Why was she so nervous around this woman?

"Great. How was coffee?" Gabriel's hand on Lily's lower back brought her comfort.

"Very nice. Such a lovely little place. Books everywhere." Iain chuckled. "And if you get there early enough, you can get yourself a great comfy seat."

Morag unloaded her groceries—two loaves of country bread, a thick slab of cheese and some red pears. She smiled. "You should see Iain running for that couch. He nearly knocked down Mrs. Freeman this morning."

"I certainly did not," Iain said.

"I beg to differ. You had your nose buried in your old manual, ignoring everybody," Morag said before leaving the room.

"Well, I do like that couch." Iain gave them a sheepish smile.

Morag returned. "By the way, Lily, we just stopped by your friends' house and brought back your overnight bag." To her surprise, she gave Lily her handbag. "I told them you would be staying here. Brianna said, 'Have fun!' and that someone will drive your car back."

"Thanks. You didn't need to do that." She clutched the bag to her chest. Though it was a thoughtful gesture, Lily couldn't help bristling a bit at the intrusion into her life. Just what were Morag's intentions?

"It's no problem, really. It will save you the trouble of having to leave the lake today."

Iain turned to Gabriel. "Can you help for a bit this morning? The trapdoor to my lab is almost off its hinges. And with fall coming, I'd like to get that fixed."

His eyes twinkled at Lily. "Gabriel is very good at fixing the household. I'm rather useless, I'm afraid."

"No problem. Let's do it now." Gabriel drew Lily tight to brush his lips on her earlobe. "I'll have to leave you to fend for yourself. I'm sorry, I'll make it quick."

She returned his smile, tingles traveling down her neck at his kiss. "It's okay," she said as he let her go. "I have a paperback in my bag. I'll just read on the back porch. It's so beautiful over there." She glanced quickly in Morag's direction.

"No worry, boys. I'll take care of her." Morag smiled widely. "I'll show her my studio. She might find it fun. Go, go." She held on to Lily's elbow as the men left the room. "We'll be just fine."

Five

Lily caught the faint caustic smell of chemicals as soon as she entered Morag's studio. Canvases of all sizes leaned along the bare walls. The paintings didn't represent anything she could recognize. They were covered in large blotches of various colors, as if someone had tried to draw the impression of emotions or a dream. The paintings' hues were dark and faded, contrasting vividly with the bright sun shining through many wide windows.

"Have a seat." Morag pointed to a stool next to a large wooden table covered with diverse types of paper, containers full of pencils and brushes.

As Lily sat down, she examined the few paintings near her. They were a study of gray tweedy tones, speckled with washed-out rose and lavender. On closer inspection, Lily distinguished a barren land where tall erect forms lay. The painting had been splattered with a crude bright red, as if an afterthought.

"What is that?"

"Oh, just an experiment. It did not work quite the way I wished. I cannot seem to be able to finish it."

Lily turned away from the unpleasant images.

"I saw some of your cards at a gas station on my way here." She dragged a container full of pencils toward her and started to rearrange them. "They were very nice."

Morag showed Lily a small sketchbook. "Do you like this?" The black-and-white etching depicted the face of a young woman asleep. Morag had captured her vulnerability well. Her relaxed features and her full mouth made her look fragile, unsuspecting.

Discomfort seized Lily. The sleeping woman appeared too familiar.

"Yes, it's you, sorry. I hope you don't mind." Lily's breath shortened. Morag took a little too much space.

"Let's try another one, shall we?"

"I don't know." Lily tried to reason. This was Gabriel's aunt, after all. She should just go along until he returned. But without him near, she started to regret her decision to stay for the weekend.

Morag flipped her sketch pad to another page and reached for some charcoal. She studied Lily, then started to draw while Lily shifted on her stool, rearranging the container in front of her.

"Please try to stay still."

Lily dropped a pencil and settled her hands on her lap. She resigned herself, hoping Gabriel would return soon.

"Your last name is Bellefontaine, yes?" Morag's large strokes slashed the paper loudly.

"Yes."

"It reminds me of an old story, about an Evangéline Bellefontaine."

"Really? That's my middle name, Evangéline."

"That's odd."

"Is it? It's common in our family. My mom thought it too ancient for me. But my dad really liked the name, so they kept it."

"The Evangéline in the story lost her fiancé during the Acadian deportation, in the eighteenth century. The English had conquered Acadia, in eastern Canada. They took all the local settlers, put them on ships and sent them away to other French colonies. Everyone got separated in the confusion of the boarding, mothers on one boat, children on another. It tore families apart."

"Is it a true story?" Lily was surprised by Morag's melancholic tone.

"The deportation is true, yes, sadly. Some ships landed in Louisiana, others in Canada."

"Is that why New Orleans is so French?"

"Yes. There was already an established French settlement there, but the Acadians, or now the Cajuns, brought their own flavor to the area." Morag paused to study Lily, then returned to her drawing. "So, the story said that Evangéline and her fiancé were made prisoners on their wedding day, locked in the church with all the other villagers. Then they put him on a ship and left her behind for the next one. Some say they never saw each other again. Gabriel spent is life looking for her, first in Louisiana, then all over America."

"Gabriel?" The name had caught her by surprise.

"Yes, just like our own Gabriel."

"What a strange coincidence."

"Yes, I thought so too." Morag looked up from her sketching. "Such a sad story, don't you think?"

"They never reunited?" The concurrence of the names made her even more interested. It felt almost personal in an eerie way.

"Others said that he finally found her on his deathbed. In fact, this version has been written in a beautiful poem."

"I think I like that better, don't you?"

"I suppose everyone would like tragic love stories to have a happy ending. But you know, life can be harsh and cruel. Regardless of Evangéline and Gabriel, think of all the other families. They were decimated. You were lucky to be born in this century." Morag appeared to want to say more but didn't.

"Yes, I guess we all forget sometimes."

Morag stopped sketching for a moment. Her eyes narrowed. "Do you believe in soul mates?"

"I don't know." Lily tried to stay still as Morag returned to her drawing. "I never thought much about it. I guess it would be ideal—a lot of people dream of that—to meet someone you feel was destined for you, to live together forever after. But if I have a soul mate, I haven't met him yet."

"So you haven't met the one?"

"Definitely not. Most guys I went out with were not ready to settle down. I've only dated friends from the hospital. Maybe I should meet other kinds of people." She tried not to think of the gorgeous man she'd just gone to bed with.

"Maybe you should." Morag stopped drawing to examine her artwork. She didn't appear willing to bring Gabriel in the conversation either.

Lily wanted to ask whether Morag saw Iain as her true soul mate, but the general coldness in Morag stopped her.

"There is another tale you may find interesting." Morag looked up. "Most people don't know about this one, but my family is very old and kept a lot of legends through the centuries. This one tells of the fate of soul mates."

"Really?" Lily's curiosity rose. Morag was fascinating.

"My people say that true soul mates were separated centuries ago by a dark force, Taranis, a Celtic god of thunder. They shall be reunited when the time is right."

"Reunited?"

"Yes, it makes a nice story, don't you think?"

"So you're a romantic?" Lily stretched her legs now that Morag had finished drawing.

"Sometimes. Are you not?"

"Well, not really." She'd seen firsthand what misplaced love could do to the small ones left behind. "Thanks for telling me about the Acadian story. I'd like to learn more about it, especially if they may be my ancestors."

"I will lend you a book if you wish. It includes the

poem of Evangéline and Gabriel. You will find it truly beautiful."

"I'd like that, thank you."

Morag put the sketch down and, as she examined it, pulled her sleeves up past her elbows.

Lily's gaze settled on a curious tattoo in the cradle of Morag's arm. The plain black image was thick and well-defined, as if she'd been branded in ink. It showed two crescents separated by a circle.

Morag caught her inquisitive look. "You seem surprised." She lifted her arm so Lily could see it better.

Lily stared at it, then at Morag. "What does it mean?"

"The moon—they are old symbols representing the moon, waxing, full and waning. They also represent a woman's life, maiden, mother, crone. You can draw a lot of power from the moon." She gave Lily an unusually gentle smile.

Lily looked again at the symbols on Morag's smooth skin. Was she dreaming? The moons seemed to swirl around, changing colors from a blue-black to a dark bloodred.

"Do you believe in the power of the moon?" Lily's voice had become hesitant.

"There are a lot of unseen and unexplainable forces out there, wouldn't you say?" Morag stared at her now. "And yes, I do believe and do draw some powers from the moon."

"I find it hard to understand."

"Really, yet the moon affects us all—the tides, women's cycles. Did you know the earth's crust itself shifts because of the pull of the moon?"

Lily didn't know what to think, suddenly very curious to know more about Gabriel's aunt, even though part of her still mistrusted the woman.

"Here, look." Morag turned the drawing around.

Yes, it was definitely her, but she didn't really recognize herself. The woman in the picture stood, looking strong and determined, very powerful, commanding even. "It doesn't look like me much."

"Maybe not, but it will." Morag smiled at Lily again. "It will."

"What are you up to, Alchemyst?" Gabriel examined a series of glass beakers in Iain's dark lab, the familiar pungent smell of herbs rising from them. "I should be outside with Lily, not here helping you."

The lab's dampness made him wish for some fresh air. A feeble light shone through the small frosted window above their heads, but did nothing to ease the feeling of confinement creeping in his body.

"*Solas.*" Iain made a quick flick of the hand.

The five white candles around the pentagram on the floor lit at once. Their flame reflected on the flagstones covering the wall.

"Red mercury, Gabriel. That's what I'm up to, boy, red mercury." He walked to the center of the room then, grabbing the marble mortar and pestle from the altar at the heart of the pentagram, and started pounding some dark crystals. "Ah, the red soil of the Soul."

Gabriel dragged himself next to Iain. "Why don't you wait until Loïc comes? He's much better at these things than I am."

"No, no, I want to try this now, impress him a little. And you're not that bad." He handed Gabriel the pestle. "Here, take over."

Gabriel started to crush the crystal.

"*Teine, flamm teine,*" Iain commanded, and the athanor furnace behind him lit up.

"Morag did something to Lily last night." Gabriel

gripped the marble rod tight as he pounded. The black crystals soon pulverized into a fine powder.

"What could Morag possibly have done?" Iain seized a large amber-colored flask. "Here, give me the powder."

"You know exactly what I mean. She cast a spell." Gabriel poured the powdered black crystal into the flask, trying to control his fury. "I won't let her use Lily like that."

Iain hung the flask over the athanor. "Calm down. Morag does like to experiment, I'm afraid." He gripped an iron poker and moved the logs around in the furnace.

"*Islich.*" Gabriel flicked his hand and the flames lowered.

"Thank you. Here, pass me the universal quicksilver."

Gabriel reached over to a shelf full of small glass containers. He took one filled with a thick liquid, then passed it to Iain. "I'm not going to be one of her experiments."

Iain took the amber flask and added a drop of quicksilver to the crushed crystal. "You have to let Morag do as she wishes." He swirled the flask. "We have her now, your Evangéline. We know she is the one."

Gabriel wished it were that easy. How would he tell Lily the truth?

"I believe she is, but I have to do this on my own. I don't need Morag pushing Lily into my bed and getting her scared."

Iain added more drops to his tincture, swirling the flask between each addition. "Gabriel, listen to me. You have to trust Morag. She knows more than we ever will." He put the flask over the low flame. "Ah, the Earth element, almost there. Let's get ready."

"Morag may well know more than I do, but I won't have her forcing things on me." Exasperated, Gabriel lifted the sleeve of his T-shirt over his shoulder, exposing the Priory mark tattooed on his skin. He hated that part. It always reminded him of his allegiance to them.

"Give me the wee bottle over on the altar. Quick."

Gabriel passed him the glass vial filled with pungent green oil.

"Perfect." Iain admired the amber flask. "Look at these shiny crystals forming . . . just beautiful." He took his jacket off, exposing a multitude of Celtic knots drawn on the tanned skin of his entire forearm. "Ready?"

Iain started to intone an incantation in a language nearly as ancient as the earth itself.

Gabriel followed him with his own spell, reciting different words and intonations, yet completely in tune with his old master.

Gabriel's power built up as they focused on their polyphonic chant.

The tattoo on his arm burned his skin now. Then the slithering started, like many thin snakes winding around his arm. He focused on his spell, while the Celtic loops rose and slid along him, intertwined.

The sorcerers' voices echoed louder and louder. The many lines on Iain's forearm also twirled, a complicated lacy lattice of minute filaments enclosing his entire arm.

Suddenly, the coils on their arms froze to solid shiny silver metal, a thick brace around Gabriel's bicep and a full lacy sleeve on Iain's forearm.

"Now." Iain dropped the oil into the amber flask. *"Flamm teine muioc'h."* The flame in the athanor grew taller. The solution started bubbling. A strong smell diffused through the lab. *"Echuiñ, cuir crìoch air."* The flames died. A dark compound had settled at the bottom of the flask.

"Now, the Air." Iain took it to the few rays penetrating the lab. With his free hand, he drew some symbols above him in the air. The air turned into a small breeze circling around him, playing with his gray hair.

It then blew faster and stronger, until it enclosed Iain in a swirling wind closely contained around him. Gabriel, untouched by the small tornado, could see only a blurred image of the sorcerer.

"*Echuiñ*." Iain's strong voice commanded the air.

The wind stopped and the whole room returned to calm again.

Gabriel shook his head. "Don't you think that after two hundred and fifty years I know exactly what I want and what's good for me? I don't need Morag to mess with my life."

Iain wobbled the flask in the light. "Look at that. The Celestial Fire of Life." The liquid glowed bloodred in the light. Iain looked hard at Gabriel, flask still in his hand. "See, Voyager, the alchemist must separate the true soul from the body. Your soul is not fully free. This is where you need to work harder."

"My soul is not mine to free. It has always belonged to Evangéline. And now that Morag has interfered, it belongs to Lily. I have no choice but to mate with her at the next Beltane rites."

"Well, you have a while until then, but please handle this matter carefully. I would hate to lose your soul to Taranis." Iain's gaze softened. "You know, maybe Morag had nothing to do with last night. She may not have used a spell. Perhaps the connection between you two is so strong, it happened naturally."

"I'll never know, will I? Morag has all her little plans and never tells anyone anything. Damn, I hate that."

"Voyager, you're the first one. The others—Phoebus, Renaud, Loïc—they're not even close. We have no experience on how this is supposed to work. Morag only wants to help you."

"Well, I don't need help."

"Unfortunately, I now have more concerns than just your reuniting. Theuron is close again. He will be a threat to us all."

"I know, Morag told me."

"He surrounds himself with some sort of bodyguards."

"Bodyguards?"

"Yes . . . Keepers, he calls them. But let me worry about him. I've called the others. I won't be alone. Focus on Lily."

"I will." Gabriel sighed. That was all he wanted, to spend all his time with Lily, to convince her that they were meant to be together. "Just tell Morag to stop messing with me."

"I will do what I can. We have two months until Samhain. Theuron will be stronger. I fear he will become bolder." Iain's brow furrowed. "It may be possible that Lily needs to be protected from him. She's vulnerable, now that she's been with you."

Gabriel was painfully aware of the meaning of Iain's words. Now that they'd made love, she was bound to him. And he didn't want to think of his own fate if he failed to convince her to mate at Beltane.

"She does have some powers of her own," Iain added. "But she doesn't know much about it. And I fear Morag has not found her worthy."

Gabriel clenched his fist. Lily had priestess powers? "The hell with Morag. If Lily has abilities, she must be taught."

"It's for the High Priestess to decide, not me."

"Don't give me that, old man. You have complete control over her."

"Yes, I do, but I can't risk breaking the balance between us. It could have dire consequences. Remember that, Gabriel, balance. You're wild and bold. You must seek balance."

Gabriel stared at Iain, who was studying his red mercury again. He shook his head. The old sorcerer made too much sense. He'd heard that line before. The Abenaki natives he'd lived with after learning of Evangéline's death had always lectured him.

Balance, Voyager, balance.

But he didn't want balance. Fate had run his entire life and he wanted control. Now that he'd found his lost soul mate, he could finally leave it all behind. He didn't need the Priory, Morag's power. He would teach Lily, protect her.

Gabriel touched the markings on his arm. The thick braided metal had subsided.

He rolled his T-shirt sleeve back down. The Priory had found him the last time he fled. What would happen now if he tried again?

Powers of the moon . . . What had she meant? Lily knew some people used nature and multiple gods as their higher power, but did Morag actually believe this?

Sitting alone on the porch, she tried to forget about the swirling colors of the moon symbols on Morag's arm. She dismissed it as a sign of fatigue, convinced she hadn't recovered completely from the ordeal in the woods.

Lily was grateful Morag had suggested she go out for some fresh air. Her head was bursting with unanswered questions. What about Morag's moon powers? Could they be real?

And would she understand Lily's own abilities?

No, she didn't want to think about that. It had been too painful then and would still be now.

That sketch of her had been disturbing. Lily shuddered.

To settle her worries, she crossed her legs in the comfortable wooden outdoor chair, closed her eyes and slowed her breathing down, reaching for a filament of strength. Familiar peace soon settled over her.

But something in the distance of her mind caught her attention, troubled her. The symbols—they were still present in her consciousness. The symbols branded on Morag's skin shimmered in her mind now, three entwined moons.

Voices, many feminine voices, suddenly whispered in her head. *Maiden, mother, crone,* the voices repeated over and over, drowning Lily's thoughts, overtaking her mind.

Six

"Happy?" Gabriel, in the leather jacket he'd worn for the bike ride, looked impressive standing on the crowded beach that stretched miles before them.

"Very." Lily took in a big breath of clean maritime air. The sounds of crashing waves and blowing wind helped clear her mind.

Dark clouds gathered in the distance, announcing an approaching evening storm. People were packing their belongings and trailing down toward the parking lot.

"Thanks for the stop." She took off her flip-flops and dug her toes in the sand, reveling at its warmth on her feet. She felt like her old self again, the vast ocean bringing her reassurance.

"No problem." He pulled her close as they walked to the water's edge and sat down on the beach.

"I haven't been here in years, yet I live so close." Lily trailed her fingers in the sand.

Gabriel kissed the top of her head. Something bothered him as he studied the water, where tireless surfers waited to catch the next wave. An abnormal darkness in the air disturbed the elements.

As a huge wave crashed on the shore, most surfers struggled to stay upright. But one of them, a shaven-headed man in a black wet suit, glided effortlessly. He blended so well with the elements that he appeared to be floating with them. Smooth and in control, he brought his board to shore with each single wave. The other surfers laughed as they crashed, having a good time, but this man appeared bored as he landed on the beach.

Why were so many shadows emanating from him? As if he were not quite human. Gabriel's skin started to prickle with worry.

"The surfers, they're good." Lily nodded toward them. "Look at that one with the shaved skull."

"Yeah, I know" The man really bothered him.

He was gesturing to three guys surfing along with him. Their skulls were also close shaved, covered in tattoos. All were bare chested, despite the cold water. Their skin was tanned and their bodies muscular, with large runes inked on their upper backs. Gabriel was too far away to decipher them. But he had a bad feeling. This couldn't be good. He needed to find out more.

He focused his consciousness.

He made everything still around him, the presence of Lily's warm body helping him concentrate. He looked deeply at the man bothering him. With his mind perfectly quiet, he merged with the elements surrounding him.

His mind touched the air and water molecules mixing at the sea surface. He felt the minute bubbles transferring the air continuously back and forth between the ocean and the atmosphere.

The sun's warmth became alive. He sensed the heat variation creating the pressure difference driving the air, the momentum of the wind creating the waves, building them first, then sending them to a crash.

Earth's gravity sucked down his whole self, as it did to the water and air around him. The cyclic force of the moon pulled gently on the water's edge as the tide slowly rose.

Spirit was the last element to build on, his soul now melding in tune with it all. Awareness filled him. All was one, his body made of small particles interacting with the elements of the entire world.

His heart pounded, drumming in his blood.

There, he was in the man's mind. Yes, this was no ordinary man. He felt the mental barrier erected around the consciousness he probed. But so far, his target seemed unaware of Gabriel's invasion.

Images suddenly rushed in: Darkness, Taranis symbols, yearnings and desire, the desire to be alive. Lust, a young dark-haired woman, brutally forced to her knees. Fire, steel slashing through flesh, blood splattered, people screaming, dying.

In shock, Gabriel felt the man's pleasure at the intense pain, delight at the chaos he'd generated.

Who could be this twisted? Despite the horror, Gabriel had to know. He forced himself to dig further into the cruel mind.

That's when he saw Lily. Or was it Evangéline? He saw the small face framed by tumbling dark hair and he froze, the vision nearly ripping his bond with the man's thoughts.

She sat next to a blonde woman he didn't recognize. Someone had tied them together. Half-naked, the creamy skin of their bare arms and shoulders pressed against each other, their dark nipples showing through the flimsy pink lingerie they wore. Many shiny pendants hung between their pushed-up breasts. Thick black leather boots covered their thighs. Their hair was tangled and wild. Tears messed the heavy black rimming of their eyes.

The image tore at Gabriel's heart.

Theuron Keir.

The dark mage was here.

His companions were Keepers, creatures conjured in forbidden necromancy.

Drawing comfort from Lily's warmth on his body,

he extracted his consciousness from the black sorcerer's thoughts. Protective feelings surged through him. He wanted to shield her with his very blood. No one would have her. Lily would never be in contact with such darkness. She must never know. He wouldn't even let Morag and her magic taint his love.

Returning fully to the present, he slowed down his breath. He had to get away from here. He hated to drag Lily into his world. But she was his soul mate. Fate had decided. He would protect her from evil.

Tightening his hold around her, he brushed a tender kiss on the crook of her neck, just under the hairline.

A dark look flashed in his direction before returning to the crashing waves. Theuron. The mage had sensed something.

"Let's go," he whispered to Lily. The more distance between her and Theuron, the better.

Seven

Gabriel's broad shoulders flexed as he plunged the paddle in the slick water, the tattooed Celtic symbols accentuating his muscular arms.

Lily admired the ripples of his bare stomach as they tightened through the whole motion, his navel exposed by his low-slung cargo pants. The lake surface behind him was shiny and sleek in the midday sun, the canoe gliding smoothly across it.

He was mesmerizing. Rocked gently by the canoe in this secluded part of the lake, Lily enjoyed the vision Gabriel presented much more than the scenery.

A hint of small dark curls trailed beneath the buckle of his black leather belt and Lily's cheeks flushed as she imagined where they led. The gentle breeze, warm for this time of year, played with Gabriel's hair, brushing it over his golden and well-built shoulders.

The gaze of his smoky green eyes lingered on her, his expression happy and relaxed, with maybe an edge of possession.

They'd spent the previous night wrapped in each other's arms. He'd seemed unusually nervous when they left the beach and had only loosened up at dinner, touched by stories of her little patients.

That night he'd taken her to his bed and made love to her passionately, almost frantically. He'd ridden her hard, sweeping her with his demanding need, over and over as if he would never tire of her, as if she held the key to his own self. Over and over, she'd been filled with contentment as he persisted in leading her body to ecstasy.

She'd known him for two days, yet it felt like forever—two days spent in each other's arms, sharing a passion she hadn't known before and couldn't understand. What would happen when she had to say good-bye?

Tomorrow he would drive her back home, only one more day, one more night together. She wondered what she'd tell Brianna and John at work on Tuesday. Brianna would surely be full of questions.

Just as Lily was.

Three days with a complete stranger, baring body and soul to him, and then what?

Go back to her responsibilities? Her regular life felt so far away. How would Angèle react if she brought Gabriel over for dinner, untamed in his dark clothes and biker boots?

"What makes you smile like that?" Gabriel drew a powerful stroke through the water.

"I don't know you at all." She let her fingers drag in the cold lake.

His lips curled into a half smile. "Really? I think I'm starting to know you pretty well."

"I've known you for what? Thirty-six hours?"

"Thirty-six hours is a pretty long time."

"Maybe in your world, but not in mine."

"My world?" He raised an eyebrow at her. "Are we from different worlds?"

"Oh, I don't know. I usually don't spend my weekends in bed with strangers."

"Neither do I, usually." He gave another effective paddling stroke. "But if I meet someone I like, no reason not to indulge."

His response shocked her. She hadn't wanted to hear that. "See, that's what I mean." She frowned. "Casual encounters are not really me."

"Why are you here then, spending the weekend with a stranger?" His expression was impossible to read.

"You're not exactly a stranger."

"So, now I'm not a stranger." He flashed his charming smile at her.

"You're teasing me again. What I mean is that I usually don't spend my weekends in bed with men I've just met."

"So, you don't go out of your way to get lost in the woods, just so you can get rescued?"

"Right."

He stopped paddling. "Lily, I know that." He stared at her, a serious look on his face. "There is no need to explain yourself to me. Life starts here. It's just you and me, that's it."

"And what about the part where you indulge with someone you like?"

He laughed. "It's not about indulging here." He looked at her with intensity. "You're my life, sweetheart, until the very end."

He put the paddle down in the bottom of the boat, slowly, still looking at her. His smoky eyes flashed as he started to undo his black leather belt, his gaze on her dark and brooding.

"You're the one I'm marrying."

Her heart fluttered. "Stop kidding." She lowered her lashes and drew one leg closer, setting her chin on her knee. "You'll hurt me, you know." She had to be honest with him.

He took off his pants and stood above her, entirely naked and glorious.

She couldn't help but gasp at the sight of his perfect body.

"Hurt you? I'll never do that." His face was dead serious. "Never."

He plunged into the cold lake in one smooth motion. Not a drop of water rained on her.

Swimming under the dark depths away from the boat, he disappeared from her sight.

She sat there alone for a long minute, then crawled to the back of the canoe to check if she could see him. She sighed with relief when he reappeared in the distance and hollered at her.

"Come and join me."

"No thanks. I like it nice and dry for now." She observed him as he swam away with perfect masterful strokes.

Her mind was still full of mixed emotions. She didn't know him, yet she wanted him. His intensity had shaken her. She should be scared that he'd said she was his life. Marriage . . . he must be kidding. This was all happening way too fast.

What frightened her more was that deep down, it was exactly what she wanted, a lifetime with him. How could she have such feelings when she'd known him for only a few days? And what would Angèle say?

Sure, her attraction to him was physical. He did things to her she'd never experienced before. Every time he stepped away from her, her body ached, hungry for his. She craved his closeness constantly.

But it was more. His crazy strength attracted her. She felt drawn to his foolish assurance. Life seemed an adventure for him, and she sensed nothing would go wrong in his world.

And he needed her, she knew that. There was this torment in him, something behind his casualness, his teasing smiles. Now and again, she saw a glimpse of it in his eyes.

She was drawn to that, wanting to be the one who would soothe his anguish, make him happy.

She looked at Gabriel swimming back toward her and felt her body arouse at the sight of his nakedness, of his powerful arms cutting through the water. Her need for him scared her. What if, no matter what he'd said, she was just another casual encounter?

She watched him emerge by the boat, water glistening on his sculpted chest.

"Nothing like cold water. It makes you feel alive." Gabriel climbed in, then flashed her a quick grin. "I guess I forgot a towel."

Turning his back to her, he stood naked and dripping at the front of the canoe. He grabbed the paddle and guided the boat toward the shore.

His back was broad, well defined and smooth, his buttocks firm and tight, individual muscles flexing with each stroke. She was dying to reach and trace them, cup his backside with both hands, but instead she just looked at him, filled with longing.

They were alone, surrounded by the still water and the rugged trees. An eagle circled the sky in the distance, high above the tall pines. Gabriel moved like a predator, completely at ease as he maneuvered the boat within a small cove. She felt as if she were back in time.

He belonged here, in the wilderness. He was part of it. They were all connected: the natural elements, the animals and the man before her. She felt like an outsider, sitting here in her modern summer dress. She longed to be part of his world, was urged to complement his strong masculine spirit, sensing her yearning clearly, at a very primitive level.

Gabriel sat down to put his jeans back on. "I think I'm dry now." He smiled at her over his shoulder.

Soon, Lily would be back to her old life. And she

honestly had a hard time picturing Gabriel in it. It was as though a spell would be broken as soon as she left the lake. But at least she'd have this image of him to cherish.

He fastened his leather belt as she kept her eyes on him.

"No underwear?" she said.

He shook his head. "Nah, too uncomfortable."

Eight

Screams pierced the calm of the day. The urgency of the shrieks unlocked Lily's first-response nursing training.

A girl on the lake shouted. "Mommy, come quick! Jayden, grab the paddle, come on." Lily heard more panicked screams. "Mommy, it's Jayden! He's in the water!"

Lily searched around her, focused on the echoes of the shouts. Then she saw them, two children and a small kayak, in the distance, near a small public beach. The children's small shapes were shadowed by the dark clouds that had started to gather overhead.

In a flash, she kicked off her flip-flops and dived into the lake.

"Lily!" Gabriel shouted behind her.

She hit the cold. The dress clung to her instantly, but her limbs moved freely.

Ripples started to build on the lake surface as the wind rose, but she swam fast, powerful strokes, similar to Gabriel's.

Reach, pull. She focused to get maximum speed. As she got closer to the children, she switched to a breast stroke to keep her head out of the water. Her heart steady, she surveyed the scene.

A little boy splashed in the lake, gulping water. An older girl knelt in a red kid's kayak, her long hair plastered on her face by the gusty wind, while she tried to get the boy to grab onto a small paddle. She cried and screamed for her mother. Neither child had a life vest.

When the girl saw Lily, she redirected her shouts. "Help! Help him, he's drowning!"

The little boy struggled more and more, trying to stay above water.

Soon Lily was upon him. "It's okay, sweetie, I've got you. Calm down." She saw the panic in his eyes, the fear, the instinct to fight.

A large wave threatened to swallow him.

She grabbed him by the arm, and he kicked her hard in the stomach, sending searing pain through her. He couldn't have been more than five, and his fighting instincts were strong. Like a wildcat in her arms, he smashed Lily with a few more kicks and struck her with his small fist. She didn't know how long she could hold on to him.

"Lily, you got him?" Gabriel was right behind her. "I'm bringing the boat around."

The boy still thrashed all over while Lily tried to keep her grip on him.

"What's his name?" Lily shouted at the little girl, her voice drowned by the gust.

"Jayden." She shook with sobs. "His name's Jayden."

"Jayden." Lily tried to bring the boy closer to her. "I'm Lily. It's okay. I'll take you to your mommy, sweetie. Relax."

The boy was still kicking and started to slip from her. Despite the pain mounting from his repeated blows, she remained calm. Without a second thought, she summoned the familiar power within her.

She grasped the small thread of strength rising into her and hung on to it. Focused on building it, she ignored everyone except the frightened little boy beside her.

Female voices suddenly filled her ears. This was different. She was somewhere else, still holding Jayden, and could no longer feel the water. In her consciousness, she saw a misty field, stones, things that were new to her.

But she also felt the well-known energy exploding in her, washing through her body. Channeling it, she sent serenity to the little boy.

All was still.

She looked at Jayden. He grinned, his whole body relaxed in her arms. The mist left her mind and she was back in the water. She heard Gabriel's strong voice mixing with the girl's sobs and felt the wet fabric of her dress clinging to her skin. "It's okay, Jayden. I'm taking you to your mommy."

"Bring him in," Gabriel said. She noticed the canoe right beside her.

Cradling her hand under Jayden's head, she kicked the water under her to keep herself straight. As she raised the boy with both arms toward the boat, Gabriel reached down and lifted him in.

"Wow, kid, you're a good swimmer." Gabriel rubbed the little boy's back. "You kept your head out of the water the whole time."

Shivering, Jayden looked at Gabriel with a tentative smile.

"Great job," Gabriel added.

"You held on really well, Jayden." Lily climbed on the canoe and collapsed to the bottom, exhausted. Her dress dripped and stuck uncomfortably to her back.

Jayden beamed now. "I'll tell Mommy I can swim," he said as his hand clutched Lily's dress and he settled his head on her lap.

Lily rubbed his back as hard as she could, trying to warm him up.

"Jayden!" The girl shouted at them, still in the red kayak. "Jayden, are you okay?"

"Poor kid, she must have been so scared." Gabriel shook his head as he navigated the canoe toward her plastic boat. He found a rope and used it to tie up the kayak.

"Come on, come here with us. We'll take you to shore." Gabriel grabbed her arm and the girl hopped into their boat.

"Jayden, I was so scared."

"Lucy, I was swimming. Did you see that?"

Lucy sat down and looked at Lily. "He was standing in the boat," she said in a small voice. "He was fooling around, and then he just fell." She started crying again.

"It's okay, sweetie, he's fine." Lily said. "You did what you could. Come sit with me."

Lucy sat down and Lily wrapped her arm around her. Relieved they were safe, she felt the girl's tension ebb as she held both children close.

"You were quick," Gabriel said to Lily. "One minute you were with me and the next you're swimming toward these kids."

"Emergency training." Lily smiled at him wearily.

Gabriel started to paddle toward shore, where a group of people waited, talking with animation, probably the parents and friends. He looked at her with the children. The wet yellow dress had plastered to her body, revealing the smooth curves of her hips. She must have been freezing, yet she held the children, thinking only of them.

For a brief moment, all thoughts of Evangéline left him. The woman who'd saved this child was different from his lost love. She was stronger, more resilient. Maybe he didn't know her at all.

Nine

"Those parents should have watched their kids a bit more." Gabriel sounded exasperated as they walked back to the boat from the lakeside picnic area, the children now reunited with their family.

Lily couldn't agree more. "At least they should have put life jackets on them."

"They seemed grateful at least."

"And they did give me a towel." She wrapped the colorful terry cloth around her dripping body.

They stopped to look at each other and burst out laughing. Gabriel suddenly scooped her into his arms and started walking.

"Put me down."

"Come on, you're like a wet cat, you're freezing. Let me help."

She was indeed freezing. Her head on his powerful chest, the heat from his body radiated through hers. The adrenaline rush had left her and she felt drained.

"You were amazing over there. I have never seen someone swim so fast."

She didn't answer, enjoying being in his arms.

"It's a shame those people didn't realize what you did. That little kid could have drowned."

"All those years on the swim team finally paid off." She snuggled closer to his chest.

He deposited her in the bottom of the boat with her back leaning on his seat. She pulled the beach towel closer to her, slumped like a rag doll.

Gabriel dragged the canoe into the water, then sat down with his legs around her while she rested her head on his thigh.

He paddled back home in silence, his legs keeping her warm. She enjoyed the quiet moment, grateful for his presence, for his strength. How nice to be able to let go, to lean onto someone you trust.

She caught a glimpse of what it'd be to have a lover in her life who would be there for her. For a moment, her days seemed empty. She'd always been independent. But Gabriel showed her another side of life.

"You really have the touch for calming panicked children, don't you? It was strange. For a while there, Jayden was screaming and kicking, and then he just calmed down."

"It's always like that. I tell them to relax, and they just do it. It never fails."

"Does it work on adults?"

"Don't know. I've never tried it." And she knew she never would.

"My girl with the magic touch. You're a witch."

"A witch?" The word took her aback.

He pressed his thighs harder around her. "Yes, my beautiful, caring, lovable witch. You're a sorceress. You've trapped me with your charms."

"Come on, Gabriel, I'm not exactly the type to bewitch anyone."

"Maybe you don't know who you really are."

She smiled in dismissal.

"I need to get you back. You'll catch something."

She felt conscious of her hair plastered down along her neck and over the towel. She must be a sore sight.

Gabriel paddled harder and they soon approached the Callans' house.

"Well, look who's here." Gabriel voice was low.

Lily glanced up and noticed two men on the shore.

She sensed a change in Gabriel, tension maybe. His strokes got longer and slower.

As they neared the shore, Lily got a better look at the men standing on the beach.

They were both tall and broad shouldered, dressed in black overcoats similar to Gabriel's.

Their expressions were flat, neither friendly nor unpleasant. All they spelled was danger and cold, incredible, raw power. They were perfectly still, not the smallest hint of movement about them except their coats flapping gently in the breeze. Their presence caused a strange prickling at Lily's neck.

One man had long golden hair flowing over his shoulders and sharp facial features. He wore all black: black boots, jeans and a fitted black T-shirt. His silver belt buckle with intricate symbols was the only interruption of his monochromatic look.

The other man's hair was dark and close-cropped. He had a hint of a smile that softened his deadly appearance and similar black clothes.

They stared at Gabriel and Lily, seeming to take in every detail, without any sign of strain from being so still.

"Hey," Gabriel said as the canoe hit the shore. "Look what the cat dragged in."

"Gabe, such a pleasure to see you." The blond man had a sophisticated British accent with a hint of French. "A nice little boat ride to soothe your nerves? I see you're taking good care of Morag."

"Morag doesn't need taking care of." Gabriel's voice sounded flat and dangerous, different. He planted his paddle in the shallow water and leaned on it. Then, he turned to the other man. "Loïc," he said with a nod. "What's up?"

"Gabe." Loïc smiled at Lily. His eyes were a deep black, completely unreadable.

"Lily, meet my cousins, Phoebus and Loïc."

Lily gave them a weak smile as they both nodded at her.

"Now, Voyager," the blond man said. "Are you done? Morag is waiting. We have some family issues to discuss."

"Phoebus, stop being an idiot. Lily's freezing." Gabriel got out, bare feet in the shallow water. "Now, help me with this boat."

Phoebus shook his head, walked directly to the canoe and grasped the rope handle. The murky lake water soaked his sleek black boots and the bottom of his oil-cloth overcoat, but he didn't appear to notice.

He looked up at Lily, his hand on the canoe, and in one swift pull hauled the boat halfway onto the beach. His abs bulged under the tight black T-shirt.

He smiled at her, a bright smile echoed by his eyes. She'd never seen a gaze of such striking ocean blue. It was gripping. "You look like you had a bad day." His voice was rich, enthralling.

"Yes," Gabriel said. "She got bored with me and decided to jump in the lake."

Phoebus raised an eyebrow, then turned to Loïc.

Loïc was expressionless for a moment. Then his face relaxed in a half smile as he studied the flock of geese paddling on the lake. Dark clouds obscured the sky. The breeze had picked up.

"Lily just saved a little boy." Loïc still surveyed the lake. "He was drowning." He spoke slowly in a deep soothing voice, without trace of an accent.

Lily stared at Loïc. Who could have told him that?

Phoebus stood. "That explains everything, then. Well, Gabe, hurry up. The lady's freezing."

Gabriel ignored him and helped Lily out of the canoe.

Her bare feet hit the moist sand. She craved a hot shower and dry clothes, and had no energy for polite conversation.

Phoebus took off his black coat and with a flourish, wrapped it over her shoulder. She felt instant relief. The coat brushed the ground, heavy and warm on her damp body. It enclosed her with its sophisticated scent, thick and spicy with a faint aroma of crushed herbs.

She gave Phoebus a grateful smile.

Gabriel tied the canoe to a low tree trunk and was soon beside her. His strong arm embraced her over the heavy coat.

She caught the dark glance he shot Phoebus.

Loïc gave a small sigh, almost undetectable, and turned away from the lake. "Not good. We need to talk."

"I know. I wish Roan was here." Phoebus shot Gabriel a somber look. "What's wrong with him, anyway?"

"Leave Roan out of this. Let's go."

They all walked up the hill, Gabriel's arm still tight around Lily's shoulder.

"I bet the old man showed you his red mercury," Gabriel said to Loïc.

"He did. Fascinating."

"Yes. Although I have better things to worry about." Gabriel flashed a teasing grin at Lily, then scooped her up in his arms. She let out a small scream, surprised by his quick gesture. As he picked up his pace, she held tight around his neck, her face buried in his shoulder.

"You'll have to stop carrying me everywhere like this," she whispered to him.

He laughed. "Why? It's fun."

All thoughts of Phoebus's refined scent left her. Gabriel smelled wonderful and tempting.

He strode ahead of the others and shouted, "Come on, guys. Morag's waiting."

Ten

The motorcycle pulled over in front of Lily's apartment building the next morning.

Her backside was numb from the half-hour ride, but resting against Gabriel's back and feeling his heat so close, she didn't want to let go. A few more seconds and she'd have to.

She hadn't seen much of Gabriel's cousins the previous evening. They'd departed soon after Lily emerged from a long restoring bath after the events at the lake. And she'd spent one last delicious night in Gabriel's arms.

But tomorrow, she'd return to work, settle back into her routine.

Angèle would be there, waiting for her. The pile of real-estate listings would still be on her desk for her to study.

Yet there was Gabriel, now warm in her arms, between her legs.

He eased the bike onto its stand. Lily slowly pulled away from him, then took off her helmet. Gabriel still straddled his bike as he removed his helmet and balanced it on one of the handle bars.

"There you are." Gabriel turned around to strap the helmet she'd handed him onto the side of his bike. "You're all set."

Lily looked at him. "My handbag."

"Right." He got off the bike to open one of his saddle-bags. "Here you go." He gave her the bag and leaned back on his bike to stare at her, still looking dangerous in his low-slung dark jeans and black leather jacket.

She clutched her bag to her chest. Would she see him again? He said he'd call soon. Did she want him to?

"Well, good-bye."

He didn't reply and gazed at her for a long time, without a move.

She just stood there, waiting, not quite knowing what to do.

He finally grabbed the collar of her cardigan and pulled her close to him, his legs straddling hers. As he clutched her sweater, he rested his forehead on hers. He sighed and closed his eyes.

Was he as upset as she was?

Trembling with emotion, Lily felt the warmth of his breath on her lips. He didn't move, as if he wanted to get his fill of her.

Then his mouth met hers, his lips tasting so familiar now. Responding hungrily to his kiss, she leaned even closer into him, grasping the rough leather that covered his back.

He wrapped his arms tight around her, the intoxicating scent of his jacket making her dizzy.

His kisses got deeper, full of passion. She welcomed them without a thought, her lips parting to meet his need. His tongue took possession of hers, tasting her, invading her sweetly.

His hands spread wide on the small of her back as he pressed her hips toward his hard bulging crotch.

Her lips burned for more. She couldn't get enough of him. All her emotions were bound in her kiss, surrendering to his insistence. Their tongues twirled, the cold autumn air making her seek his warmth even more. His lips crushed hers, marking her, taking her very soul.

Searing waves of passion descended though her whole body, her knees barely able to support her.

Her duties had receded into the back of her mind

again. She didn't want it to stop, didn't want him to go. She wanted to fold herself in his embrace forever. Oh, why did he have to leave?

He cupped her face in both hands, pulled away slowly from her mouth and gazed at her with tormented eyes. He then gave her one precious kiss on the mouth, brushing her lips with tenderness. He smiled as he edged her gently away from him.

She felt a sharp pain inside her as she let him push her back. He had to go. This was not meant to be. She didn't want him to call.

Stepping farther out of the way, she watched him as he straddled his bike and put his helmet on. He turned on the ignition, revved the engine a few times and gave her one more look.

Then he took off.

Lily stood there on the sidewalk, looking at the man riding away from her.

She sighed, a heavy burden descending upon her. Then she hiked the strap of her bag onto her shoulder and slowly headed to her apartment building.

"Angèle, have you ever taken a big leap of faith?" Lily hiked the handmade quilt over her as she nestled on the corner of her couch. "Done something bold?"

Watching her great-aunt walk in from the kitchen later that day, she yawned a little, fighting sleep in the familiar surroundings of her apartment, the place a little too warm as usual, the scent of Angèle's baking wafting in the air.

It was still early in the evening, but she was exhausted. How would she manage the whole work week ahead of her?

Angèle handed her a steamy mug of coffee before sitting down in the armchair beside her. "You mean like how you spent this whole weekend with a stranger?" A hint of mischief warmed her voice, while a twinkle gleamed in her eyes. "Gabriel, is it? A nice name."

"Yes, Gabriel." Frowning a little, Lily peered into Angèle's pert blue gaze. "Have you ever done anything like that, though?" As she cradled the mug in her hands, the events of the past few days played in her mind. She didn't know what to make of them.

"Well. It's not something we would have done when I was your age. Times were different." Angèle, prim as always in her neat wool skirt, cardigan and tiny slippers, laid her hands in her lap as she gave Lily her full attention. "It doesn't mean we didn't think of it." Her lips curled into a little grin.

Lily tilted her head and smiled kindly at her great-aunt. Warmth filled her to think of Angèle as a young girl. She must have been as full of life then as she was now.

"It was a big deal, this, wasn't it?" Angèle nodded with concern at Lily.

"You mean me and Gabriel?" Lily shrugged "I don't know." It was still so fresh in her mind, she hadn't had time to think it all through.

"When you called from his house you sounded different, excited, happy."

"I did? Well so much had happened. You know, I thought I'd die in the woods. And him rescuing me . . ."

"I know, dear." A show of concern played on her aunt's expression, and Lily felt bad for bringing up her ordeal again.

"I'm fine. Don't worry," Lily said.

"I know. I'm so grateful he found you." Angèle let out the tiniest sigh, and with her eyebrows raised, she carefully added, "You know, he could be the one."

"The one? You think?" It seemed quite unlikely at the moment.

"Why not?"

"Oh, I don't know," Lily said, a wave of fatigue over-taking her. She set her mug on the coffee table and tucked her knees under her. "Sometimes this whole relationship thing just sounds like too much work."

"You are always so serious, Lily. A boyfriend is a good thing."

"Maybe, but for now I just want to be here for you. That's all." Lily smiled at Angèle, meaning every word.

"Am I so much work that you can't have a boyfriend?" Angèle tried to speak lightly, but Lily knew she was serious. This was not the first time she'd expressed those feelings. How could she think Lily minded living with her?

"Of course not. You're not work, you're my whole fam-ily." Lily stretched to rest a hand on her aunt's knee over the thick wool of her skirt. "And with a boyfriend, it's dates and nights at each other's place. Where would you fit?"

"Oh, I'd find a place."

Lily knew what Angèle would say next, and cut her off before she had a chance. "Assisted living? No, not while I'm alive." She shook her head forcefully.

"Jean Desmarais is thinking about it. I could go with her."

Lily knew it was the last thing Angèle wanted to do. She wanted space, a garden. That's why she was working so hard for them to find a home. But Angèle would never admit it out loud, always careful not to put any more pressure on her niece, who worked so hard.

"Not another word on this, Angèle." Lily pushed her blanket away and sat straight on the couch. "You're stay-ing here with me. I'll buy us a house and it'll be just like when I was a kid living with you."

"But you have to live your own life, dear."

"I have my own life, and you're in it." She set her shoul-

ders back. "I don't need some guy messing everything up.
I'm perfectly fine without him, no matter how handsome
he is."

"That handsome?" The twinkle reappeared in Angèle's
eyes.

Lily nodded grimly. *Gabriel.* He would be hard to forget. "Yes, very."

"Sounds awful." Keira patted Lily's hand as soon as the
waitress left them with their usual drinks. "What a weekend. You must have been so scared."

The small bar where they often met after work was
quiet at this time of day. A few gilded mirrors on a background of jade green walls broke the monotony of the
dark wood paneling surrounding them. Bowls of dried
hydrangeas in faded blues and pinks had been arranged
here and there, enhancing the place's sultry atmosphere.

"Well, yes." Lily looked at her best friend as she circled
the smooth edge of her glass where the crystalline white
wine reflected the dim candlelight. "Being lost wasn't so
great. And those wolves were freaky." In truth, she'd almost forgotten about the woods. Her mind swirled with
the memories of Gabriel's possessive hands exploring her
body.

Keira nodded. "But not Gabriel. That wasn't bad."

Lily sighed. "No, not Gabriel." She hadn't heard anything from him since his motorcycle roared off, but then
again, it'd been only one day since he'd said good-bye.

But before Keira had a chance to probe further, Lily
said, "New outfit?"

Keira Black almost always dressed in business suits or
elegant dresses, but tonight she wore a slinky knee-length
lavender skirt that revealed every curve of her hips and
thighs. The skirt was topped with a pink mohair cardigan adorned with a fluffy leopard-print collar.

"Yes, do you like it?" Keira gathered the edges of the cardigan in attempt to cover the tiny purple push-up top she wore underneath.

"Well, it's different," Lily said.

Keira did look different in the dark atmosphere of the bar. Her usual sleek white-blonde hair had turned messy and wild. Her eyes were thickly rimmed with black, her lips pale but appearing bee-stung.

Keira laughed, sounding like a little girl suddenly. "It is, isn't it?"

She toyed with the bloodred oblong pendant that swung in the valley of her cleavage and started to slide it along its black silk cord. "My new boyfriend bought it for me."

She extended her foot. "The shoes, everything." She admired her black shiny leather pump, the large gold-studded leather straps wrapped around her fragile ankle.

"Oh." How unusual for Keira to have a boyfriend pick out her clothes. "How long have you been seeing him?"

"About a month of so." Keira shrugged. "I'm meeting him later. He told me to wear this."

"Told you?"

Keira bit her bottom lip. "Yes, told me." Her voice dropped lower, and pushing the frosted candle aside, she leaned over the table. Her unusual heavy floral scent enveloped Lily. "I've never had a guy instructing me what to wear before. Isn't it sexy?"

"Sexy? I don't know."

"What if Gabriel surprised you with a really sexy outfit and ordered you to wear it. Wouldn't that be exciting?" Keira's eyes were bright.

"I don't know, Keir. Gabriel is a strong guy, but he doesn't seem the type to order women around."

"No?"

"No, and besides, I don't think I'll be seeing him

again." Frustrated, Lily tried to push the memory of Gabriel away. What were the chances that he'd really meant all he said to her?

Keira shook her head. "Why in the world not? The man seems perfect. And he's obviously crazy about you. Are you dense?"

"The weekend was amazing. But it was also pretty intense. I'm not really ready for that. I just don't have time for a boyfriend."

"He doesn't want to see you again?"

"No, it's not that." In fact, he had said he'd call. "I'm busy, you know."

"Busy? C'mon, that's not an excuse for saying no to a guy you like. You're afraid, Lil." Keira stared hard at her. "You do this all the time. You're afraid that the men you meet will turn out to be like your father."

"No, I'm not afraid. It's just not the right time." With her thumb, Lily collected cool droplets from the side of her chilled glass.

"You need to let go, Lily. It's never the right time." Keira leaned back and crossed her legs, hiking the skirt high on her thighs. Lily flinched slightly to see the black ties of a garter belt crisscrossing Keira's skin, which shone so pale in the soft light. "Go with the flow," Keira added.

"With the flow?" Her jaw slightly tensed, Lily shook her head. "What, like you and your new guy?"

"Not just any guy. He's on the hospital's board of directors. A foreign businessman, from London. Extremely wealthy. He drops in on meetings now and again. You wouldn't know him." Keira took a slow sip of wine, then let it linger in her mouth. "And yes, you do need to let go, Lil. There's something really hot about letting a boyfriend lead for a while."

"Lead?"

"Yes, lead. The things we do, such a turn-on."

"Keira, are you okay?" Her friend ran the big human-resources department at the hospital. She wasn't the type of woman to be led and controlled. "You're not letting this guy do kinky stuff to you because he's rich and powerful, right?" Lily wondered suddenly if Keira could use this to get ahead.

Keira laughed. "No, don't get any crazy ideas. I haven't even slept with him yet."

"When you said 'things,' you know, you got me worried."

"Well." Keira giggled. "He did see me naked already."

"Oh?" Lily turned her gaze away from Keira for a second.

"Yes." She lowered her voice. "He likes to take me out to top-tier restaurants or a show now and again in Boston. And he asks me to do sexy little things for him, like wear a garter belt under my clothes." She displayed her lace-clad thigh again. "No panties, that sort of thing."

"Really?" Lily stared at her friend, while embarrassed by the slow tide of heat building inside her. She truly didn't want to know any more.

"It's so sexy how he tells me. Not asks me, tells me. He likes to touch me in public. But very discreetly, you know."

Lily shifted in the wooden bar chair as she grew more and more uncomfortable. "Are you okay with that?"

"It's a total turn-on. I love the illicit thrill." She rested her elbows on the small table and tilted her head to the side. "And oh, I don't know if I should tell you this, but . . ."

Lily sat up straight and raised an eyebrow, waiting. She definitely didn't want to hear this, but Keira obviously needed to share.

"He brought me to his place a few times. It's so beautiful. You can see the whole city from the living room. At night, it's gorgeous."

"So he is very rich."

"Very." Keira pressed the pendant to her mouth; then, with the smooth curved surface, she slowly traced her bottom lip. "Anyway, he sits back and watches me undress, then walk for him."

Lily swallowed. "Naked?"

"Yes, or just wearing something sexy."

Lily crossed her legs higher, still surprised to feel so flushed.

"That's it?"

"Yes, that's it. I once tried to go down on him, touch him, but he said it wasn't right yet." She frowned. "He was quite domineering that time. He pushed me away, hard."

"Sounds scary." Lily slid her drink aside, her breath a little short from Keira's confessions. She wasn't sure whether to be embarrassed or slightly turned on herself.

"No, Lily. Not scary, liberating. That forced delayed gratification . . . I don't know. It's so sexy." She sat back again. "He creates this incredible lust in me that just won't go away."

For a moment Lily felt she had a stranger in front of her.

"Keira, I'm not sure. Are you careful? You don't know this man."

"No less than you knew Gabriel. And from what you tell me, things got pretty heated last weekend."

Lily looked at the dark and rainy street through the bar's window. She took in a deep breath, disturbed by both Keira's lush perfume and her own thoughts. Must Keira remind her how little she'd known Gabriel before sleeping with him?

"Don't worry about me, Lil. I'm just having fun, exploring. I'm in complete control." Keira leaned back and recrossed her legs. "You should see his eyes when he looks at me. Theuron is totally in love with me."

"Theuron?"

"Yes, that's his name." She lifted her chin with pride in her voice. "Almost like mine. Sir Theuron Keir."

Lily finally drifted to sleep.

When she'd left Keira, she'd been troubled. Something had bothered her, that unnatural lust her friend had mentioned. It was vaguely familiar. Hadn't she experienced something similar for Gabriel?

Her time with Gabriel had been so beautiful and pure, though, no controlling or posturing. Just pleasure.

And now it was a nice memory, nothing more. She'd just brush Gabriel off when he called. If he called.

What she needed was a good night's sleep.

But as she slept, voices and faces kept dancing in her mind. First, it was Angèle, telling her to go back to the Callans' house and tell Morag about Keira's new boyfriend.

Then Morag herself, who lulled Lily with a soft and soothing voice.

The two of them strolled through a woodland clearing. The moon shone full and bright. The forest felt peaceful and welcoming, almost as if the trees were telling her she belonged there, that she was one with them.

Morag's red hair flowed loose, thick and curly all the way down her back and held by a braided cord circling her head. She wore a long fluid gown, reminiscent of those of Greek goddesses. Crossed golden bands, embroidered with black writing, sheathed her chest.

The dress itself was pure black, shiny and silky, made of a thin material that clung to every curve of Morag's perfectly proportioned body. The dress danced gracefully with each of her movements and brushed her bare feet.

A sword lay flat in her open palms, a large steel broadsword with intricate symbols carved on the naked blade. The hilt was adorned with twisted metal knots. Morag offered it to Lily.

"This is your destiny. Come, child, take what is yours. Come back to us."

Lily didn't want to move, but an unseen force, stronger than her will, drew her to step toward Morag. She reached tentatively for the sword.

"You are home now. You are safe." Morag's gaze lowered to the ground.

Lily glanced down. She stood in the middle of a five-pointed star surrounded by a circle—a pentagram, its appearance oddly bringing her comfort and joy. She took the sword by the hilt and laid it by her side, its tip to the ground, the weight too heavy for her to lift.

Morag smiled encouragingly at her. "Know your enemies." She pointed to the dark.

A shadow emerged.

An extremely handsome man strode toward them like a panther, tall and muscular with a strong, chiseled face. His head was shaved and Lily could see a black tattoo on the left side of his neck. He wore a black robe covered by a flowing cloak of the deepest red, evoking dried blood or dead red roses. Thick black bands covered in dark red symbols edged the cloak.

He was so magnetic that Lily started to walk toward him, almost stepping outside the circle.

Morag put her hand to Lily's shoulder to stop her. "Watch his true form."

The man's skin suddenly dissolved, flesh rotting, drying, exposing the bones underneath. The creature seemed unaware of the transformation of its body. Its eyes filled with longing, with deep secrets untold, until at last, they no longer looked human.

An incredible chill descended along her spinal cord, and her heart hammered in her chest. The handsome man had become a vision of pure horror, a rotten skeleton covered in a black robe and velvety dark red cloak.

"He wants you," Morag said.

Lily screamed in terror, dropped the sword and scrambled into the woods, away, as far away as she could from the horrible sight.

Moments later, she couldn't move. She lay flat on a cold hard surface, hands pinned above her head. As she tried to free herself, she realized her feet were bound too, her body naked under a plain white linen shift, the fabric coarse on her skin.

Tall, flickering candles were everywhere around her, blinding. Black shadows circled the platform upon which she lay. She felt incredibly weary.

The handsome man in the bloodred cloak was beside her, his hand on her forehead, soothing her like a child. She could see his face through her eyelashes and was fascinated by his neck tattoo, a triangle made out of intricate knots. The man was so powerful and enticing, she just wanted to please him, obey him.

He talked to her now. "Sleep, my love, sleep and you won't feel a thing." His hand caressing her hair, he smiled kindly at her. "Soon you will live in me."

Yes, I will. She wanted to believe him. Soothed by his deep black eyes, she just wanted to rest, feeling so close to sleep.

But something caught her attention as she was about to drift, something above his head. His hand was raised high and strong. He held something, something silver.

She strained to look. It was a dagger, ancient and sharp. And it aimed straight at her heart.

She recoiled in fear.

"Gabriel!" she screamed as she tugged at her bonds, twisting and thrashing.

The man disappeared and she was surrounded with smoke. She couldn't breathe anymore. All she saw were flames, tall and bright, dancing around her. The heat was intolerable. She couldn't move.

She kept screaming Gabriel's name.

And finally, she saw him, far in the distance, behind the fire embracing her. He strode toward her, dressed in fringed deer *hide, wearing a fur cap on his dark curls and carrying a musket on his shoulder.*

Hope filled her. Gabriel, the only one powerful enough to save her. "Help me." Her pleading voice was a raspy whisper. "Gabriel."

Lily suddenly woke up, her heart pounding.

She lay in her own bed. All was well. She listened to the familiar sounds around her: the fridge humming, the faint traffic noise in the background.

That had been truly scary.

She didn't usually have nightmares, but then again, it had been a disturbing week—the wolves in the woods, the strange Callans, Keira's unusual behavior. She really needed to go back to her simple routine.

Lily got up and went to the kitchen, poured herself a glass of water. A dose of reality, that was what she needed. The sooner she would go back to her routine, the better. Tomorrow, she'd go for a swim at the community center after work, one hundreds laps, no less.

She set her glass firmly on the kitchen counter. With a little willpower she could erase Gabriel from her mind forever.

Eleven

"Lily, did I wake you?" The voice on the other end was deep and sensuous, sending shivers along her skin, dissolving all resolutions of pushing Gabriel away.

"Gabriel, hi." She struggled to get her bearings. What time was it?

"I'm sorry, baby. I had a dream about you last night."

"Oh?" She shuddered, remembering the rotting creature and the flames around her. "Did you have a nightmare?"

"How can I have a bad dream about you?" His voice purred in her ear and erased the visions of last night. "No, it was more . . . intimate."

"Really?" She didn't quite like where this was heading.

"Are you still in bed?"

She glanced at the clock. Seven. Crap. The alarm hadn't gone off and now she was going to be late. "Not anymore."

"A shame. What are you wearing?"

"What do you mean? Right now?" She rolled her eyes.

"Yes. Are you naked or wearing something sweet and sexy?"

Her face flushed. His comments had started to arouse her. The thought of wearing something sexy for him shortened her breath. Her breasts felt heavy, and warmth started to spread between her thighs. Is this why Keira had given in to her lover's demands? Did she feel this too?

Lily frowned, irritated with herself. How could he make her feel so needy so fast? He wasn't even in the

room with her. "I'm wearing boxers and a tank top."
She hoped he'd cool off a little.

"What color?"

"What?"

"The tank top—what color is it?"

Her cell phone glued to her ear, she headed toward
the kitchen. The apartment was quiet, Angèle being a
late riser. She had to get to work and definitely didn't
like the turn this conversation had taken. "Why did you
call?"

"Please, tell me the color?"

"Pink. Gabriel, I have to go to work."

"Pink, sweet." He paused on the other end of the line
and she poured herself some orange juice. "I'm calling to
see if you want to go out to dinner with me on Saturday."
The question was so normal, it took her by surprise.

"You mean, on a date?"

"Yes, a date, a man and a woman, they go to dinner,
get to know each other."

She was grateful he'd stopped talking sexy. "Oh, that
kind of date. Did we not skip that part?"

"I guess we did." His voice purred. "But you felt so
nice, I couldn't resist you."

There we go again. I'll never be ready. She put a slice of
bread in the toaster.

"Yes, well, we did have a nice weekend. Although . . ."
She grew uncomfortable now. It was easy to tell Keira
that she couldn't see him again, but even on the phone,
he managed to affect her.

"What?"

"I don't think it's wise to take it further." Her hands
trembled. There, she'd said it.

"You don't want to see me again?" She cringed at the
shock in his voice.

"You make it sound so definite." She paused, setting her toast on a plate. "But I guess, well, I really can't see you again." She let out a deep breath.

"You can't, or you don't want to?" His tone turned icy.

"Both, I can't and I don't want to. It's too fast, I'm confused. You're not good for me."

"Not good. You can't say this weekend was not good."

Lily didn't know what to say.

"What we did was special, Lily. You had to know that. Surely you felt it too."

"I did, I did feel it. It scares me." She had to be honest with him. "I don't know how to explain it."

"Well, try." She could hear him trying to control his anger.

She stood barefoot in the kitchen. Her toast lay untouched on the plate. She'd grown so upset, she wanted to cry. "Gabriel," she started. "I like my life simple."

"What does this have to do with not seeing me?"

"Listen, during the week, I go to work, then go for a swim. On the weekends I clean the apartment, buy groceries and spend Sunday reading a good book. The biggest excitement I ever get is to go over to Keira's place to watch a movie. I've never traveled."

"That's all right, we can fix that."

"You don't get it, Gabriel. I don't want it fixed. I like my life just the way it is."

"Don't you want a family, someone to love?"

"I don't know about a family, mine was so messed up. I have Angèle. That's plenty, she's great. And I was thinking about getting a dog."

"I love dogs." His tone was lighter now. "And I'll love your great-aunt too."

"You don't understand. I don't have space or time for you. I have work and house searching and . . . I'm busy."

"Baby, all I know is I want to be with you. I can't stop thinking about you. We're meant to be together."

She could sense the angst in his raspy voice. It shattered her heart. Deep down, she felt the same, that she was meant to be with him.

But that was scary. She didn't want to repeat her mom's life.

"I am not asking for a big commitment, just dinner. I know you feel the same as I do. Give us a chance, please?"

Her defenses started to crumble. "I don't know. It's such a bad idea."

"Just dinner, come on. Pretend I'm an old friend, a buddy from the hospital."

Lily smiled. She imagined him working at the hospital. He was so incredibly different from her colleagues. "Dinner."

"Yes, just dinner. We'll talk. I won't put any moves on you, and if you decide to stop there, I'll never bother you again."

Her tensed muscles relaxed. He wanted to talk, in a public place, over dinner. She owed him that much.

She already knew what the outcome would be. They would part after dinner, like two civilized adults. She'd make him see her way.

Then she'd be free to go back to her old, reassuring life.

Shaking with mixed emotions, Gabriel flipped off his cell after she'd settled on a time for dinner. Why was she being so difficult?

He'd worked all night on a problem with Roan. Their distributer of aqua regia had shut down and they'd searched all over the web for a new one. Gabriel had finally found someone in Europe who could supply them with the acid, and he'd started the long process of filling out customs forms.

This morning, he'd been drained. The thought of Lily had been such a comfort. His longing for her had prompted him to call right away.

But the conversation had taken a strange turn. He didn't know how long she would persist in pushing him away. He wasn't used to being turned down. He found it slightly amusing, but then, digging deeper, he started to panic.

Dread returned in force, feelings long buried came back to haunt him. Evangéline, the hurt, the incredible pain as he'd watched her on the shore. He could still feel the humiliation of being beaten by an Englishman in front of his family.

He'd loved her with all his heart. They were young then, barely twenty, a young love full of promise, destroyed by a horrible twist of fate. And he'd wanted to believe Iain when the old man had told him he would see her again. He would have done anything to make it so.

And he did.

But still there had been no sign of his soul mate. Furious at having been deceived, Gabriel had escaped the Priory. He'd started his long search for Evangéline alone, first looking in the lush swamps of Louisiana, where the English ships had taken most of the Acadians. Then he'd made his long way up the eastern shore, back to the thick snowy woods of Canada.

An endless search, until he heard of her death.

Happiness. The word no longer meant a thing to him.

Morag had put Lily in his path. Or was it fate?

All these years, his heart had been in turmoil. And now, being in Lily's arms, he'd felt peace again, hope.

She was perfect, so like his Evangéline. He could almost believe they were the same. Lily was more modern, maybe, but still they shared an identical essence.

It enraged him to think that Morag had any part in that. He wanted their reunion pure, untouched. Lily should be shielded from all that was his life.

His fist tightened. *The Priory.* Both a blessing and a curse. There was no running from them. The only family he had.

He relaxed a little as an image of Lily crossed his mind. He recalled the softness of her skin on his fingers, her smile, the way she frowned when she was determined about something. He liked how methodical she was, all in control of her life. He would love that, an orderly life with her. How could she accept him?

She worried about his lifestyle. But how would she feel if she learned of his immortality, that he could alter the elements, that he engaged in an ancient battle of the souls?

Fear of losing her crept into his heart. Could he just keep her in the dark about that side of him? Or would she accept all of him? Join with him at the Beltane rite?

He would have to take it slow, court her. The weekend had been too fast.

She deserved more.

What do I wear on a break-up date? Lily stared at the pile of clothes on her bed, drumming her fingers on her naked thigh.

He was picking her up on his bike, so a dress wouldn't work. She wanted to feel in charge and confident. Plain black fitted pants were an easy solution. She discarded a top with spaghetti straps as being too bright, too sexy.

Finally, she settled for a clingy white long-sleeve shirt. The outfit showed off her body without revealing too much skin. There, not bad: urban and elegant.

On impulse, she grabbed her black high heels, a good four inches high. Definitely impractical, but they gave her more assurance. She let her hair loose, tumbling down her back, added silver hoops to her ears and put her tiny wallet and lipstick in her pocket.

Gabriel was due to arrive in a few minutes, so she sat down in the empty living room, Angèle having gone for the evening.

She fidgeted with the cushions. What if he made a scene?

She did want to see him again. She had to be honest with herself. But she shouldn't. She'd always known what was best for her, but this time it was hard to follow the voice of reason.

Almost seven o'clock—he'd be here in minutes. She grabbed her favorite novel and tried to concentrate on reading, ignoring the palpitation of her heart.

She'd just started to settle when she heard knocking.

This was it. Time to gather her courage.

Taking a deep breath, she walked to the door, catching a quick glance at herself in the mirror in the entryway.

But upon opening the door, all sensible thoughts left her.

He leaned on the door frame in his usual black jeans, with a faded gray T-shirt and motorcycle boots. With his full-length black coat, he looked like a modern Jesse James, dangerous but with tremendous sex appeal. No one would want to mess with him.

"Hi, baby." The twinkle in his eyes and his charming smile offset his dark appearance.

She wanted to run into his arms, where she knew nothing bad could ever happen, but she restrained herself. This was turning into a difficult evening.

"You look beautiful," he said.

"Thank you." That was all she could say.

Both were quiet while they looked at each other.

He broke the silence. "Do you like Italian?"

"Love it."

"There's a little place I know downtown. It's really good."

"Sure. Let's go."

Before she could react, he got hold of her waist and his demanding lips took hers with possession. Her knees buckled as his kissed her furiously.

He then slowly released her, a burning look full of promise in his eyes. "Now we can go."

Still shaken, she vowed not to let herself be caught off guard again. This had felt much too good. It would definitely be a complicated evening.

Half an hour later, they sat at a quiet table at the back of a small restaurant. Only a few tables filled the place. Paintings of popular Italian sites hung on the wall. Music filtered through some hidden speakers, making Lily loosen up a little as she recognized the rich baritone voice of an Italian singer over a background of smooth jazz.

"Tell me more about this house you want to buy."

She had told him of her project shortly after the young hostess seated them.

"I've been working for six years now. Each month, I put a little away. Now I have enough for the down payment, the closing cost and all that."

"Wow, you've really planned this."

"Yes. It's important to me."

"You're smart."

"Well, buying makes so much more sense than renting. It's better financially. I know a few single women who own their own homes."

"Smart and practical." He smiled at her.

"Well, I do have to look after myself. If I start paying off a mortgage on a house in my late twenties, I'll feel much more secure."

"You don't feel secure now?"

She sighed. Did she really want to explain herself to him? "Well, it's more than financial. I'd love to have my own place, you know, paint it, fix it a little. I dream of a big flower garden and a nice patio." She gave him a little smile. "I watch all the home-improvement shows on TV."

"Lily the builder." His expression filled with tenderness as he took her hand in his on the table, his touch warm and comforting.

"You know, I never really had a home growing up. My father left my mom when I was a baby and he never wanted me around. I only started seeing him later, when I was a teenager and had stopped asking to go live with him."

"Sounds terrible. So you still see him?"

"Now and again. He lives in California."

The waitress came back. As she set their drinks down, she completely ignored Lily, her attention focused on Gabriel. When she left, her hips swung seductively in her long clingy black dress.

"I think she likes you." Lily nodded toward the waitress.

Gabriel squeezed her hand, his thumb slowly rubbing the sensitive skin of her wrist. "How about your mom, what is she like?"

"My mom died a few years ago. Cancer."

"I'm sorry."

"Thank you." She was silent for a moment. "I miss her. She had a hard life. In fact, she was really hurt when my father left her." Lily took a sip of wine, then said, "After the divorce, she kept getting new boyfriends, one after the other. She would cling to them, so desperate for love."

"What about her child? She must've known you loved her."

"I think she loved the excitement of falling in love. She would meet someone and become so happy. She'd be a lot of fun then. The new guy would move in and after a few weeks she would send me to my great-aunt Angèle. I guess Angèle felt responsible for me. She's really my dad's aunt. And she doesn't have any kids."

"Did you stay there long?"

"Depends. Sometimes I was there for a few months. Once, it lasted a whole year. I got tired of packing and unpacking. I had to change schools many times. I hated having to make new friends."

"That's a terrible way to treat a child."

"I know. I can't blame her, though. I loved my mother and she suffered in the end. Her life was short and difficult."

"Somehow, I can't see you doing that to your child."

"I'm different from my mom." She frowned, then looked at him. "I don't know if I'll ever have children. I'd have to be married for a long time. And I'm settling down in a house before I can think about any of that."

"No love at first sight, then."

He'd brought up the touchy subject. Her attraction for him had been strong the minute she'd laid eyes on him. As if she'd known him forever. But could she tell him that?

"No, I don't believe in it. I think you have to take a lot of time to get to know each other, before even thinking long term."

"Isn't that a little too reasonable?"

"Maybe, but it's much better to make sure you can handle the long haul instead of burning up in an intense few weeks." She was relieved when the waitress brought their plates of pasta.

They ate in silence for a moment. Then he said, "What's your great-aunt like?"

"She's great, full of life. It was wonderful to live with her when I was little. Her house was beside a small river. I used to sit in the garden and watch the water run. The Callans' house reminded me a lot of that time I had at Angèle's. Maybe I'll look for a property along a river."

"Then you'll need my help if you get flooded." He raised a teasing eyebrow at her.

She smiled. "Lily the builder, remember?"

"Actually, I can believe that. So, what will I help you with?" He raised his eyebrows playfully. "I guess I'll think of something."

Remembering what he was so good at, his hands on her body and his mouth tasting her, she felt her cheeks flush. "Gabriel, why did you come in and mess up my life?"

"Why do you say that?"

"I don't want a relationship right now."

"I know, you told me, the house first. But life doesn't always run the way we want. Sometimes you have to change plans."

"How do you know?"

"I was in love once. I was much younger. We were perfect for each other. All ready to get married, and then we were separated."

"She left you?"

"Well, not exactly." He paused. "Let's say that I never saw her again."

"Did you look for her?" Lily really wanted to know what had happen to Gabriel. There was this shadow in him that never quite left him.

"It's complicated." His eyes were dark. "I shouldn't have brought it up." He sat back in his chair. "My point is that life takes all these turns, and you have to adapt to them. Like now, you and I have met. Maybe there's a reason. You have to hold on to the few beautiful things life brings you."

Lily stayed silent for a moment. "You have a lot of secrets."

He looked at her and she couldn't read his expression. "Some things are better left unsaid."

He sounded angry—or weary, maybe? She couldn't

tell. Had his girlfriend died? She felt terrible for him. But then, she had to protect herself. "Gabriel, it's too hard for me to see you right now."

"Why?"

"It's too fast. I've had this dream for so long, to get this house and settle down, just me and Angèle."

"There's nothing wrong with your dream. In fact, it sounds wonderful. I'd love to be in a house that you set up. I'd help you look after your aunt. Old ladies love me."

He was insistent, but she couldn't see how it would work. "But what about *your* life? You like to travel, your job. You'd be bored after three months with me."

He signed. "Lily, I'd never be bored with you. I can work from wherever I am. All I need is an Internet connection. That's easy enough to do. So I can be part of your life. I'll take you around and we can travel."

"What about my work?"

"Don't you have holidays? You can work abroad too, you know?"

"You're forgetting Angèle."

"Don't worry. We'll take her with us. I can afford to hire a caregiver for her. Our family has a lot of resources."

Lily smiled. She bet her aunt would love that, to go to Europe and visit the Old World. She'd always dreamed of visiting Paris, and also Normandy, where her ancestors had originated.

She shook her head. "Gabriel, let's be realistic. I've known you for a week."

He looked at her for a while, his expression full of tenderness. "Really? I feel like I've known you forever."

Twelve

Moments later, Lily winced at the ringing of Gabriel's cell phone.

He glanced at the screen. "Sorry, I know it's rude, but I've got to pick this up. It's Phoebus."

Gabriel put the phone to his ear. "What?" He picked up his knife and rubbed his thumb along the blade.

"Where, here? What the hell is he doing?" He sounded angry, squeezing the knife handle.

"Well, I won't let him." He'd almost shouted that. "You guys just keep an eye on him. I'm bringing Lily."

Lily looked at him, puzzled, as he turned off his phone. Where did he want to take her?

"Want to go clubbing? Phoebus is over at the Blue Circle by the docks. He wants me to go over for a bit. Normally, I'd much rather be alone, but I think it's important. Sorry."

They really hadn't sorted out all she wanted to discuss. But he seemed nervous about something. She knew the call hadn't been casual. And they couldn't get too intimate if they were around other people. "Let's go then."

He seemed relieved at her answer.

They paid for their meal and headed for his bike.

A few minutes later, he parked in a deserted lot. A large sign with a neon blue circle was the only thing announcing the club, a plain brick building with no windows.

They took their helmets off and clipped them to the bike. She still wasn't too excited about going to a nightclub. She'd never felt comfortable in them.

He reached for her hand as if he'd sensed her hesitation. "Let's go, baby. You're with me tonight."

She said nothing but felt a bit better as they reached the entrance. People stood in a long line, wanting to get in.

Gabriel ignored them and went straight to the door. "What's up, Frank?" The doorman was heavy built, dressed in a dark suit over a black shirt.

"Hey, Gabe, my man." They high-fived each other. "What's going on tonight? Your cousins are here."

Thumping music resonated through the door entrance.

"Yeah, a family reunion."

"Who's the lovely lady?" Frank admired Lily.

"Lily, and keep your hands away from her. She's mine." Gabriel could have said, "She's with me," but the way he said she was his, possessively, made her body tingle.

"Have fun, guys."

"Sure." Gabriel put his hand on the small of Lily's back to lead her in.

The club was dark, the dance music so loud Lily couldn't recognize the song being played. She could only sense the heavy beat echoing through the floor.

Beautiful people stood everywhere, especially women, with their perfectly groomed hair and faces, and wearing incredible shoes. Most had on pastel little dresses that stretched seductively every time they moved and showed legs tanned to perfection. The latest handbags dangled from their toned arms.

The air smelled of expensive perfume and repressed sexual urges.

Lily was glad she'd chosen heels to go out in. They hadn't been too comfortable on the ride over, but now they made her feel confident.

Women turned toward Gabriel as they walked through the crowd. They smiled seductively at him, trying to catch his attention. But he didn't seem to notice, his hand holding hers tightly.

Her gaze was suddenly drawn to a mane of blond hair and a dark long coat.

Phoebus was there, still impossibly handsome. A hint of relief eased within her. She was glad to see his familiar face.

He was talking with an extremely sexy black-haired woman in tight leather shorts. She wore knee-high black boots and a black tank top that left her flat navel exposed. Her thick hair was braided down to her backside. A long black leather coat lay folded in the crook of her arm.

Celtic knots braced her bicep. She was superbly attractive, the large tattoo on her arm giving her an air of danger.

Gabriel noticed Phoebus and the woman. "Phoebus," he yelled.

The music blasted too loud for anyone to hear his call, but Phoebus turned his head toward them.

Gabriel bent down toward Lily. "That's my cousin Tara next to him."

They approached Phoebus and Tara.

"Lily." Phoebus flashed her an intriguing smile, his ocean blue eyes full of secrets. "A pleasure to see you again."

Lily nodded and smiled politely as she edged closer to Gabriel.

"Lily, my cousin Tara," Gabriel said. "Tara, this is Lily."

Lily became speechless suddenly, intimidated by the incredible woman in front of her. People only looked like that in magazines or in action movies.

"Lily, I'm so glad to meet you." Tara's voice was friendly, with a faint foreign accent. She took Lily's hand in hers and Lily sensed both caring and a lot of confidence. "I've heard a lot about you."

"I'm glad to meet another cousin of Gabriel's."

"She's already met Loïc, last weekend." Gabriel said.

Tara smiled. "We do like to keep in touch."

"He's right there." Phoebus sounded more serious now as he nodded toward a corner, where two men sat with a group of women who had a lost look about them. They had black-rimmed eyes and long hair and wore an odd mix of lingerie, fur and black leather. An eerie feeling overtook Lily from just looking at them.

"Has he seen you?" Gabriel asked Phoebus.

"We're a bit hard to miss, don't you think?" Phoebus said.

"He's watching us now," Gabriel said. "Bet he thinks we're scared of him."

"And we're not?" Tara said.

Gabriel just smiled.

What had Lily walked into?

A group of people passed by them, careful not to bump Gabriel or Phoebus. Tara drew a lot of attention from some of the men, but as soon as they got closer, they seemed to lose the courage to approach her and left.

Lily suddenly wished she were sitting back home in her sweats, reading a good book. The music was too loud and her companions seemed definitely worried.

Gabriel pulled her close in front of him. He wrapped both arms around her shoulders as if to shield her from the club atmosphere.

"I'm sorry, Lily. You must wonder what's going on. See that guy over there?" He gestured discreetly at the group sitting in the corner. "The one in the suit? He's an old business rival. He's English, Theuron Keir."

Lily froze. Theuron Keir, Keira's new friend. "My

friend Keira knows someone by that name. I wonder if it's the same person."

"Probably is. I bet no one has the honor of sharing his name," Phoebus said with contempt.

"Please do a favor for your friend, Lily," Tara said. "Tell her to stay far away from him. He's very dangerous."

Lily would have liked to ask more questions, but Tara's expression was dark, frightening. For a moment, Tara hadn't appeared quite real.

Lily shivered and leaned back even closer in Gabriel's arms. "I thought you worked in shipping?"

"I do, but I'm also involved in the family business. Morag and Iain are independently wealthy—lots of old family money that's invested all over the world."

"Theuron's an old enemy of the Callans." Tara still examined Theuron and his entourage.

"And he never bothers to come to America," Phoebus said.

"I'd really like to find out what he wants," Tara said.

"Simple, I'll just go ask him." Gabriel gently took Lily by the elbow and started to take off toward Theuron's table.

"Gabe, wait. Don't be stupid," Tara called after him. "Phoebus, what's he doing?"

Gabriel ignored her.

"That's my boy," Phoebus said. "Come on, leave him be, Tara. It will be fun."

Gabriel, all muscles and black clothes, soon stood in front of the businessman. He held Lily close and she could feel unnatural power radiating from his whole body.

"Theuron." Gabriel appeared calm, his hand around Lily's waist. "What the hell are you doing here?"

The man sitting on a couch before them lifted his eyes slowly, then stopped to fix them both in a deadly stare.

Lily's blood ran cold. The shaved head, the tattoo . . . If it weren't for his dark business suit and the crisp white shirt, she would have sworn he was the man from her dream.

One of the women sitting next to him stretched. She had on black stilettos, a short peach silk skirt and a loose silver top that left her back bare and exposed her dark nipples through the fabric.

To Lily's astonishment, she lowered herself and put her head on Theuron's lap, her long legs lying on the dark velvet couch. Then she curled up like a toddler near the man's thigh.

Theuron slowly stroked her naked back, his long elegant finger trailing on the perfect white skin, while the other women gazed blankly around, apparently not noticing Gabriel or Lily.

The man who'd been sitting near Theuron stood up without a word and edged toward them. He was completely bald, his head covered in intricate tattoos. Lily looked at him nervously.

"Bear, leave it. They're acquaintances." Theuron return his gaze to Gabriel as Bear sat still again. "Now, who do we have here? One of Iain's little protégés. Gabriel, I presume. I heard you like playing with the wind?"

"Got to love the weather. I did pick up a few new tricks, though. All those years, one gets curious. I should show you someday." Gabriel appeared relaxed, but Lily could feel his tensed muscles ready to uncoil at any sign of trouble. He pushed her gently as if to shield her and added, "So, what the hell are you doing here?"

Theuron ignored him and turned his attention to Lily, who was already paralyzed with fear. She had no idea what the men had been discussing, but she was anxious to warn Keira about the man in front of her.

Visions from the dream rushed back at her, the dagger

raised above her still vivid in her mind. His eyes smoldered pitch-black, like a deep bottomless pool. She remembered Keira, the bloodred pendant between her breasts. Her confessions, how she'd walked naked, knelt in front of him.

He now stared at her, her only. She felt his gaze, deep, intense, like he was undressing her. And suddenly a deep yearning swelled in her. She wanted to reach out to him, wanted to know more.

There was so much darkness emanating from him that she ached to merge with it, neutralize it. Her core became very warm as she craved his touch. She took a step toward him.

"*Cuir crìoch air,*" came a whisper in her ear.

She blinked. She was back in Gabriel's arms again, safe, away from the dark.

What had just happened? She turned to Gabriel, troubled.

Looking hard at Theuron, he folded her tighter in his arms. "Don't even think about it," Gabriel said to Theuron.

"Just a little amusement."

"Words of warning: stay far away." Gabriel's voice remained dead calm. Then he suddenly turned away, and they walked back to his cousins. Something had shaken him, and yet she knew it wasn't fear.

"What does he want?" Phoebus said when they returned to him.

"Not sure." Gabriel still held Lily close to his chest, as if he could lose her.

Something passed between the cousins.

"We have to see Morag," Phoebus said. "And you need to come with us."

Tara turned to Gabriel as she put her coat on. "Sorry, it's best Lily goes home."

"You're right. I wasn't thinking." Gabriel shook his head. "Lil, sorry, I have to get you back."

Something was seriously wrong and they wouldn't tell her.

Part of her was glad to go back to her place, but she felt dismissed by them all, like she stood on the outside of their tight group.

She looked at her companions. First Gabriel and Phoebus, tall and broad in their black coats. Then Tara, even more fearsome and enticing, her coat brushing the floor and partly covering her extremely sexy outfit, all naked thighs and black leather.

Lily said nothing as she let Gabriel lead her out of the bar, Phoebus and Tara following close behind.

She held tight through the whole ride back to her apartment. She was shivering and confused by what had happened at the club. She needed to call Keira right away to warn her about Theuron.

When they finally climbed the steps inside her building, her tension ebbed slightly.

Gabriel left her on her doorstep after a passionate kiss and a promise to contact her soon. Lily closed the door behind him, then leaned on it to compose her thoughts.

And that's when she remembered she'd completely forgotten to break up with him.

Thirteen

"Hello, beautiful."

The sight of Gabriel, wearing cargo pants and nothing else as he opened his door, caught Lily's breath. She clutched the heavy grocery bag in her arms.

He reached out to relieve her of her burden. "Welcome to my place." An apologetic grin curled his lips. "Not much of a place, really."

"Hi." She returned his smile, waiting for the kiss she knew would come. Having admitted to herself she could no longer resist him, she'd again agreed to another date, their fourth, her first in his apartment. He'd asked her to dinner tonight, and she'd volunteered to cook.

A voice interrupted them. "Oh, hi, Lily."

Tara? What was she doing here?

Gabriel edged aside to make way for the beautiful woman. In plain jeans and a simple black T-shirt, she still managed to look incredibly sexy. Had Gabriel invited Tara as well?

Lily gave him a puzzled look.

"Tara's on her way out." He shifted the grocery bag to his left arm, then led her in, his hand splayed wide in the middle of her back. His firm touch spread luscious warmth down her backside and around her hips.

"Yes, no worries." Tara took the brown bag from Gabriel and disappeared into what appeared to be the kitchen. "We'll soon be gone."

We? Who else was there? Lily peeked inside the place with caution.

"It's fine. I don't mind," she said as Gabriel led her to the living room.

Everything was stark: wooden floors, black leather couch and not much else, except for the impossibly handsome blond man in a dark suit leaning back in a black armchair as if he owned the world.

Phoebus.

Caught for a moment between Gabriel's strong touch at her back and Phoebus's sensual gaze, she was at a loss for words.

Phoebus jumped to his feet. "Ah, the very beautiful Lily." His British accent seemed more obvious than she remembered from last month.

"Please." He gestured to the seat that still retained the imprint of his tall and powerful body. "Have a seat."

Gabriel shot him a warning look. "Hey. This is my place. Lily is my guest." The possessive tone in his voice was impossible to miss.

"Just making her comfortable, that's all," Phoebus said while Lily settled in the leather chair, where his sophisticated scent still lingered.

She stared at both of them.

"Right." Gabriel's look was dark.

"What?" Phoebus turned to Gabriel and his smile vanished, replaced by a somber expression.

Lily made herself still, caught off guard by the sudden change in Gabriel's guest.

"Don't push, Falconer." Gone also was Gabriel's usual playfulness. A ripple of muscles descended from his wide naked shoulders and along his powerful arms, emphasizing the Celtic brace inked on his left bicep. His controlled anger was palpable in the small living room.

Phoebus held Gabriel's gaze for a few seconds, then said slowly, "I do what I want, Voyager." He'd said the last words carefully as a feral smile curved his lips.

Lily held her breath, hoping Tara would soon make an appearance.

Gabriel was dead calm at Phoebus's words. "Not with me here," he said.

Power emanated from him. He looked bigger and more lethal than ever, his temper ready to explode.

Phoebus, in his well-cut suit and immaculate white shirt, looked equally deadly, with maybe a hint of viciousness. He held his gaze steady, his stance wide, arms at his side.

Both men stared at each other for what felt like hours.

Tara walked into the room. "Okay, honey. Let's go."

Lily let out a slow breath of relief.

Phoebus broke the deadlock and raised his eyebrows at Tara. "Honey?" A slow grin reappeared on his lips.

"Come on, Phoebus. Let's leave the two lovers alone." She smiled warmly at Lily. "We'll get out of your way." She picked a black leather messenger bag from the floor and hiked it across her shoulder.

"Yeah, good idea, Tara." Gabriel's tone turned light as if the tension Lily had witnessed had never occurred. Yet it still betrayed an underlayer of hostility. "Time's up, guys."

Lily remained silent, anxious to have him all to herself away from his cousins, relieved as he sat on the floor beside her and placed a hand on her thigh. His fingers traced the seam of her jeans.

Phoebus took out a sleek black cell phone from his pocket while he flashed Gabriel another hostile look.

Then he smiled at Lily in a most delightful manner, without a sign of the heartlessness his expression had revealed earlier. "Mademoiselle," he said in his deep sensuous voice.

Lily nodded, not sure what to make of him.

Without another word, Tara and Phoebus disappeared and Lily found herself alone with Gabriel in his apartment.

The tension between them became suddenly more palpable. This was the first time they'd been by themselves since the Labor Day weekend at the Callans' house. Their dates had been great: a movie, dinners . . . He'd even once taken her on a small country road to teach her how to ride his motorcycle. Yet she'd always avoided this, them alone together, close to a bed.

He caught her cautious look toward the open door that obviously led to his bedroom.

"Baby, I missed you," he said, even though they had seen each other just a few days before.

She knew what he meant. He missed their time at the Callans' house. They had kissed frequently since then, while he'd run his hands intimately over her body, leaving her in a flush of heat. But they had not taken it further.

"So did I." Her voice shook a little as she slid her fingers through his hair, pushing the dark strands away from his eyes.

Warmth mixed with caution rose in her heart. She couldn't guess how he felt about her. He hadn't professed his love yet. She kept expecting it, but so far, nothing. Too soon perhaps?

He knelt up in front of her and rested his hands on each side of the armchair, hovering over her, practically trapping her.

She looked up at him, his smoky green eyes full of darkness somehow. How could she forget the power he had over her?

Her breath shortened and she suddenly blushed. "Should we put the groceries in the fridge?"

He laughed. "Nervous?"

She smiled at him. "A little."

"You haven't yet been caught all alone with me, have you?"

She swallowed, deliciously aware of his strong arms solidly anchored at each side of her, making any escape impossible.

"No, we haven't been alone in a while." She glanced at the tensed muscle of his forearm, blocking her way.

"I'm not letting you go this time." He bent closer, his familiar scent reaching her at a deep level. When he brushed his lips on her forehead, she sighed involuntarily. Perhaps she didn't need to hear he loved her. Perhaps this was enough.

"When do you go back to work?" he added. "Monday?"

She nodded. Her nervousness edged away.

"Then I have two whole nights to seduce you."

"You plan to seduce me?"

"Oh yes, babe. It's been too long. I've had a wonderful time with you these past weeks, but I want more." His expression showed his care but also his power, his urge. This time, she would not be able to sidestep the inevitable.

"I needed time." She had. Still not sure where this would lead, she hadn't been ready to sleep with him again.

"I know. I gave you time. But now you're ready." His words shook her a little. The way he'd said them didn't give her much leeway to contradict him, yet she also found this strangely comforting. He cared for her, she knew that much.

His lips brushed hers gently. Then he pulled away a little, his taste still on her lips, making her want more.

"You want me," he said. "Don't deny it."

"I won't." It had taken her a while to let her defenses down, but in the past weeks, her attraction for him had grown to a level where she knew she had to take that risk. She could no longer deny the love growing in her heart.

He bent down farther, and this time his lips brushed her neck, sending a trail of shivers down her breasts, her belly, lower even. An incredible desire burned in her. He knew her well; she wouldn't deny him this time. Whatever the future held didn't matter. She wanted him—now, in this moment.

His lips rose to her hairline. He nibbled the sensitive skin just below her ear.

She moaned as she stroked his naked chest, then slid her hands down his sides, tracing the curve of his muscles, so tight under her fingers.

"That feels nice, sweetheart," he whispered. "Your hands on me. I did miss you."

"I know," she said.

"You want this? With me? You do, right?" He pulled back to stare at her, his expression suddenly serious.

She nodded. "I do, yes." Her heart swelled with emotions. This was more than pure lust. She wanted to be with him, feel him close. She was being drawn deeper into his pull and just didn't know how to stop.

She raked his hair away from his forehead again and let a silky curl weave around her finger. "I so want you."

He smiled. "Say it again."

Slowly, she said, "I want you."

He took a deep breath, then hovered over her again. "Kiss me," he breathed close to her ear. Tendrils of pleasure descended from her sensitive earlobe down to the cradle of her neck.

With her head thrown back, she reached for his lips, so incredibly soft and yielding under hers.

"You taste so good, babe. I want to taste all of you."

She drew in his masculine scent. "You do?"

"Yes." His voice was soft in her ear. "Kiss me again."

She did. This time, he grasped the back of her head and pressed her toward him, his mouth forcing his way into hers, his tongue swirling inside her, invading her.

Her body, already aroused just by his presence, shot to another level of need. Her core grew hot and moisture spread between her legs. There was nothing she wanted more now than his warm naked skin on hers, his powerful hands all over her body, leaving nothing untouched.

With eagerness, she traced his skin. She wanted to explore all of him, make him hers. Make him forget everyone else before her. Make him love her.

She could no longer deny her feelings for him, couldn't deny that she loved him.

He let go of her mouth and looked at her, fever burning in his eyes. She shook to the core, mesmerized by him, by the power he had over her.

"I want you, Gabriel," she said, yielding to his force.

"Oh, baby, I love you." His hand descended along her hips. He leaned back and pulled her against his chest. "I love you so much."

She closed her eyes for a second, reveling in his words. A powerful passion surged in her.

Love her. He did love her.

She rested her head on his shoulder. "You love me?" she whispered.

He pulled back and cradled her head gently between his palms. "I love you. Do you doubt it?"

She looked into his smoky eyes to see the sincerity in them. "No. I don't. It's just . . ." She lowered her gaze.

"What?"

Placing both hands over his at each side of her face, she stared at him. "You never told me. This is the first time."

"It is?" He let go of her head to grip her shoulders, drawing her hair back.

"Yes."

"I never told you I love you?"

"No." The thought that had lingered in the back of her mind was now out in the open.

"Oh, babe." He embraced her again. "I've loved you since I first saw you at the gas station." He squeezed her hand and looked hard at her. "You love me too, don't you?"

His question caught her off guard, and she paused for a few seconds, then nodded silently.

"See, I knew it." His lips curled into a charming smile.

"Yes, I love you." There, she'd said it. She loved him. A peaceful feeling washed over her. All this time, she'd waited for him to say so, when it was all simple really. She loved him, no matter what.

"I love you, Lily." His featured softened. He stared as her as if he wanted to brand her image in his mind.

He leaned his lips to her ear again and his sensual voice made its way steadfastly through her core. "Come, let me show you."

"So you have come for her, at last."

Gabriel's blood ran cold as he stared at the kind face of Angèle Bellefontaine in the cozy kitchen she shared with Lily.

Later that week, he'd finally gotten to meet Lily's great-aunt. And now, after some introductions and chit-chat, Lily had left them alone for a few minutes.

Mrs. Bellefontaine set her teacup down. As she lay a gentle hand on his, a strange tingling ran through his veins. "Gabriel LaJeunesse."

Speechless, he stared at her. No one had used that name in centuries. Morag had said nothing about Mrs. Bellefontaine knowing them. Did the old lady also have powers?

Gabriel glanced at the doorway where Lily had disappeared minutes ago. Did she also know his real name?

Mrs. Bellefontaine shook her head. "She doesn't know anything."

Her grip on him tightened. "*Mon cher Gabriel*, you see, my grandfather was very fond of legends." She now stared at him with intensity, her bright blue eyes sparkling. "He used to tell us all kinds of stories when I was a little girl, ghost stories mostly, the seven o'clock monster, the loup-garou—you know, werewolves. We were so scared, it was great." She chuckled a little, which highlighted the laugh lines etched at the corners of her eyes.

"Sometimes, when he drank a little too much gin, he told us how our French ancestors first settled in Acadia, then were deported to Louisiana by the English. And how some had rebuilt in Québec. He said our family was special. We have the gift, *Le Don*. Have you heard of that?"

Gabriel shook his head. He knew some Acadians had gone to Québec, but most were from Port Royal, not Grand Pré. He said nothing, waiting for her to continue.

"My grandfather said that the Bellefontaines were caught in an ancient battle of the souls, and that we were Protectors. We guard one of them," she said. "Legends are often built on truth." She let go of him and gave him the sweetest smile. "It's about time you came, isn't it?"

A rush of emotion surged in him. Visions of the rough ocean and red coastline of his homeland overtook him. He couldn't say anything.

Acadia, the Celtic sorcerers, the petite lady facing him with her tidy short silver hair, everything was tied somehow.

Morag hadn't told him. Had she known about Mrs. Bellefontaine?

Lily startled him as she walked back, her voice jolting him out of his daze.

"You two aren't eating my coffee cake." She sat beside Gabriel and filled everyone's plate, her movements serene while, smiling, she handed out plates.

He was surrounded by her fresh scent, her domestic gestures bringing him joy. As he watched her, he became suddenly happy.

Her smile enchanted him and he delighted in watching her silky hair dance with each movement, her hazel eyes sparkling in the sun.

He could relax. Mrs. Bellefontaine knew him, knew the soul connection he had with Lily. She'd been waiting for him, but hadn't told her niece yet.

He had time.

Between the two women, in their busy and cheerful apartment, he felt as if he was coming home. Leaning back in his chair, he allowed himself the enjoyment of this moment of grace, wishing to hold onto it forever. It may pass, but at least for now, for the first time in centuries, he could rest.

And then he'd have to find a way to tell her the truth.

Fourteen

Lily was having lunch alone in the hospital cafeteria, looking outside at the busy highway, when the sound of a lilting voice surprised her.

"Do you mind if I sit here?"

Lily stopped eating at once. "Morag?"

She couldn't have been more stunned. Gabriel's aunt stood beside her, dressed in a long raincoat, her thick red hair flowing along her back.

"What are you doing here?" She caught herself. "Sorry, please sit down. I'm on lunch break."

Morag took a seat in front of Lily. She set her Styrofoam cup on the table and edged her canvas tote under her chair. Pushing her hair away from her face, she gave Lily a quick smile.

What could Morag be doing at the hospital?

"I'm in the process of donating some paintings to the Cugini-Leduc Foundation." It was as if she'd guessed what Lily was thinking. "Their committee wanted to meet me." Morag took a sip from her cup. "I went up to the pediatric wing and asked about you."

"Oh."

Morag appraised the clean and modern cafeteria. "You have a pretty decent work environment here."

"Well, it's a good hospital, hard work but satisfying."

"Why nursing?"

"I don't know. I've always been good at taking care of people."

"Yes, I do sense that in you. You did save a life back at the lake last month."

"Oh, that wasn't a big deal." Lily shrugged. "I was a lifeguard for many years."

"I wouldn't be so dismissive if I were you. You did save a life all by yourself. You have a gift, you know."

"A gift? Well, I've always been pretty calm."

"No, I mean you have powers, psychic powers. They're pretty weak, I'm afraid, but still, they're there."

Lily quickly sat back, her arms clung to her chest. Where was Morag going with that? "I don't have any special powers."

Perhaps at one point she had. But not anymore.

"Oh, yes you do. I feel them. But suit yourself, ignore them if you wish." Morag gestured toward Lily's cup. "Have some coffee. It's getting cold."

Lily ignored her, hoping she would go away and leave her alone.

But Morag wasn't finished. "Anyway, I didn't come to discuss your gifts. I just have this book for you." Morag searched through her canvas tote.

"A book?"

"Remember, the one about the Acadians' history? I forgot to give it to you when you left our house. Gabriel told me you worked here, so when the people from the foundation called, I thought of it."

She fished an old book from her bag. Faded gold writing adorned its spine. "Here, the poem about Evangéline and Gabriel is at the end. I thought you may want to read it, with that odd name coincidence."

Lily took the book from Morag, relieved she'd stopped talking about psychic powers "Thank you. If you don't mind, I'll show it to my great-aunt. She has always liked all that family history."

"You read it too, Lily. It's good to know where you come from."

Lily put the heavy book next to her coffee cup. "Morag." She suddenly turned brave. "Tell me something: what happened to Gabriel? He won't tell me anything about his past."

Morag smiled. "That's my Gabriel, very secretive." She shook her head a little. "He is not our real nephew. He came to us when he was twenty or so. Iain became his mentor. He doesn't really like me, I think. He resents my intrusion into his life. Anyway, it is not for me to tell you about him. He will tell you when he is ready."

"It's hard to have secrets between us. It's not right." Lily was surprised by how she confided in Morag all of a sudden.

"Give him some space. He has become hardened; his youth wasn't easy. He is impetuous sometimes, but very determined, and solid. Don't put conditions on him. He needs a woman who will accept him as he is." Morag clasped her hands together under her chin and looked hard at Lily. "Are you really that person, though? I hope you are, because he will be devastated if you reject him."

"I haven't known him that long."

"Maybe, but how do you feel about him, really, in your heart?"

How did she feel about Gabriel? Just thinking about him made her smile. Her body warmed at the thought of him all over her the night before. In fact, she couldn't wait for her shift to be over so she could run back to his place. Was it just lust?

"It's more than lust, dear," Morag said. "What you feel, it's a lot more than lust."

Lily stared at Morag in shock. Was she reading her thoughts?

Morag laughed. "Of course, I told you before. Why are you so scared?" She edged closer. "I can read you, yes. You can't hide from me. But that's not important."

She put her hand on Lily's, her grip solid.

Lily's heart quickened. She wanted to run away as far as she could from Morag. The woman unnerved her.

Morag then seemed huge, taking up the whole space around Lily. She swallowed everything with her presence, her powers. Lily had never felt so much unnatural force surrounding her. She looked at Morag with horror, her breath short. How could Gabriel be involved with such dark energy?

"What's important is that you love Gabriel for what he is. He deserves it. Search your soul, you'll find it's more than lust. Oh, I know you burn for him when he puts his hands on you. That's good, very good."

Morag patted Lily's hand. Her touch was icy and her aura pinned Lily to her chair, as if it sucked part of her soul. "But you also can't live without him, can you? Be honest with yourself." Morag let go of Lily's hand and looked normal again.

Lily breathed more easily but she still couldn't say a thing. Had she been dreaming? Did Morag really have powers that strong?

"Read the book I gave you. Try to imagine the pain those people felt, their despair. Search your feelings, lass." Morag got up and left the cafeteria as quickly as she'd come.

With dread, Lily examined the ancient book lying on the cafeteria table in front her. She was almost too scared to touch it.

"You brought a drink?" Gabriel watched Phoebus retrieve an antique silver flask from his long black coat and set it on the ground beside him. The engraved metal shimmered in the light of the flames from the nearby bonfire.

"Single-malt whiskey, the best." Phoebus laid down a delicate crystal tumbler and began pouring his drink. "Just arrived from Islay, oldest vintage. Got a whole case of the stuff."

"Nice." Loïc sat in complete stillness on a flat rock nearby. Overhanging oak branches cast giant shadows over him.

"I need all the help I can get." Phoebus admired the amber liquor, angling it to let moonlight shine on the fluid surface. "We're camping."

"I hardly call this camping." Gabriel flung another log into the fire. The three sorcerers had gathered in the clearing behind the Callans' house, and Gabriel would likely be the only one left to sleep in the dark night.

"It looks like camping to me. Woods, bonfire, uncomfortable seats."

"Come on, Phoebus. Didn't you ever rough it in France?"

"Never. I prefered to conduct these little rituals in the comfort of the lavish ceremonial rooms of my homes."

"Don't believe him, Gabe." Loïc still gazed at the fire. "Falconer had his fair share of battles to protect his lands, especially just before the Hundred Years' War."

"Couldn't have been much fun." Gabriel couldn't help but be a little impressed. Phoebus was indeed quite old. "Probably never bathed much."

"No worry, I did. A French count got many privileges in the battlefield. Including enough ladies of small virtue to scrub my back." Phoebus grinned, then took a sip of whiskey. In appreciation, he let it linger in his mouth before adding, "And it certainly wasn't as bad as hanging out in the woods with you two."

Gabriel sat down and watched the bonfire in front of him, the moon above. He inhaled the crisp air. His tension eased. He didn't like Morag's magical rituals, but this, outside, with only the sorcerers for company, it thrilled him every time. This connected him with the soul of nature, made his spirit soar. He could almost feel the one they called Cernunnos, the Horned God, the Warrior King. The essence of this wilderness.

"Sorry, Falconer. But this is important." He reached in his pocket and brought out a tiny ring.

With care, he laid it in his palm. A surge of emotion overcame him. The woman who would have worn this ring centuries ago had returned. And he would use all he knew to protect her.

"Pretty," Loïc said. "You made this?"

"Yes, in my father's forge. I was his apprentice."

"A nice life you'd have had."

"Yes a nice life. A simple life, really."

"Not meant to be." Loïc shook his head so slightly it was almost undetectable.

"Doesn't look like it."

"Nope." Loïc's expression grew dark as if he was also speaking for himself.

"And now we're stuck here with you," Phoebus said.

"I'm not forcing you." Gabriel slowly traced the edge of the ring with his thumb.

"I'm here because I'm curious," said Loïc.

"Oh."

"First time one of us has found his soul mate. I want to see how it turns out."

"Fun," Gabriel said. "Well, enjoy the show."

"Actually, I'm worried you'll screw it up."

Gabriel ignored Loïc and placed the ring in a small pewter cup in front of him. He stared at it for a moment.

He'd carried the ring all this time, never able to let it

go. The ring that would have been Evangéline's wedding ring. He'd had it in his pocket the day they were wrenched from their land. All these years looking for her, he had dreamed and anticipated her expression of surprised pleasure at his handiwork.

He shook his head and cleared his thoughts. Not meant to be.

He retrieved the bag of rune stones from his coat. This was his life now, surrounded by ancient artifacts, some so old Iain couldn't even remember where they came from. But the runes had belonged to an alchemist Iain knew, a sorcerer who'd studied with Nicholas Flamel in France and died horribly under the Inquisition.

Gabriel blindly picked three of the ancient carved stones and, asking the question in his mind, threw them on the ground at his feet. The spidery symbols he'd selected glowed silver against the amber background of the small rocks upon which they were drawn.

"You're good at that." Phoebus bent closer to the stone.

Even Phoebus was impressed by Gabriel's divination skills. No, he couldn't shift to a bird of prey yet, as could the others, but rune casting had been natural from the start. It reminded him a little of the animal-bone readings he'd learned from the native Abenaki.

"Gabriel's good at many things," Loïc said. "Have you ever seen him fight?"

"He's not that good. Just crazy, that's all."

"No fear, Voyager?" Loïc ignored Phoebus to address Gabriel.

"No fear." Gabriel kept staring at the stone.

"See, he's crazy."

"Yep."

"And I wouldn't trust you in the lab either." Phoebus casually threw the last of his priceless whiskey into the flames.

"Never been good at cooking," Gabriel said.

"Alchemy is not cooking. Only a strong mind can do it. You just can't control your emotions."

Gabriel looked up from the runes. "And you can?"

"Yeah." Phoebus's mood was dark as he stood up.

Whatever Phoebus hid, it wasn't pretty. Morag had said he'd driven his last wife mad, locked her up in her room out of vengeance. She'd never seen daylight until her death.

Gabriel was grateful for his emotions. At least he had no dark deeds on his conscience.

"So." Loïc barely glanced his way. "What do they tell you?"

"Fire. Just as I'd guessed." Gabe scooped the runes into his hand. "Fire and a bunch of other stuff."

"Falconer?"

"Here." Phoebus passed along a few small pouches, each of the finest embroidered velvet, their lavish colors like those of a handful of precious gems. "Sage, belladonna, comfrey."

"Monk, you want to do this?" Gabriel returned the bag of runes to the inside of his coat and took out two tiny glass vials. "You're good at enchantment."

"Nah, it's your project." A half smile curled Loïc's mouth. "I'm only here in case something goes wrong."

Nothing would go wrong. Gabriel shook his head as he reached for the pewter cup containing the wedding ring. He popped open the vial of deer blood and let it dribble over the ring.

The black-red liquid swallowed the fleur-de-lis pattern he'd carved centuries ago while dreaming of a life with his love.

No time to become sentimental. His life was no longer innocent, but consumed by darkness as surely as the ring was now tainted by the animal blood.

The mystic ritual was working its way inside him, the god calling to the male in him. Power of the wild. Yes, a good protection for his love.

He added a few drops of myrrh oil, then crushed the brittle herbs between his fingers before letting them fall into the bowl. He covered the entire mixture with salt.

Toitriú luibh reizh. As the snakelike tendrils of the cuff at his bicep sprang to life, he watched the blood absorb the spell components. The mix of colors and textures twirled and meandered as the substances fused together.

Flamm teine. The solution started to boil of its own accord. Bubbles of various sizes popped, slow and viscous, releasing an acrid black smoke into the air.

Conscious of the two other sorcerers' focus beside him, he repeated the chant. *Flamm teine, muioc'h.* The words came easily to him. All his heart went into insuring that this spell would succeed.

As he watched the solution continue to boil madly, the persistent call of an owl in the distance echoed in his ear. Iain perhaps? Looking over his disciples?

All were silent as they waited for the solution to evaporate. The disturbing smell of burned blood and pungent herbs soon filled the air, overtaking the soothing scent of oak smoldering in the bonfire.

Gabriel picked up the ring gently between his thumb and forefinger. It was coated with a red-green shell.

"Fire," Loïc said, as if he'd sensed Gabriel's hesitation.

Gabriel stood up, followed by the other sorcerers. No choice now, really.

Facing the bonfire, they stood side by side, all three of them. Powerful, carrying secrets untold for centuries. The power of the Ancients.

"Now," Loïc said.

"Yes." Gabriel threw the ring into the bonfire. The last untouched part of his previous life now tainted by the magic that would never leave him. All of this for Lily, leading him to his true love.

The sorcerers remained still as they watched the flames swallow the tiny ring.

"Have you told her yet?"

His black coat floating around him, Gabriel took in a deep breath and let it out, slowly. "Tell her what? That I'm not what I seem?"

"Yes, and that she's Evangéline, reborn."

"No, not yet."

"You have to do it sooner or later."

"I'm not like you, Falconer. I don't take pleasure in ignoring women's feelings."

"You know nothing, Voyager. Grow up."

"Phoebus is right, Gabriel. You have to tell her."

"I know."

They all watched silently for what seemed to be forever, until the flames subsided.

The ring was there. Clean, shiny, purified by fire. It glowed brightly in the dark night.

Satisfied with his work, Gabriel bent down and picked it up gently. The glow dimmed. The ring looked just as it always had.

He traced the engraving with his index finger and sighed. Evangéline's ring, now Lily's. Now enchanted.

Yes, he would have to tell her.

Fifteen

Her heart pumped hard. Twenty more laps and she'd be done. The familiar rhythm of exercise restored her feeling of self-control.

Lily had finally managed to squeeze a workout into her busy schedule. Gabriel had been wonderful, volunteering to take Angèle to the cardiologist today to give her more time to look at houses after her shift at the hospital.

She still couldn't find one that felt right. Buying a house turned out to be much harder than she'd thought. It had all seemed so simple: save the money and buy her dream. But the listings she'd considered had been awful, either too shabby or cookie-cutter new. A wave of apprehension crept through her. What if she never found the warm home of her dreams?

Lily hit the side of the pool and stood up to rearrange her goggles while she caught her breath. She shouldn't be so negative. Surely, there was a home for her out there somewhere.

Happiness soon replaced her frustration as she thought of Gabriel. How silly she'd been to believe that having him in her life would be complicated. She had packed days but cherished every minute spent with him.

Eighteen more laps. Her mind wandered as her body glided through the chlorinated water.

What of Morag? The woman had read her thoughts. Lily had no doubts about it. She had real psychic powers. And that was the last thing Lily wanted in her life. A trickle of dread seeped at the base of her neck, thinking of her own powers. She could no longer live in denial.

They may have been much weaker than Morag's, but they were real and somewhat frightening. Or at least they had been. She'd worked hard at suppressing practically every occurrence.

Her breath became more regular as she tried to block her thoughts and concentrate on her swimming. But the memories came back to her, fighting with her focused effort to be in the moment.

As a child, she had been able to read minds, as Morag did. Maybe not as easily, but when she'd concentrated hard, she'd achieved it. It had been fascinating, and horrifying.

When she was six, she'd read people's consciousnesses regularly. At first, she'd assumed everyone else could do the same, but as people became more puzzled by her conversations, she realized that she had a special gift. And she'd learned to keep quiet about it.

A strange curiosity had pushed her to read her mom's thoughts regularly. And she had to live with the knowledge that her mom had resented taking care of her, that she'd hated her little daughter.

Lily fought a tight ball of pain in her throat as she remembered the burden of being aware of her mom's feelings toward her, a shadow that had always hovered over her, brought her tremendous sadness.

Her young mind had been confused and hurt, and yet at first, she'd been unable to discipline herself to stop reading her mother, always hoping the feelings would change to motherly love. But eventually, she grew up knowing she needed to protect herself and had succeeded in blocking her psychic abilities almost entirely.

Lily finished another lap, then stopped again, in the deep end this time. With one hand, she readjusted the strap of her bathing suit, which was cutting into her skin. She'd swum hard today. Maybe she should end right now, shorten her workout. The exercise drained her body; her shoulders ached with the dull pain of muscle fatigue.

No, she'd keep going.

Catching her breath, she pulled her bathing cap lower over her forehead, then propelled herself through the water. Nine more laps.

She'd do it, just one at a time.

More memories rushed back as she cut through the water. By the time she was nine years old, Lily could no longer read minds. She could only reach for threads of powers to soothe herself. And she'd needed that.

Her mother had been fun, but hadn't known how to respond when Lily had confided her small childhood hurts, seeking solace. So Lily had learned to keep it all to herself.

She could have leaned on Angèle, but by the time she lived regularly with her great-aunt, it had been too late. A third-grade child, she'd become completely self-sufficient.

As she grew older, she'd found out she could help the children around her by soothing them, as well. It had helped her as a lifeguard and then as a pediatric nurse. But her gift scared her and it didn't feel right to try it on adults. Even when her mom had been in a lot of pain in the final days of her illness, Lily had relied on conventional medicine to help her.

Now Morag was here, bringing it all back to her. Lily felt invaded, but a part of her had turned curious. What if she'd been trained to use her gifts? What if, when she was six, she had known someone like Morag?

Lily focused on the contraction of her muscles to find the energy to complete her hundred-lap workout. Exercise always cleared her mind. Something she could count on, the power of her own body.

She'd been truly frightened when Morag had visited her at the hospital the day before. It was as if Morag had bullied her into loving Gabriel. But Lily didn't need to be persuaded—she did love him. She wished he would tell her more about his past, but deep down, she knew she could give him the space he needed. She'd wait until he was ready.

Stretching her arms farther, she felt a small burst of energy from within and switched to alternate breathing, three strokes for one breath. She picked up some speed.

Last night, she'd finally read Morag's book. She'd been swept away by the tale of Gabriel LaJeunesse and Evangéline Bellefontaine. She wondered if they'd really existed, if she was related to Evangéline. It was not impossible. Her father had given her that name, told her it had been in the family for centuries.

How hard it must have been for Evangéline to be uprooted and never marry, to spend her life as a missionary, to have waited for her Gabriel all that time. The poem had them reunite in the end on his deathbed, but still, what a wasted life.

Lily couldn't imagine being so emotionally strong. Evangéline had been a model of patience, of devotion. And what of Gabriel the Acadian, being taken away from her, roaming the forests of America in the eighteenth century, forever looking for his love? The chatter in Lily's mind quieted, replaced by a mist of sadness for the two ancient lovers. Her happiness with her own Gabriel made her feel for their tragedy.

She got out of the pool, then fetched her towel and water bottle. She was exhausted but felt great, the familiar endorphin rush kicking in. Walking carefully on the wet tiles, she headed toward the changing room.

Lily knew what Morag meant by telling her to search

for her heart. Life had handed her a beautiful gift. As
Angèle kept telling her, she had to seize it.

Not a soul had ventured that far out onto the beach.
They were miles from the parking lot. The ocean waves
crashed violently and the wind swirled around them, but
Gabriel loved the elements bursting free, loved the wild-
ness of it all.

He brought Lily closer, content to be simply walking
along the deserted beach with her. Feeling cooped up in
the city, he'd needed the fresh air and it'd seemed a good
way to spend her day off. "Are you cold?"

"No, not really." She snuggled up to him, looking beautiful as always in a black peacoat and loose knitted hat.

Feeling a little guilty at dragging her into the cold, he
kissed her temple and inhaled her fresh scent.

He kept her close as they turned to retrace their steps.
"Ready for a hot chocolate?"

She didn't have time to answer, startled when he
stopped dead in his tracks.

Three huge strangers stepped out of the mist to block
their way.

What now? He braced the muscles of his shoulders and
tightened his fist.

"Gabriel?" Lily tensed in his embrace.

Damn. Not them. Not now, with her here.

Anger ripped in him to see the three Keepers striding
toward them. Where had they come from?

They were massive, almost indistinguishable with their
tattooed bare skulls, and apparently oblivious to the cold
in T-shirts thinly stretched over their muscular torsos.
Their faces were expressionless.

"It's okay, baby," Gabriel hugged Lily, then gently let
her go. "I'll just go talk to them."

He winked at her. "If things go bad, just head for the dunes."

"What?"

He could see the fear in her eyes and it killed him inside.

"I'm joking. Just stay away, stay safe. It'll be fine." He carefully pushed her away and strode toward the Keepers.

"What do you want?"

"Just checking you out." The Keeper who spoke narrowed his eyes at him.

"Oh, well hey, let me check you out too." Gabriel tried to remember what Iain had told him about Keepers.

Some were magic-users but most were just thugs, and all not human. Theuron knew some powerful necromancy.

"Being a smart-ass?" The second Keeper brandished a hunting knife.

Lily gasped behind them.

"I wouldn't joke if I were you." The Keeper swirled the knife forward. The weapon itself wasn't that lethal looking, but runes were carved along its blade.

Enchanted?

"Just having a nice time with my girl here." Gabriel strode openhanded, his steps relaxed. "Be cool. Just let her walk."

"What makes you think it's not her we want?" The Keeper who had first spoken rolled his shoulders back and stretched his massive arms to his sides. He closed in on Gabriel.

But it was the third Keeper, quietly staying back, who caught Gabriel's attention. Studying his hands, he detected a small motion, a pattern traced in the air.

Yes, you're the magical one, aren't you?

Gabriel narrowed his eyes at him.

"Samhlchaitheamh cosc." The discreet holding spell rose to Gabriel's lips. No time to wait for whatever the spell-caster had in mind.

Gabriel stretched out to the Keeper in front of him.

He grabbed the collar of his T-shirt. Then he yanked the guy toward himself and sucker-punched him the gut.

The Keeper gasped and hunched over.

One down.

Gabriel kneed him in the face. His opponent yelped and collapsed in the sand, holding his bloody face in his hands.

A slashing burn seized Gabriel's chest. The knife-wielding thug had hit his target. Gabriel swiveled and grasped the Keeper's free wrist.

"Cosc samhlchaitheamh cosc." Still holding the Keeper struggling to slash him again, Gabriel kept the magic-user at bay.

"Lily, get away!" he screamed.

Fear for her made him catch his breath. The magic-user raised his arms high in the air and sand started to rise around him.

Hell, no. Gabriel grabbed the arm he held with both hands. He anchored himself, then kicked the knife out of the Keeper's hand.

Adrenaline pounded in his blood. They were after Lily. That was all he could think.

The Keeper was still not down. He charged again at Gabriel, then swung with massive fists.

Gabriel ducked, but the punch caught him on the shoulder. Searing pain spread out over his arm and neck, but he repeated his holding spell again. He couldn't let the spell-caster free.

The magic-user gave him a smile and walked toward Lily. Gabriel's spell wasn't strong enough.

Agony for Lily's safety distracted him. Another punch

hit him on the chin. This time the pain flew to his skull. He tasted blood in his mouth.

There was no time. *Focus.* He tore his eyes from Lily and slammed the Keeper in the face. He punched once, twice. Soon Gabriel hammered at him.

Blood poured out of his enemy's nose. His left eye was shut tight.

Gabriel located the magic-user in his mind. With a simple spell, the Keeper could vanish with Lily, gone to Theuron.

Gabriel had no choice. Fists alone would not get rid of them. Rage swallowed him. He was forced to use offensive magic. And Lily would witness it.

With a frustrated roar, he swiveled and smashed his boot in the Keeper's face to finish him. The thug slumped and Gabriel slammed the back of his neck. Bone cracked under his hand.

"Gabriel, no!" Lily screamed.

Gabriel wasn't thinking.

"Flamm." A flick of the hand and a ball of fire hit the spell-caster square in the back.

Gabriel caught Lily's look of horror. She stared at him, then at the Keeper.

He clenched his jaws in frustration. Not fast enough. Fire had vanished from the Keeper's chest.

He pointed at Gabriel. *"Scrab."* The deadly word escaped the Keeper's lips and resonated in the air.

Gabriel was catapulted back. He crashed down on the sand. Red heat stung his back.

Ignoring the pain, he kept Lily in his line of vision. *No.* Horror drenched him with cold sweat. The magic-user pointed a finger at her.

Gabriel rolled to his side and spit out his spell. He hurled another fireball at his enemy.

Lily screeched.

This time the spell hit. The magic-user howled in the cold air. He slumped to his knees on the ground.

Good. His shield was down.

Lily screamed again, rooted to the spot as fire consumed the magic-user's chest.

"Lily, run!" Gabriel shouted as he shot to his feet.

But she wouldn't budge. She couldn't take her eyes from the burning body, which dissolved like melting solder in front of her.

"Gabriel!" The air filled with her screams, shrieks mixed with sobs. "What's going on?"

Fury at the attackers would not leave him. Striding toward Lily, Gabriel pointed at the two Keepers unconscious beside him.

One word and they both burst in flame.

Still sobbing, Lily walked backward from them all, then sank to the ground.

Gabriel ran to her. He held her tight as her sobs turned to whimpers that tore Gabriel's heart.

"It's okay, sweetie. It's okay." He wrapped her closer to his body, protected her with his coat, his arms. "You're safe."

"But those men. What you did . . ."

"They're not human, baby. Don't worry." He knew it was a stupid thing to say, but couldn't think of anything else.

She didn't answer as he rocked her gently in his arms.

Theuron's creations burned as he continued to hold her silently. Soon there was nothing left, just black and acrid smoke, carried away by the thrashing wind and leaving both of them hugging in the sand.

As her sobs receded, Lily pulled back to look at him. Suddenly, it hit her. The power. What he'd done.

Unnatural dark power emanated from him, similar to

Morag's. She could feel it now, hitting her strong, hard, waves and waves of it. The things he could do. He was loaded with it. Something out of this earth itself, radiating from him, striking her full force.

She stared at him, her heart frozen.

Now she knew.

But it couldn't be. The unfairness of it was not possible, too horrible to contemplate. Pain coursed through her chest.

She shoved him away. "Gabriel," she howled. "No, not you." The wind carried her voice away.

He put his hand gently on her arms, his expression pained. "Sorry." She couldn't hear him but saw his lips mouthing the word. *Sorry.*

She shook her head hard. "No." Her voice was loud in the blustery weather. Not that, not him, not that strange unearthly power from him. She couldn't deal with that. All she wanted was normality.

A huge weight slid onto her, squashed her. The weight of her childhood flashed in front of her, draining her. "You can't do this to me."

He said nothing and pulled her close to his chest.

She couldn't breathe. She couldn't move. He was too close.

She'd let her guard down for him, let herself fall in love with him, and now this. She didn't want any part of it, the mind reading, the power over others.

And this.

Her whole body recoiled in horror. Nothing seemed right. She wanted to run away and hide, away from from her memories, from the weirdness.

She'd been so blind. Morag, Keira, that sinister Theuron Keir and now Gabriel. How could she have been so stupid?

Gabriel now invaded her space, his psychic powers all around her, like a sticky web trapping her, preventing her escape.

She closed her eyes, haunted by the images of burned bodies on the sand.

He was doing it, doing that to her. It was all his fault. He wanted her to feel his power. But she wouldn't let him. She would stop him.

His hands were on her shoulders, heavy, restraining her.

She pushed hard at his chest. "Stop it." She screamed again. "Stop doing that to me."

He shook his head. "I can't, Lily. It's who I am." His voice was audible now, calm but strong.

"No. Stop it now. Get away from me." Her fingers dug into his coat and her muscles coiled tight as she pushed him.

He let go of her, his expression wounded. "I can't stop it. I can't hide who I am from you."

She grabbed him by the collar, wanting to hurt him. "You lied to me." Her knuckles turned white from her tight grip. She looked into his eyes and searched for answers.

"I wanted to protect you. I didn't want to scare you."

"You lied." Her eyes were narrow slits, her body bursting with rage. "You hid it from me." She shook him with all her strength and he did nothing to stop her. "So what trick can you do beside burning people to a crisp?" she shouted in the wind. "What other great powers do you have? Any more subtle ones? Can you read me? You know all my thoughts, don't you?"

"No, I don't.

But she didn't want to hear him. "Can you move things, control people? What have you forced me to do?" He'd used her as surely as Theuron had controlled Keira. She shook him harder and he staggered.

"Lily, I didn't do anything to you." He recovered his balance. "I didn't mean this."

"You could have told me right away." Her voice came from somewhere else and she felt herself grow cold. Quiet anger took complete control of her.

"It wasn't time yet."

"Time? And when was it going to be time?" She shoved him hard, then turned away, her whole body trembling.

She stared at the long stretch of sandy beach. Why had he come to her? He should have left her alone after that fateful night, driven her back to her friends' house right away. He should be with another woman, someone like him, and leave her in peace with her quiet life.

"We're fated." His voice echoed behind her. "We're made to be together. I can't love any other."

She turned to face him again and narrowed her eyes. "You're reading me. Don't do that. Don't ever do that to me." Her voice echoed strong and slow.

"I'm not reading your mind, Lily. I never have. I love you. That's all. I love you. There's nothing I can do about it." He stood there, so broad and dark, covered with his rugged black coat, so dangerous.

Yet his expression was soft, defeated. His eyes were the lightest green now. His black curls danced in the wind.

She loved him. God, she knew she loved him. Her rage disappeared as quickly as it'd taken her over. Her eyes filled with tears.

"Why Gabriel? Why me, why us?" She put a hand on his cheek. He was the same to her now, except for a hint of something else. "You don't seem real, not human." She stroked his unshaven chin as a tear rolled onto her cheekbone. "What are you?"

"I'm like you, just like you. But I can't die." He leaned his face gently in her hand.

"You can't die." It was not a question, but just a horrible, mind-numbing statement.

He cupped the hand on his cheek with his. "No, I can't die."

"Gabriel." She sobbed now, big hard sobs that shook her torso and resonated through her body. Letting go of his cheek, she held on to him, both hands on his shoulders. She couldn't talk.

He laid his hands on her back, lightly, as her forehead rested on his chest. The world shattered around her. He couldn't die. What did he mean?

Her legs shook. She knelt down, sinking to the cold ground, her hands sliding along his body, her palms raking the coarse fabric of his coat. She lay down on the gritty sand.

And she couldn't stop crying. She leaned her head against his solid thighs, her hands clutching his jeans. She cried for her lost illusions, her lack of control, this unnatural life she couldn't seem to escape.

As the wind swirled around her, howling and lifting the sand, she vaguely felt his hand resting on her hair. The rolling sound of the crashing waves deafened her and it was as if the elements had gathered to crush her.

Gabriel bent down to her, tried to lift her up to her feet, but she let herself fall even lower. She wanted to stay down, as low as she could, flatten herself to the ground, never get up.

He wrapped her in his arms, in his coat. His masculine scent reached her from far away.

He put his chin on her head. "We will deal with this together, sweetheart."

We. He'd said, "We." Yes, she was not alone. She lifted

her head from his chest and looked hard at him. "I hate you for this."

"I know."

"But I can't help loving you too. God, how I love you."

She saw the hint of tears in his eyes. "And I love you, Lily. Forever."

Slowly, she took his head with both hands and brushed his lips with hers, the salt of her tears stinging her tongue. Her kiss trembled, soft and pure. Pulling back from him slightly, she said, "Together?"

"Yes, together."

She sat on the sand next to him, pulled her knees close and took his hand in hers.

They stared at the ocean, side by side, holding hands.

There was so much more to say, so many questions, but not now. She was weary; the weight of his revelation still pinned her to the ground, paralyzing her will. She looked at the waves crashing on the shore, at the few surfers braving the cold, small black dots on the stormy ocean.

Fate had ruled their lives and it was just the two of them now, and the wide ocean, the stormy wind and the large bleak sky.

Sixteen

"I can alter the elements," Gabriel explained as they sat in his apartment. They'd driven back from the beach separately, he on his motorcycle and Lily left alone in her car with her thoughts.

She had many questions for him, but could only let him talk. The intense hopelessness she'd felt on the beach had been replaced by a surreal calm—her forte—and an extreme curiosity.

Oh, she did believe all he'd said. She didn't understand why, but she did. The impossible appeared natural around him.

"The elements?" She curled up on the black leather couch of his plain living room, her bare feet tucked under her.

"I can control the wind, the rain, fire. Change matter, people's body structure even." Gabriel faced her, sitting cross-legged on the hardwood floor.

"Like healing?" She tried to understand him, keeping her mind open.

"Yes, a little."

"And you can't die." She understood the psychic abilities, but how could someone be immortal?

He shook his head, then said, "What do you know about alchemy?"

"Alchemy? Change metal into gold, the philosopher's stone? That kind of thing?"

"Yes, there's that. But some alchemists can create the water of life, *Uisge Beatha*."

"Water of life?"

"Yes, the path to immortality. Have you heard of Nicholas Flamel?"

"I think so. Was he not an alchemist?"

"Yes, he was born in the fourteenth century. He drank the water of life during a powerful ritual, and now he still walks among us, immortal."

"He created it?"

"No. He met Iain." Gabriel gave her a slow smile.

"Iain?"

"Yes, good old Iain Callan. The most powerful alchemist on earth, older than any I know. He recruited me, you see. Taught me sorcery. Over two hundred and fifty years ago, he found me. I was on a ship sailing for Louisiana, deported by the English." His eyes turned dark as he spoke. "I was called LaJeunesse then, Gabriel LaJeunesse of Grand Pré, Acadie."

"The poem."

"What poem?"

"The one about Gabriel and Evangéline. Morag made me read it. That's you?"

"Well, not anymore. I'm still alive, am I not? All thanks to Iain and the Priory."

She flinched at the bitterness in his voice. "What's the Priory?"

"The Priory of Callan, Morag's little project, her sorcerers. We're a bunch of cursed souls. We can't escape our destiny, or her."

"How many more like you?"

"Twelve, all immortal. Iain's disciples."

"So Phoebus, Loïc . . . ?"

"Yes. Tara too."

"And the others?"

"There's Roan, Tris, Renaud—a lot of them are in Europe now."

"What about Morag? Is she immortal too?"

"Morag." He let out a cutting laugh. "Morag is many things, some I don't even understand. She claims she's the High Priestess of the Callanish Coven, and it seems her priestesses are lost to her. She has more magical power than any of us, never equaled as far as I know." He shrugged. "But let's not talk about her now."

Morag a priestess—Lily had guessed right. The memory of Morag at the hospital made her shiver. "And I thought I was the only one who was psychic." She flashed him a sad smile.

"Ah, you too. I knew it."

"Yes, not much, but I used to be able to read my mother's thoughts."

"Used to?"

"It was too painful, so after a while I stopped. She didn't love me much, you see." Lily hugged herself.

Gabriel rested a hand on her knee. "You must be quite strong if you can suppress it. Even after all these years, I can't always control it. But mostly I do okay. I know some pretty potent spells."

"Spells? Like what?" She covered his hand with hers and traced his fingers, reassured by their strength.

"I can control people, to a certain extent."

"But never me?" Even as she asked, she knew he'd been telling the truth on the beach.

"No, never. Not yet anyway, but I could."

"How?"

"Well . . ." He flashed her a devilish grin. "I could show you how I love you in a very special way."

"Sex? You mean when we are having sex?" She couldn't believe she'd just said that.

He laughed. "If I use my powers when I make love to you, it will be a whole different experience."

"Show me." She stared at him with intensity.

"Aren't you a little afraid? I'm very powerful." A twinkle shone in his eyes as he linked her fingers through his. "I'm a sorcerer. I'll make you entirely mine." He still radiated the unnatural power she'd felt on the beach.

"Show me." She was very curious now and, she had to admit, a little fearful. But the hint of fear crawling through her bones suddenly made her body tingle with lust. She was flirting with danger and she knew it, finding that speck of darkness in Gabriel strangely enticing.

Keeping his fingers twined with hers, she got up and led him to his bedroom.

He followed without protest and sat on the bed as she stood facing him. He looked at her eagerly, waiting.

Her raw emotions from earlier on the beach needed a powerful release and she felt compelled to show him her love. As if possessed by an uncontrollable force, she wanted to be naked for him, wanted to let herself feel vulnerable in front of him.

Where did this wild feeling come from? A sorcerer . . . he was a sorcerer, immortal. What would he do to her, what would his love feel like with magic?

With her gaze fixed on his handsome face, she worked on the buttons of her shirt one at a time. She unzipped her jeans, then wiggled out of them while he sat on the bed, hands together, desire written all over his face.

She stood in front of him, clad only in a lacy black bra and matching thong. She loved the power she held over him, loved seeing the admiration in his eyes. Stripping in front of him made her feel extremely feminine and wild.

She brought her hand to her back, unfastened her bra and let it fall. Her nipples hardened from the cool air and from the intense emotions running though her.

After sliding her fingers under the black lace at her hips, she pushed the thong down to her feet. She stepped out of it and stood motionless, letting his gaze trail over her entire naked body. She was all ready for him, for his magical power.

Conscious of her nakedness and his fully clothed body, she knelt down to his level and cupped his head in her hands.

"Make love to me, sorcerer. Show me your powers." Her voice purred in a whisper as her body heated with anticipation.

He grasped her wrist gently. "As you wish, my lady, as you wish." He sounded unusually solemn.

Still sitting at the edge of the bed, he pushed her up to her feet and brought her between his legs. He pressed his lips to her belly as he pulled her closer. She felt his rough jeans around her naked thighs, the warmth of his bare arms encircling her waist and his soft T-shirt at her navel.

His hand cupped her naked buttocks. "You're so beautiful. Your skin so perfect." A passionate fever burned in his eyes.

"Don't you have to say some weird words like *hocus pocus* or something like that?"

Gabriel laughed. "No, it just comes to me as I go along." He got up to face her, then guided her to the bed. He eased her down on her back so she could lie on the immaculate white sheets.

Then he stood, all lean muscle and raw power, looking at her, full of desire.

She felt his physical power but also something more, something about his will, as if he wanted her to submit to it. She was not scared but awed and a little docile about what may happen. This was Gabriel, whom she loved and trusted.

She didn't move, and waited for him as he knelt at the bed, holding one of her feet by the ankle. He brushed the top of it with a kiss.

"*Reizh leski*," he whispered, his breath warming her sensitive skin. He then blew softly on her leg.

A tingling started where he'd kissed her. It spread along her leg, an incredible sensation flowing upward— first through her thigh, her hip, then to her belly. It ended at her tightened nipples in a hot explosion.

She moaned with pleasure. *How did he do that?*

Kneeling at the edge of the bed, he grasped her other ankle, and she felt pinned by the strength of his grip.

"Now you're all mine, baby." He flashed her that charming smile again, then laughed. His laugh was playful, but she sensed a hint of something inhuman in it. There was no turning back now. She was already entirely under his control and she found herself enjoying the small thread of powerlessness she felt in being at his mercy.

"Did you just do something to me?"

"Of course I did. I just kissed your foot." She heard the playful laugh again, and then he blew on her skin once more. The hot sensation surged through her, creeping up both thighs, invading the needy area between her legs as intense desire burst to her core.

She let out a small cry of surprise. She would come, right now, from the sensation alone. But no, not quite yet.

He'd left her panting, wanting more, much more.

She needed him, now, on top of her. She was dying to feel his weight.

His gaze on her was dark. He had detected her agony, and she sensed he didn't want her to reach for him yet.

"Relax. We have all day." His lips curled into another teasing grin. Then she felt one more kiss, heard one more incantation murmured in an ancient language she didn't know.

Again, an excruciating wave of pleasure consumed her. Her nipples ached now, begging for his touch. The need in her body was incredibly strong, unnaturally strong. She would do anything for release, anything.

But Gabriel took his time.

He trailed his lips up her leg. His mouth found the cradle of her right inner thigh and he kissed it softly, the tip of his tongue occasionally licking her as he spread her legs gently. He licked her hot sensitive skin, getting closer and closer to her neediest spot.

His hand finally cupped the crest between her legs and he brushed her soft curls, parting her slightly with his callused fingers.

She gasped.

"So beautiful, perfect." His thumb was slow and gentle as it explored her slit, but it didn't quite reach where she wanted yet.

She arched her hips toward him.

"Easy, baby, easy." His hands moved up and caressed her stomach.

She whimpered in disappointment. Why was he drawing away from her now?

He gazed at her and she saw the intense fever burning in his eyes, his desire to possess and claim her.

She sighed, resigned to let him have his way with her, to take his lead.

He whispered the magic words again. His hands left her body and drew symbols in the air just over her, not quite touching her skin. *"Reizh leski, muioc'h leski."*

The sweet pain of need hit her. She writhed with uncontrollable lust as it washed all over her body. Her feet dug into the thick mattress as her hands grasped the sheets. She arched deeply, lifted her bared chest toward him in yearning.

He knelt on the bed next to her hips and trailed his fingertips in slow and tender circles on her breasts, occasionally flicking her tight nipples.

Her body was lost in sensation. She yearned for the hardness she could see bulging though his jeans. His caresses on her body were familiar, but the spell made him nearly a stranger, made her ache for him almost painfully.

She wanted him now. She wouldn't wait.

Reaching for his shoulders, she tried to pull him close, but he denied her. He restrained one side of her hips with one hand, then lifted her leg to open her wider.

He was playing with her, having fun. Using his incantations to enhance her desire for him and then taking it slow and leisurely. It killed her.

The desire she'd felt the first night with him at the Callans' house had been strong but nothing like now. She would do anything for him if he asked. For him, just for him, to be blended with his body and soul, to feel his essence all over her, in her. She was his, to do his bidding, for his claiming. The loving trust she felt for him made her light-headed and pliant.

As his kisses lowered to her wet core again and both hands anchored her thighs, she felt her love for him surging though her.

His lips lay right where she wanted them and he flicked his tongue at her dripping slit, directly on the pulsing nub so ready for him. She cried. Finally a small release. She wanted to beg for more.

"You like that?" he asked.

"You're amazing."

"You want more? Tell me you want more."

"Please, Gabriel." She moaned for him.

He brought his mouth down again, his hands opening her legs wide. His elbows rested on her open thighs, restraining her. She felt his tongue playing with her, small fast licks, then slow circles. She was so close to release, dying for him, her strong, loving boyfriend, dying for Gabriel, who swept her over the edge.

While his tongue pleasured her, he put one finger inside her, shallow at first, sliding in and out, then deeper and deeper. She gasped at the sensation, swallowed in deep, sweet waves of pleasure. So close, she was so close.

He stopped and slowly lifted his head to look at her.

She whimpered. Where was he going?

He smiled, the twinkle back in his eyes. "I have you for the whole day, remember?"

She wanted him back all over her again, but he whispered the ancient words once again.

"No." She couldn't take more. He was killing her.

"Oh, yes, baby."

Need washed over her again, need and a hint of submission. She was swallowed whole by him. How would she survive this?

He stood at the edge of the bed, dark, immense, towering over her. He brought his hand to his black leather belt and started to undo it. The simple gesture was so deeply erotic, so manly, that she watched, fascinated. He was coming to take her.

As he removed his belt, his gaze pinned her . . . filled with something? Desire, possession? No, love. Filled with love.

He slid his pants down and she couldn't take her eyes away from him, from his need of her, solid, thick and ready.

He lay above her, trailing the tip of his erection on her thigh. She felt the sweet moisture on her skin, his intoxicating scent just above her. He had to bring her release.

She took him, wrapping her fingers around the erect, hot skin, stretched fully and felt his very life in her hand. She stroked him up and down and rubbed her thumb at his wet tip. She heard him moan as she touched him in all the ways she knew he liked.

He let her toy with his shaft for a moment. Then he

gently grabbed her hands and pinned them high above her head, his face close to hers.

She met his gaze. "Take me now. Please take me."

He just smiled at her, the gentlest smile, full of tenderness. Still restraining her hands, he rubbed himself on her wet opening, nice and slow, stroking her where she felt so neglected. He kept his rhythm and she balanced on the edge again, panting hard.

Then he slid himself inside her. Intense closeness, finally. He ground himself into her, rubbing her hard, stimulating her most sensitive nerve endings, knowing her rhythm. Close—she was getting there.

She thrust her hips in time with him. All that intense need of him overpowered her. She would burst from it, really soon.

"Come, baby." His expression was intensely focused on her. "Come now." A command? A prayer?

Yes, for you, anything.

Suddenly, there, the explosion she'd been waiting for so very long. Shattering her, shaking her all over. Tears welled in her eyes as she wanted to cry from the intensity of her release.

As he slid in and out of her, he carried her through the full sensation, until there was nothing left. Then he let out a faint low groan full of love for her, a caress within her very core.

"I love you, sweetheart." He lowered his whole weight gently on her. "I love you." His voice was a whisper in her ear.

She embraced him and shook at the intense need for him still lingering on her skin, the memory of the incredible shattering sensation when she came.

She rested her head on his, feeling his soft curls on her cheek. They both remained quiet for a moment. Shifting her arms around him, she felt hard metal on his bicep.

"What is that?" She pointed to a thick silver cuff on his arm.

"Oh that, the mark, don't worry about it." He rained small kisses at the crook of her neck.

"What's the mark? Don't you have a tattoo right there?"

He didn't answer and continued to kiss her, caressing her thighs.

"Wait. Your tattoo, it's solid metal now?" She grasped his head with both hands and turned it toward her.

His lips curled into a slow smile. "You're in my world now, baby." The twinkle had returned to his eyes. "Welcome to the dark side."

Suddenly she started laughing. "My sorcerer. Full of surprises. You did that to me, didn't you, with your magic?"

He shifted on his side, pulling her with him. "Did what?"

"Make me crazy with desire for you."

"You mean that's not how you normally feel for me?" He played with her hair, sliding the strand on her naked shoulder.

"Yes, silly, I do, but this was maddening. It was torture."

"Was it too much?" He dropped the strand of her hair, sounding concerned.

"It was more like sweet torture. I didn't have much control. But it was amazing. Can you teach me how to do that to you?"

"No, I'm sorry, I'm afraid you can't. Only Iain's sorcerers can do that."

"You guys make a pretty lethal bunch."

"I won't use that spell again on you if you don't want me to. I was having a little fun today. Because you were curious. But I'd never force you."

"Oh, you can do that anytime." Her tone turned serious. "I trust you. I know you'd never do anything bad to me, even with all that power you have."

Gabriel looked at her with love. She was right. He wouldn't. He only wanted her happiness and her pleasure. He enjoyed watching her writhe with desire and being the one to satisfy it. He wanted to see her coming for him over and over again.

A warm glow spread through him as he realized how much she trusted him, how she hadn't rejected him now that she knew all about him. Well, almost all. He hadn't told her about Evangéline's essence running in her blood yet. But there would be time for that later.

She also didn't know that when he'd used magic on her, he'd felt the same as she did. He'd experienced the same burning agony, and it had taken all his self-control not to bury himself in her right away.

"So, I can do this anytime?" He didn't need the magic between them, but she'd seemed to enjoy it.

"Sure, anytime." She rested her head back in the pillows.

"Reizh leski." This was too tempting. He would never get enough of her. His fingertips traced a rune on her belly.

"Gabriel, no." She screamed in surprise.

He felt the waves of need building in them again as she wrapped her legs tightly around his waist and hungrily pressed her wet core toward him. Lily was all he'd ever wanted—sweet, loving, burning for him. His love, all ready for him, making him mad with desire.

As he took her again, he vowed to show her how she was all that ever mattered. No matter what happened now, he'd be there to love and pleasure her—forever.

Evangéline has returned. They were both the same to him now.

Seventeen

My boyfriend is an immortal sorcerer. She walked to the library somewhat taller, loving to carry such a secret. How quickly she'd adapted to her new reality.

It had been only a week since Gabriel revealed his nature to her. Everything since then had been oddly normal. They were like any other couple in love. The same, really, except for their lovemaking. She'd insisted he use his spells on her again and had reveled in the experience of such binding pleasure, such delicious torture.

Her steps became lighter as she remembered the little loving words Gabriel had whispered to her in the midst of passion. How thoroughly he'd possessed her just this morning. She'd felt vulnerable as he used magic with her, yet so incredibly safe.

But she was not ready to give her old self away. So she'd dropped Gabriel at a local coffee shop with his brand-new laptop before heading to the library for her weekly ritual.

It would take him a couple of hours to load up new software. He'd warned her that she should leave him alone as he'd probably curse through the whole process. It seemed he couldn't find a spell to speed things up.

Lily unloaded her book tote in the book-drop slot by the door, then stepped inside the historic building. The entrance had been decorated for Halloween. Cutouts of cheery ghosts and mischievous witches on broomsticks adorned the walls on the way to the children's section.

Smiling at the festive sight, Lily walked straight to the

counter and handed her card to the librarian. "I have a book on hold."

The girl swiped Lily's card in the scanner, then checked the computer. "Yes. It's here. I'll be right back." She disappeared into a small room behind the counter.

The place was busy this afternoon. A few people worked on the computers in the middle of the main room. A tiny lady talked to the middle-aged librarian at the reference desk, and a mother searched through DVDs while trying to keep her toddler quiet.

Lily's gaze stopped on a tall man perusing the new-books section beside the check-out counter. She couldn't see his face but noticed his shaved head and confident posture. He wore elegant dark wool pants and a charcoal gray sweater over a pristine white shirt. Lily couldn't take her eyes off of him.

The call of the librarian jolted her out of her daze. "There you are."

Lily turned away from the man and waited for her book as the librarian scanned it and put it on the counter. She'd finally be able to read this. It had stayed on the best-seller lists for weeks.

"What a wonderful book you chose." The rich male voice addressing her was accompanied by a strange overwhelming scent, fragrant herbs with a hint of decay.

A masculine hand rested on her book, elegant fingers drumming on the hardcover. Lily glanced up to the man towering over her.

No, it couldn't be. Her pulse quickened. *Theuron. Theuron Keir.*

"You will love it." His voice was like a caress all over her. His eyes were kind as he stared down at her. "The characters are intriguing. They are so alive." Theuron bent a little closer to her.

Lily couldn't speak, enthralled by him.

"Their struggle for love is fascinating, very noble." His lips curled into an attempt at a smile. "It's really sad when they don't make it in the end."

Lily blinked, snatched her book from him and put it in her bag. She rushed for the exit, hoping to leave him behind.

But he got there before her, appearing from nowhere as he held the door open for her. "Have a wonderful day, Miss Bellefontaine."

Lily walked outside, then stopped dead in her tracks and turned to look at him. He leaned near the doorway, on the gray stone wall.

"You know my name?" Oh, no, why had she talked to him?

"Of course, I do. Bellefontaine, one of the old Protector families. Not as old as the Blacks, but still . . ."

"Keira?"

"Yes, your lovely friend Keira. So new, so fresh, she's a constant delight to me." He stood completely immobile as he spoke.

"But she told me she wouldn't see you anymore." She'd called Keira to warn her right after the evening at the Blue Circle, but had Keira actually listened?

"Really, is that what she told you?" He raked the nail of his thumb on his sensual lips. "I suppose she couldn't stay away for too long, could she now?"

Lily stared at him. She should run to her car, get away from him.

"Neither will you, when it's time. But I'll allow Iain's young disciple to have his fun with you a little longer, I think. Let him enjoy you while he still can . . . another few months, no? I can wait."

Lily couldn't move. She couldn't sense anything coming from him, not a hint of life or warmth, just a great nothingness, and she still couldn't tear herself away from him.

•   "You'll be lovely when you join my Kyries." Theuron clasped his hands together at his chest, as if in prayer. "The girls need someone sensible around. They're such little birds. I thought Keira would be the one to lead them. She had such spirit when she first came to me. But now she has lost it all. She has amazing powers still, but not much will."

He took Lily's hand in his and gently kissed the inside of her wrist. A tide of incredible cold ran though her arm.

A black limousine with tinted windows rolled up in front of them and Theuron let go of her.

"I'll be waiting for you, love." Theuron stepped into the limo. "I'll be waiting for as long as it takes."

"Do you know how dangerous he is?" Gabriel slapped his computer shut and turned to Lily sitting beside him. He was working hard to keep his self-control.

After Lily had told him about her encounter at the library, he'd been consumed by a mix of fear and rage that Theuron could get so close to her while he wasn't there.

"Tara warned me about him." Lily didn't seem particularly scared as she played with the rim of her paper cup.

"You don't know half of it, Lil. If he ever comes near you again, you must get away as fast as you can. Don't talk to him."

"He was very polite. Creepy but polite."

Gabriel sighed. She was so sensible yet didn't seem to understand the danger. "Listen, all that man wants is to harm us. Didn't you tell me he was after Keira?"

"Yes, and I'll tell her again to stay away from him."

"Have you ever thought that maybe it's not Keira he

wants, but you?" He didn't know exactly what Theuron wanted with Lily, but he had to be prepared for the worst.

"Me? Why?"

Gabriel took a deep breath, tried to keep his voice calm. "He said he was waiting for you. He meant it. Time doesn't mean anything for him. He's undead."

Lily looked at him with a puzzled look on her face.

"Yes, undead." He sighed.

"Wait, what do you mean by undead?"

"I don't know the whole story. All I know is that Morag is scared of him, and that lady isn't scared of anything, ever."

He seemed to have gotten her attention now. He put both hands on her shoulders, his legs on each side of her. "Theuron made a pact with Taranis, god of thunder. In exchange for his powers, he now walks among the living without feeling a thing, as if he was dead, but not quite." Gabriel lowered his hands to take hers. "And Taranis wants sacrifice. Morag and her people always refused to perform them, but Theuron does."

"Sacrifice?"

"Yes, blood sacrifice, human."

"The dream. I dreamed of Theuron. I was tied. He had a dagger raised above me."

Her vision filled Gabriel with fear for her, horror that Theuron would ever get to her. His blood boiled. "The dagger of Taranis. He stole it from Morag."

"There were flames all around me."

"Yes, Taranis wants sacrifice by immolation, his offering burned alive." She had to know what they were up against.

"Burned alive?" She was visibly shaken. "Why the dagger in my dream?"

"I think Morag sent you that dream to warn you. Theuron might be stabbing his victims before setting off the pyre. He must be using the sacred dagger, blade and fire."

"Blade and fire," she said, letting the words sink in.

Still sitting in his chair, he embraced her while looking around the coffee shop. People worked on their computers. Friends were lost in deep conversations, normal people, all around them. People who would never have to deal with his cursed reality. He wished he could be one of them, having a quiet cup of coffee with his sweetheart, then going on to mundane things.

Gabriel pulled back to see her face. "Lily, this man is your worst nightmare. All the sorcerers and Morag fear him. Only Iain doesn't, but I don't think the old man is all there mentally. I've got to keep you safe." His hands caressed her hair, protective feelings surging through him.

"He did say he wanted me."

"I'm worried, Lil, that he'll try to do something to you."

"What about Angèle? He mentioned something about Protectors."

"Yes, the families that guard the third-blood souls. Not all of them know their importance, though. The Bellefontaines are Protectors."

"And the third-bloods are . . . ?"

"You, Lily, reborn three times. I'm second blood. Morag is first." He knew he was just confusing her. "Don't worry, you have me to protect you, and Morag summoned the Priory sorcerers to watch over Angèle. They've been doing it for a while now."

"I've never noticed anything."

"You wouldn't." He smiled at her. How could she ever understand the full extent of their powers? "Some of them can shift their appearance."

"Like a disguise."

He laughed. If he weren't so worried for her, he'd have

found it adorable that she was so naive about them. "No, they can take the form of animals, raptors mostly."

She said nothing for a moment, apparently pondering what he had said. "Like hawks?" He could see she was trying hard to believe him.

"Hawks, yes. Phoebus transforms into a falcon. And he is very proud of it."

She was quiet for a few seconds; then she looked at him with a shocked expression. "And you?"

"Nothing." He didn't want to admit that he remained the only sorcerer that couldn't transform. "I'm too young yet. Phoebus is seven hundred years old, and Loïc older still."

"When will you be able to do it?"

"Don't know, soon maybe?"

"Gabriel." A determined look settled on her pretty features. "I need you to help me. I've always denied my own powers, but now it's time to reclaim them. I have to see what I can do with them. I have to protect Angèle." She sat straight back.

He didn't say anything, not sure he liked the sound of that.

"What?" She frowned at him.

"Lily, sorry, but I don't think you can even protect yourself from Theuron, let alone protect someone else. I know you did great with that kid in the lake, but Theuron is too strong."

She looked straight at him and he recognized that face. She wouldn't back down. "At the very least I have to try. I can't just sit here defenseless. If Morag's so powerful, she'll be able to train me."

Great. Morag would have another pawn.

"Lil, Morag doesn't think you're ready." In fact, her exact words had been that Lily was not worthy, but he didn't need to tell her that.

"Ready?" Her eyes narrowed. "I'll show her what I can do. I'm ready—take me to her."

He sighed. "Somehow I don't think I have a choice here."

But he wasn't sure that he wanted Lily to be an apprentice to Morag. Wouldn't that give Morag even more power over them?

He shook his head, then stood up and put on his long dark coat. He felt the familiar gesture as an extra barrier erected between him and the rest of the world. Giving one last look at the people around of him, a hint of sadness permeated him. Why couldn't they have a normal life?

He held his hand out to help Lily up to her feet. "Welcome to hell, babe," he said to her. "Welcome to hell."

Eighteen

"So you think you want to be a priestess?" Morag settled a
dark look on Lily, her hands resting on a battered leather-
bound book.

"I need to learn more about what I'm capable of. If
becoming a priestess is what I have to do, then yes, I
want to be one." Lily sat at Morag's desk in the imposing
Callan library, filled with ancient artifacts: figurines of
deities, antique daggers, a battered cauldron nestled in a
corner. The faint music of a harp playing in the background did nothing to soothe her nerves. She hadn't expected to be questioned, assuming Gabriel had explained
her intentions.

"Why?"

Her palms lay flat on her lap and she forced herself to
appear calm despite the racing of her heart. "Theuron is
after me. I need to know how to protect myself and my
great-aunt."

"Theuron has been our enemy for centuries, resenting
our power. He has paid a dear cost for his gifts, allying
himself with Taranis. He is deranged, and that's what
makes him dangerous."

Lily said nothing, listening carefully.

Morag walked to the window opening onto the lake
and bare autumn trees. While she gazed on the quiet scenery of this late afternoon, she said, "He has lost all traces
of humanity and has spent his whole existence searching
for threads of it. He can only feel through others. Pain,
lust and despair. Love. He needs to be close to extreme

emotions in humans to feel a hint of the humanity he craves."

She turned to Lily, her expression weary. "The more souls he takes, the more powerful he becomes. He wants to destroy the Coven, the Priory. With us gone, he thinks he will obtain the ultimate prize." Morag's eyes had become a deep black. "He wants to become a god. You see, once he realized he couldn't be human anymore, his ambitions turned to higher planes."

Lily didn't know what to say.

"He's too powerful for you to stop, Lily. But we shall keep you safe." Morag leaned on her desk next to Lily. "We could send you and your great-aunt to Seattle. Highwayman could watch over you."

Highwayman—she must mean Roan. Gabriel had told Lily that each sorcerer had been given a special name as part of their initiation. Another way for Morag to dehumanize them, he'd said. Gabriel was Voyager, named from his work as a river guide to explorers in the eighteenth century.

Now Lily worried about the turn their conversation was taking.

"Seattle? We can't just pack up and go to Seattle."

"Why not? It's a beautiful city. You can take time off, leave your job for a while."

"Leave my job? I can't do that." She frowned at how casually Morag was reorganizing her life. "And what about my great-aunt? She doesn't know anything about all this."

"Oh, I suspect she knows a little more than she tells you. No, you two should leave New England, just for a while."

"This is our life you're talking about. I don't want to leave." Lily had never expected this. She'd assumed Morag would have been thrilled to train a new pupil in her ways.

"I was afraid you would be stubborn. You and Gabriel deserve each other. You could stay here with us, I suppose. A little commute to the city, but it would be safer than staying in your apartment."

Lily kept her hands in her lap, but her fists tightened. She was not going to be bullied by the woman, no matter how much she still feared her. "You can't watch us all the time. I'm going to have to learn what my powers are and how to use them."

Morag shook her head. "It takes time, and you need to be worthy of becoming a priestess. You do have some power Lily, I know. But what about your inner strength? Witchcraft is a hard path to follow."

"How?"

"There are many things. First, it is physically demanding. But you also have to suffer in other ways. You need to confront your worst enemy, yourself."

"I don't understand."

"It is a journey of the self. Only when you go deep inside and understand everything about yourself will you have true power. You have to face it all—your gifts, but also the bad and the ugly." Morag returned to her desk.

The priestess's words puzzled her. She'd expected to learn incantations, meditation techniques maybe, but not to relive her past.

"We all have dark corners deep inside us." Morag gave her a dead stare. "Are you ready to meet them?"

Lily squirmed in her chair. She'd never asked herself many questions. It'd been easier to plod along and not think too hard.

"You want security, Lily, don't you? I mean, not from Theuron, but from your past."

Lily said nothing and stared at the floor.

"Answer me. You're scared of losing your grip on life, right?"

Lily looked back at Morag. "Maybe." She was guarded now, knowing Morag could read her mind, and she resented the intrusion.

Morag sighed and sat back in her chair. She shrugged. "In the end, it is not for me to decide. If you want to try, I will help you."

"How?"

"This is the day of Samhain. Tonight the veil between the worlds will be thin and I will perform an important ritual. This is a perfect night for you to find out if you are ready for this. You shall come and then you will be able to decide if you want to continue."

Lily's tension eased for the first time since she'd walked into the library. Morag would teach her. She knew she'd succeed, although she dreaded the ritual part. "You don't give me much choice, do you?"

"The sorcerers say Morag can raise the dead at Samhain. I wouldn't want to be there." Gabriel words made her blood pump harder.

Lily didn't want to think about what she'd gotten into just yet. The ritual sounded terrifying and they'd do it in the forest, where she hadn't ventured since she'd gotten lost that fateful night.

She took a sip of wine, hoping it would relax her frazzled nerves before Morag called on her. Trying to gather a little courage, she clung to Gabriel's hand, eased at the sight of his handsome features caressed by the soft glow of many candles set on the outside deck around them.

"Why can't you be there?"

"I'm not allowed. No sorcerers ever participated in Morag's Samhain rituals. Only Tara, but she doesn't talk much."

"There are no other priestesses?"

"Not as far as I know. Morag lost the members of her

Coven a long time ago. She believes they will be returned to her. I don't know much more than that. I stay well away from her. I am a disciple of Iain. His magic is quite different from Morag's." Gabriel rubbed his thumb gently across her palm, the familiar gesture sending warmth through her whole body.

"How?"

"She talks to the deities. But Iain is an alchemist and a bit of a wizard. There are certain occult rituals that are needed for his magic, but he can alter the very basic elemental particles and channel energy from the universe. He sees the whole world as made of small energy waves. He's a sort of scientist."

"Is that how he got a professorship at Brown?"

"Yes. Alchemists dabble in chemistry and Iain is famous in the field, so the academics were only too happy to take him when he moved here a few years ago. He doesn't have much patience for his colleagues, but it's convenient. When he wants to order chemicals, no one asks too many questions." Gabriel put his wine glass down and got up, still holding her hand. "I tell you what. Let's go to his lab. It's fascinating."

"He won't mind?" She was hesitant about invading Iain's private space.

"No, no, I go in there all the time. Aren't you a little curious?" He flashed her a mischievous smile as he took her glass and set it down next to his.

"Maybe."

"Let's go take a peek now."

"We shouldn't be bothering him."

"No need to. Let's go by ourselves. It will be more fun." Gabriel helped her to her feet. With a flick of the hand and a few words, he put out the candles.

They walked down the deck to the back of the house. The wind picked up a little and Lily could hear the creaking of trees from the nearby woods. She'd felt nice on the deck surrounded by candlelight, but here in the moonless night, her heart pulsed at the unknown surrounding her.

She edged closer to Gabriel. "I didn't expect Morag to be out giving candies to the trick-or-treaters tonight. She's pretty funny dressed up as a witch."

"I guess she figures that if everyone thinks she's a witch anyway, why not dress the part at Halloween?"

"She doesn't seem the type to do something for fun." When Lily had seen the priestess in her gray wig and black hat, bending down to two little girls dressed as fairies, she'd been surprised by Morag's soft gestures and the kindness in her voice.

"Well, you never know with her. I think she wanted children but could never have them." Gabriel stopped by a trapdoor behind the house. "Come on." He pulled on the heavy panel and edged her toward the entrance.

"Down there?" Lily took a step back as dampness and a faint musty smell rose in the fresh air.

"Yes."

"Are you crazy? It's dark and smelly down there. You go first."

"Are you sure you're ready for the Samhain ritual?" She knew he was teasing her, but nothing would convince her to step down into the dark.

"Never mind Samhain, you go first."

"No problem." Gabriel walked down a few steps, Lily following close behind. "Give me your hand—the steps are pretty narrow."

It couldn't be as bad as she thought, just an old basement. As Gabriel guided her, she got used to the smell. Curiosity soon replaced her initial disgust. They went down a few more steps and found flat ground.

"*Solas.*" Five fat candles lit upon the floor as Gabriel

spoke. More glowed along the walls as Gabriel flicked his hand.

Lily examined the room. A painted black pentagram took up a large part of the wooden floor. Some sort of open wood stove was built out on the side of the lab and distillation equipment lay on a thick wooden workbench.

She approached the bench and inspected a series of small bottles filled with murky liquid. Dried snakes and lizards hung on the wall behind them. She looked away in disgust and focused her attention on a pretty plaque of green crystal lying flat beside the bottles, its surface carved with intricate symbols.

"What is this?" With her finger, she traced unusual writing, trying to figure out what it said.

"It's the emerald tablet, millions of years old. Every alchemist has a copy of it in his lab. It contains the secret formula for transforming our reality."

"Where did you find a copy?"

"Oh, we didn't." He lips curled into a grin. "This is the original."

Shaking her head, she walked to a high shelf filled with jars containing herbs of all species, leaves, bulbs, seeds, powders. She cautiously reached for one when the sound of rustling feathers startled her.

She looked behind her shoulder.

An owl. Perched on the workbench, it was many shades of gray, with a hooked beak and large eyes. His gaze fixed on her as it hooted. The owl turned its head in their direction and Lily felt unease creep along her spine.

"Gabriel?"

But Gabriel was searching though a series of herbs hanging in the back of the lab and didn't seem to notice.

The owl jumped onto the coarse floor. It spread its wings wide and a shimmering halo appeared around it.

Lily was mesmerized, filled with both fear and marvel.

The halo became a blur of swirling grays that grew larger and larger, until it reached the size of a grown man. It then dissolved slowly.

Iain materialized in the lab, his gray hair loose around his shoulders, a large black coat covering him. He stood ramrod straight, a fierce expression on his face.

Lily was stunned. No signs of the old shuffling professor remained in the mighty sorcerer standing in the center of his lab.

"Ah, Lily, did I scare you?" His stern features relaxed into a gentle smile. "I'm so sorry."

She shook her head. "No, I mean . . . Gabriel told me you could shift, but I didn't expect this."

"Yes, dear. I suspect it's always a little surprising at first." He walked to his workbench, then turned back to her. "So are you ready for the ritual?"

"As ready as I can be, I guess. Though I wish Gabriel could be there."

"So do I." Gabriel came to her side and placed a possessive hand on her shoulder.

"For now it is best you seek your knowledge alone, Lily." Iain sounded concerned.

"I suppose so."

"The study of women's mysteries are a must for a priestess in training, just as she should know of men's mysteries."

"Men's mysteries?"

"The three stages of a man's life. The young Stag, the Warrior King, the Elder."

"The Warrior King?" She looked at Gabriel.

"Yes. When a man has learned all he needs to enter the productive part of his life. And in this case, when a Priory sorcerer is mated with his soul mate. Chosen by his priestess to become her consort."

"Oh."

"The mating will solidify his ties to the Priory"—Iain's gaze shifted to Gabriel—"and also bring increased magical abilities."

Lily thought for a moment before sking, "Is it like you? With Morag?"

"Yes. A little like me." Iain leaned back on his worktable and crossed his arms over his chest. "So much to learn, isn't there?"

Lily nodded silently.

"Don't worry about tonight, dear. Morag is quite kind. Really."

Morag carried a light in her bare hand into the dark forest. It looked like a naked flame, and Lily, starting to get used to the unusual sights around the Callans, knew better than to ask about it.

"You're not cold, walking barefoot?" Lily picked up the pace, nervous at the woody rotten scent around her but not willing to let Morag know the wilderness scared her.

Morag smiled. "Not really." They reached the middle of a clearing and she stopped. "This is my sacred space."

Lily thought she recognized the large boulder at the edge closer to the lake. This must be where Gabriel had found her on that fateful night.

Morag turned to Lily. "Tonight, you will just sit and watch me perform the ritual."

Lily nodded.

"Make sure you don't disturb anything." Morag walked to the middle of the clearing, carrying her fire in her joined palms, Lily following right behind.

"Samhain is very special to me. It is the Celtic new year. As I said before, on this night the veil is thin between this world and the underworld. And we will part it tonight. Are you ready?"

Lily swallowed. She wasn't sure what Morag was talking about, but the whole affair made her too nervous to ask any questions. "Yes, I'm ready."

"When we reach the underworld, you may see things. Just let the visions go through you, let them lead you."

Lily looked around her, her heart beating at a thundering pace. Then she reached for threads of her soothing powers. They were faint, but there.

"Do not fight the visions." Morag seemed to have noticed her fears. "Nothing is dangerous here. Everything is already part of you."

"I'll do what you say, don't worry."

Morag blew on the flames in her hands and the fire jumped forward. It lit a few candles arranged on a low marble bench in front of them and two large torches planted in the ground at each side of it.

"This is my altar." Morag gestured to the bench. Beside the gold and silver candles lay four bronze containers, a few pomegranates and a small white-handled knife.

A silver ornate pendant in the shape of a pentagram rested at the center and a large sword leaned on the side. It was a powerful weapon, its blade large and adorned with unusual inscriptions. The polished steel shone in the light of the torches.

Lily looked at the artifacts with awe, still holding on to her stilling powers.

"I'll be using all these tonight. Now come and stand beside me. It's time to purify ourselves. Clear your mind as much as you can. Use what you know."

Lily forced herself to be calm. She slowed her breathing and focused on the candles in front of her.

Morag raised a hand and started to speak in an ancient language. The wind rose all around them. As it blew stronger and swirled, it played with Morag's dress and lifted Lily's hair.

When it stopped, peace descended on Lily. She was no longer afraid.

"Kneel by the altar. I will cast the circle."

Lily fell to the grass as Morag picked up the sword.

Lily suddenly remembered seeing it before. It had been in her dream. The one Morag had sent her after her first weekend at the Callans'.

Morag ran her fingers along the blade. "We call it the Cathair Sword, fit for a warrior. It was given to the Coven by a powerful blacksmith to bring us protection or to end life, even the unnatural ones."

Lily froze. What did she mean by that? Would this kill Theuron?

"Yes, it would." Morag had read her mind again. "But it would also kill me or Gabriel."

Morag walked to the edge of the clearing, pointed the sword at the ground and started walking in a large circle around Lily and the altar.

Lily could barely see Morag in the darkness, although she heard her mumbling. Sitting in the dark, far away from the priestess, she felt less brave than she'd been a few minutes ago. Sweat trickled down the middle of her back.

Gabriel's words came back to her. Surely Morag couldn't raise the dead?

Morag returned and laid the sword flat on the altar. "Now, Lily, this is for our protection. No matter what happens, you cannot walk outside the circle or it will dissolve."

"I won't, Morag." Lily's chest constricted, but she was determined to do just as Morag said. She was wary of the priestess, but knew she held the door to the full knowledge of her own powers.

"I will invoke more protection now. The guardians will come to us."

Morag stood straight, facing the altar. She whispered in the dark.

"*Pri.*" Her arms rose to waist level, her palms flat, facing the ground.

Lily felt the wind rising gently and lifting leaves and loose soil around them. Dust fell on Lily's jeans, but she was too mesmerized to brush it off, Morag's power enticing her to watch with fascination.

After turning to her right, Morag lifted her arms higher, straight in front of her, and she spread her fingers wide.

"*Aerañ.*" Her voice boomed low again, vibrating in Lily's body.

The wind picked up some speed, warm and soft against Lily's cheek. *She must be calling the air,* Lily thought.

Morag then turned to face Lily. Her eyes closed, she raised her arms high above her head, her hands in tight fists.

"*Flamm.*" Again, she'd spoken the ancient language, but loudly now. The wind became warmer and warmer, the air as hot as on a mid-August day. Lily's skin burned uncomfortably, flushed from the heat.

Morag turned toward the last direction. Her hands lowered and formed a cup raised upward.

"*Dour,*" she said in the still night. Her voice was softer, as if she spoke to a lover.

Coming out of nowhere, light rain fell on them. It was gentle, almost misty. Lily could barely sense the drops on her hands. The air had become cooler.

Morag faced the altar and threw her head back. She cut a majestic figure as her arms extended high in the air, her fingers spread, her thick hair covering her shoulders down to the middle of her back.

For the first time, Lily felt a strange kinship with the priestess with the fiery hair glowing like copper from the flames around her. No longer afraid, Lily wished Morag would accept her and teach her all she knew.

A wispy fog built up, full of the scent of the ocean laying a mile away from them. The whole clearing became thick with it. The four elemental guardians had been summoned.

Lily could no longer see the shadows of the trees around them. They were embraced by mist and the eerie light diffusing from the candles and torches.

"The goddess Cerrwiden will soon be with us. You must be calm and we will see whether she touches you in any way."

While Lily stayed focused, fighting to keep her heartbeat regular, Morag took the pentagram in both hands. Still facing the altar, she knelt on the ground next to Lily. She raised the pentagram above her head and called the goddess.

Soon Lily's consciousness filled with female voices, softly chanting. She could no longer see the altar, only mist, thin and layered this time. She wasn't sure if it was a vision or if she was still in the clearing.

Then, she saw erect stones on a barren land. She felt cold wind on her skin. No, this felt different. She was no longer in Morag's sacred clearing.

What are you seeking, child? An unknown voice rose in her mind. She was startled to distinguish a shadow in front of her among the stones.

Lily wanted to run away but couldn't. She was transfixed, paralyzed with fear but also curiosity. Who had spoken?

I am the crone, said the shadow. *Are you ready to transform?*

The shadow walked closer and, her blood running cold, Lily saw the face of a woman so old, she must have lived forever. Her hair was steel gray yet long and lustrous.

She had parched, wrinkled skin, but her lips were full and soft, her green eyes clear and piercing.

Lily gasped and the woman disappeared, as if Lily's own fear had chased her away.

Then she saw the familiar clearing and Morag still kneeling in front of the altar beside her with the pentagram in her lap.

Lily wanted to get out of there, wanted to be back at the house, safe in Gabriel's arms, not sure now if she sought any part in Morag's mysteries.

Morag got up swiftly and laughed. "Are you such a coward that you won't acknowledge what lies in your soul?"

"I'm not a coward." Lily summoned every ounce of courage she'd ever possessed, her fists tight in determination. She would see this through to the end.

"Really? Then it's time to part the veil."

Lily stayed still as Morag turned to her left and drew a complicated symbol in the air.

Instantly, Lily saw black. Gone was the fog, the altar, Morag. Darkness had swallowed her. Where could she be?

Lily, honey. A voice she recognized, but no, it couldn't be.

I'm worried about you. The soft voice again.

"Mom?"

She felt her mother's embrace, her warmth around her. She saw her sweet smile. Her heart melted to feel the love she'd always needed, but never truly got.

Follow your heart, Lily. Don't be scared, her mother said to her consciousness.

Mom, what is all this?

Live, sweetheart, live your life. Don't let your fear control you.

Her mother's presence slipped away and fog surrounded her again as she knelt on the cold ground. She blinked. Had she been dreaming? Was that what Morag had meant by the underworld? Lily was full of confusing thoughts.

Morag was cutting a pomegranate on the altar with the white-handled knife. Squashing the fruit, she collected the seeds in one hand, then offered it to Lily, bloodred juice dripping on the ground. "Eat some. Be filled with Earth's power."

Lily, still shaken by her vision, obeyed. The seeds tasted sweet and tart on her tongue and helped bring her back to reality.

"You can get up now. Take the rest of these seeds and scatter them around on the ground."

Lily got up, her legs stiff from having knelt so long.

"What we take, we must give back." Morag got busy with the bronze flasks on the altar while Lily sprinkled the pomegranate seeds on the ground and wiped her sticky hand on the dry grass.

"Our ritual is done. Let me open the circle now." Morag took the sword and went around the circle, in the other direction this time, while Lily stood in front of the altar, not sure what to think.

As Morag walked back from the dark, Lily contemplated what she'd learned. Did her mother mean that she approved of Lily's embracing her powers?

Still puzzled, Lily looked at Morag. Her heart froze.

A completely different woman stood before her. Gone were the fiery red hair and the domineering stance.

Lily faced an old woman in a thick light plaid, her gray haired tied back in a bun. On her shoulder casually leaned the Cathair Sword.

Lily's mouth opened. She couldn't utter a single word.

To her horror, the woman laughed and it sounded more like a cackle. "Are you afraid? It is still I, Morag. I wear two faces. Between Samhain and Beltane I walk as Cailleach the Hag. Do not worry. I will return in the spring as Brighid."

The old woman swung the sword high in the air with surprising force. In one swift move, she planted it in front of her.

Lily jumped back.

Morag laid both hands on the hilt. "So tell me, child, did you find what you sought?"

Nineteen

Come on. I don't have all night. Lily fiddled with her wallet as she waited for the barista to take her order. She had ten minutes left before night training class started.

Between her shift at the hospital, training with Morag and time with Gabriel, she found herself busier than ever. But once she got over her uneasiness at confronting her past during the Samhain ritual, she'd realized how much she had to learn.

Morag was indeed the one meant to teach her.

"Who's turn is it?" The big guy behind the counter looked at both Lily and the young woman standing next to her.

The blonde beside Lily, in a lace-trimmed black dress topping knee-high combat boots, smiled warmly. "You were ahead of me I think." Her voice was high-pitched and breathless.

Lily shrugged. "It's okay. You go ahead."

"Oh no, you go." The blonde furrowed her eyebrows. She nodded vigorously. "You were there before me."

"Thank you." Lily turned to the barista and asked for her drink.

"That coffee must be very sweet." The blonde inched closer to Lily. Her luxurious scent seemed odd, given her youthfulness. The thick fringe cut high above her pencil-thin eyebrows made her look like an old-fashioned pin-up girl.

Lily nodded to her. "Yes, I like it sweet."

The other barista, a wire-thin man in his fifties, set

a large paper cup on the side of the bar, yelled out a name, then turned back to the blonde. "What would you like?"

"I'll have what she's having." She beamed at Lily like a little girl who wants to behave.

"And that was . . . ?" The barista looked at Lily.

"Large coffee with a double shot of vanilla syrup," Lily said while the blonde edged even closer. Her heavy musk scent and proximity made Lily pull back slightly.

"It does sound very good." The girl darted her small pink tongue over dark berry lips.

Lily smiled back politely. "It is."

The barista called Lily's name. She fetched her coffee before heading slowly out.

The girl followed her. "You're not staying?"

"No, I'm late." Balancing her cup, she looked at her watch to emphasize her point, then edged to the glass door. A light fog had settled over downtown Providence and dimmed the headlights of the few cars driving by.

"Oh." The girl's pouting expression almost made Lily feel bad. "My girlfriends are here." She pointed to a table where two other girls waited.

It was impossible to guess their ages. One was as blonde as her friend and wore an ivory lacy dress that didn't hide her heavily tattooed chest. The other one, a redhead, was clad in a black leather ruffled skirt and matching jacket over a cropped pink T-shirt. A thick black velvet choker adorned her throat.

"I have to go." Lily took her gaze away from the seated girls to nod at the blonde. "See you around then."

"Yes." The girl beamed. "I'll see you later."

Lily stepped into the sticky air. The streets were quiet after hours and she rushed her steps.

She yawned slightly. After her tough shift today, she'd need that coffee to stay awake during class.

It was only a few minutes' walk. She took a small alley that would get her to class faster.

The streetlights shining through the fog made her think of Halloween somehow. Maybe she should pick up some cute pumpkin string lights next year for the apartment. Angèle would like it.

As she walked, she sipped her coffee. Sweet. Yes, it was good. The pouty expression of the girl danced in her mind. Lily shook her head. Odd.

She was tired, and cursed whoever had decided to schedule class right after work in the middle of the week. She wouldn't be home until after eleven tonight. No time to unwind.

Oh well, better get it over and done with.

She walked faster, securing her bag close to her body as it bounced on her hip.

The sound of hurried footsteps echoed behind her.

"Hey." The footsteps had turned into a run and were accompanied with fast breathing.

"Hey, wait."

She stopped and turned back toward the voice. What now?

It was the girl from the coffee shop.

"Oh, hi. Sorry, but I'm really late for class." Why wouldn't this girl leave her alone?

"That's okay." The girl pushed her bangs up off her forehead. "I can walk with you."

"It's just a couple of blocks. Why would you want to do that?"

"I like you. Just wanted to talk to you."

"Really?" A odd eeriness crawled over Lily.

"Yes. In fact, my girlfriends wanted to meet you as well."

"Oh." She turned, ready to ignore the girl and be back on her way.

She jumped.

Her heart pumped faster. The girl's two friends were right there.

They looked at her with vivid interest, their features softened by the cold fog suddenly thickening around them all.

Lily secured her handbag under her arm. How could the girls appear out of nowhere?

"Hi," the girl in black leather said.

The blonde who'd been talking to Lily so far seemed harmless, but she wasn't so sure about these two.

"Where are you going?" the third girl said, wrapping a thin cardigan over her lacy dress.

Lily took a few involuntary steps back and found herself edging up to a brick wall. The alley hadn't been so dark when she took it, but now it seemed as if nightfall had suddenly descended upon them, the street incredibly empty.

"Why do you want to know?" Lily slowly sipped some coffee, trying to look detached.

The redhead in black leaned one arm on the wall, standing dangerously close. "We have a friend who'd like to talk to you."

"A friend?"

"Yes. Male friend. Very sexy." She licked her full top lip.

"Yes, very hot." The other girl slowly slid her palms from her hips up to her breasts. Her motion lifted her fragile dress, exposing her panties, a tiny triangle of baby blue silk. The fabric almost disappeared between the part of her tattooed thighs not covered by her black stocking.

Lily's heart hammered in her chest now. She didn't like this.

"Don't be scared, girl." The blonde from the coffee shop said in her little girl's voice. "He's very nice."

Lily wrapped her arms closely around her as she

shivered. *Theuron.* The girls were Kyries, the mage companions that Gabriel had warned her about.

"Theuron Keir."

"Why, yes." The girl rested deeper into the wall. "He wants to see you. But first he thought we should make friends." She leaned over Lily and gently brushed the hair out of her eyes.

Lily flinched at the intimacy. The girl's dark eyes were vacant. As if she wasn't truly moving of her own free will.

"We will be very good friends," she said.

Lily forced herself to breathe in slowly, then let a breath out, keeping control over her shaking body. They couldn't be dangerous, but still, there were three of them.

Lily silenced her mind.

Peace, yes. Again, there is was. She was in control of her initial panic.

But she didn't dare push out of the Kyries' way. She didn't know how they'd react.

"That's great." Lily turned to the girl who was so close she could feel her breath on her cheek. "I'll give you guys my phone number." She dug into her bag with her free hand, looking for a pen and paper.

But the redhead ignored her. "He wants you now," she whispered in Lily's ear. She leaned her head on Lily's. "Lily Bellefontaine."

Lily flinched to hear her name on the Kyrie's lips. As she thrust her head back, her mind raced with possible ways of escaping them.

"Yes, right away, cutie." Still fondling her own breasts, the girl in front of Lily moved forward to crush her closer to the wall.

Never panic. Whatever Theuron has in mind for you, never panic. Morag's words brought calm to her mind. *You do have powers, priestess. You must use them.* Power . . . What power did she really have?

"Lily, please come with us." The innocent girl from the coffee shop looked suddenly scary as she tugged at Lily's handbag.

Where was their weakness?

"Surely you're not scared of us?" The redhead lowered her fingers to Lily's cheek, then down her neck, sending shivers along Lily's body, her touch so soft, so gentle. This was much too weird. They were all so alluring.

Lily closed her eyes for a second. A strange desire rose into her. *No, impossible.* She almost wanted to be one of them. They were chilling yet so beautiful in their lost-angels way.

The girl in front of her stopped and took Lily's hand to lift it to her breast. It was big, pliant and soft in her hand. So feminine under the ivory lace.

Mesmerized, Lily couldn't really take her hand away. No, she couldn't be attracted to them.

You do have powers, priestess, Morag's voice chimed again in her mind.

The girl took Lily's thumb and rubbed it on her nipple. The alien sensation of feeling another woman hardening under her touch released something in her.

"No." Lily jolted back. She peered into the girl's big brown eyes and saw.

She saw the world as the girl saw it: a child lost in the street begging and hungry, a handsome man taking her hand. *Theuron.* A group of young women in a dark and musty room surrounded by stone walls, the girls hugging each other. Theuron watching, his enigmatic expression always present. Pleasure and pain mixed together, teasing the girl. Pleasure from a woman's touch, always. Denied by the man who watched them.

Lily gasped at the thoughts running through her. Seducing prey. Men lured by the beautiful Kyries, led to their death by the girls. Theuron's human sacrifices.

In horror, Lily tore her mind from the girl's.

Without a second thought, she kneed her in the stomach. In one swing, she hurled her coffee at the redhead. She pushed her way out and bolted.

"Hey, wait!" the other blonde Kyrie shouted. "What did you do that for?"

Lily heard them break into a run behind her.

No, they wouldn't get her. Fast on her feet, she'd beat them. No time to dwell on the fact that she'd read minds again after so long. Yet a rush of power surged through her.

She could do it. She had done it. Her power still remained.

The main street was just a block away. She lengthened her stride, contracted her muscles with each pounding step.

She turned the corner leading to a side alley, then smacked into something solid and hard.

"Well, hello there." The scent of mold and herbs mixed with sophistication struck her at once.

She looked up at the man she'd hit. *Theuron*. His bare head gleamed in the shadows, emphasizing the symbol inked at his neck. A full-length black cashmere coat entirely covered his tall body.

He held on to her arms, steadying her.

She stayed there panting, catching her breath and too stunned to say anything.

"Are you all right, love? You look very flustered."

Lily just stared at him as her breath slowed. Her legs didn't seem to be able to support her.

"She doesn't want to be our friend." Her breath wheezy, the blonde had finally caught up.

"It's okay, Kali. We don't want to frighten her now, do we?" His smooth voice made the hair on the back of Lily's neck prickle. It overwhelmed her with both fear and fascination.

"Of course not." The redhead appeared at the corner of Lily's eye, her tiny pink T-shirt now stained from the coffee Lily had thrown over her, drips snaking down to her bare stomach. "She's so pretty."

"Go, my beautifuls." He nodded toward a car at the curb. "Wait for me in the car. There'll be plenty of playtime later." His lips curled into a smile as his gaze still held on to Lily.

Without another word, the three girls walked to Theuron's limo, parked a few feet away.

A large man with a shaved head got out. He reminded Lily of the thugs Gabriel had fought on the beach—Keepers. He opened the back door and the girls disappeared inside before he settled back into the driver seat.

Lily swallowed. It was now just her and Theuron.

She'd managed to run away from him at the library, but this time, in the back alley thick with fog, she just couldn't tear herself from the mage.

"What do you want from me?" Everything she'd heard about him came running into her mind. A mixture of Gabriel's loathing and Keira's lust. She had no idea what to expect.

"Oh, she speaks." He simply smiled at her, sounding not so threatening suddenly.

"Let me go."

"Of course, my love, of course." Theuron let go of her arms and Lily found herself fascinated by his hands as they lingered on her coat. She blinked away a thought of his fingers on her skin.

"I was just preventing you from falling. You looked quite distressed."

"I'm not." She wasn't lying. He didn't appear so fierce,

and the surge of power she felt at reading the Kyrie's mind made her stronger.

"Good. As I said, we wouldn't want you frightened. And to answer your question, I just want you to make friends with my girls."

"I have my own friends, thank you."

"Oh, yes. The lovely Keira Black."

"Leave Keira alone." A twinge of guilt rose in her. She should have been a lot more forceful when she told Keira to stay away from Theuron. She should have made more time in her schedule for her friend.

"I can't really do that right now."

Lily stared at Theuron's elegant features and focused, felt the strength inside her, power.

Yes. Oh how easy it was. The world as he saw it. She was in his mind.

Then she saw her. In his consciousness. *Keira.* Her blonde hair cascaded down her pale naked shoulders. She sat sprawled on a leather couch in a shift dress so thin it showed the black leather bra and garter belt she wore under it. Was this true or just Theuron's fantasy?

Keira played with a strand of long dark hair belonging to a girl sitting beside her. The girl wore a pink full-length dress with a tulle skirt like a ballerina's, the velvet bodice cut so low, her breasts were more on offer than covered.

The dark girl turned her face into Keira's touch and Lily froze.

No. This is wrong. This is not me.

Pain hammered into her skull at once. She opened her eyes wide at Theuron, gripping her forehead in her palm.

"No, no, no. Love." He smiled. "You can't go in there."

Lily stood trembling and stunned, as the pain slowly

subsided. She had read Theuron's mind. She could see the surprised look underneath his superior air.

"You do have power," he said. "How interesting. I can't wait for you to be mine."

She didn't answer and watched, unwilling to escape him. What was it that made him so fascinating? She held her breath, wondering if he'd force her to go with him.

"I want you willing, my dear Lily." His hand disappeared under his coat. "I wouldn't just capture you without your consent. I want you begging for me."

Her body started to tingle, causing a mix of emotions.

The memory of the Kyrie's nipple hardening under her thumb and the images from Theuron's mind swirled together in her thoughts. She shook her head, trying to ignore the heat rising within. Was that what Keira had experienced? Lily stood there almost willing to let Theuron take the lead. The mind reading had drained her.

"Sweetheart." Theuron caressed her cheek, then took her hand in his. "It's not so bad. There." He placed a business card in her palm and closed her hand over it.

He kept her hand between his. "Call me when you're ready. I know you will. You can't help it." He smiled.

Her lips parted. A mix of revulsion and lust filled her at his words.

"I know you're happy with your Gabriel now. But trust me, it won't last. It's not you he wants. It's Evangéline, his lost fiancée. He doesn't appreciate who you really are. I want *you*, love. The full, passionate Lily.

"When you realize his true feelings for you and stop denying what you really want, come to me." He let go of her hand and stepped away.

She tried to dismiss his words, but found she had a hard time doing so. Lily was still rooted to the spot when the limo drove away.

She opened her hand and looked at the card. Just a plain name and a number, a black card with white writing. She motioned to throw it away but a thought stopped her. Evangéline, Gabriel . . . Could it be true?

With a pressing need to see Gabriel, she shook her head. No, it wasn't true at all. They loved each other. They had been brought together because it was meant to be. It felt right. She fully trusted him.

But she didn't want to get rid of the card. She'd read Theuron's mind, used her power on a powerful mage. She wanted to keep something from the experience.

She started to walk again. Her night class seemed unimportant now as she recalled the hint of desire she'd felt for Theuron, the temptation even. Was he truly bad?

What was she thinking? Of course he was. She had dreamed the attraction, the lust. It wasn't real.

She opened her bag and found her wallet. With great care, she placed Theuron's number behind the rest of her cards.

There, far away from sight.

Twenty

"Oh God, Lily, I'm lost. Help me, please, help." Keira drew her legs closer to her, a pale wraith in black.

Her voice sounded very small as she rocked her body side to side on Lily's couch.

She'd stormed into Lily's apartment minutes before, looking a wreck in not much more than a black night-gown. She had lost a lot of weight since Lily had last seen her a few weeks ago. The see-through lacy fabric clung to the entire length of her skinny body. Her white-blonde hair was tied into two messy braids.

Sitting on the armrest, Lily drew one of Angèle's holi-day quilts on top of her friend. "It's okay, Keir. I'm right here. Tell me what's going on."

Keira huddled at the edge of the couch like a frightened cat. "You know what he is. Help me. Do something."

Her eyes were different, a strange dark blue color, al-most black. She clutched a bony hand on Lily's arm, her grip incredibly strong. "He made me see. I saw it all." Her horror-filled gaze made Lily cringe with dread.

"What, what did you see?"

"I'm the one. You know I'm the one. He made me see the past. They buried me alive. It's horrible, Lily. I'm bur-ied alive." Keira's voice sounded high and wheezy. She curled into a tighter ball.

"Buried alive." Keira frantically rubbed her emaciated shin; then her expression became blank, her gaze fixed on the wall as if she was looking at something that wasn't there. "The darkness, the smell. I can't move. Do you know how long it took me to die?"

Lily patted Keira's knees, trying to appease her. Horrified at the current situation, she cursed herself for not having seen earlier the signs of Theuron's influence on her friend.

She had to do something, anything, to take Keira out of his clutches.

But she felt powerless as Keira now stretched flat on the couch, her arms around her, and rolled side to side, her legs kicking the quilt.

"I'm dying, Lily, help me. I can't breathe. It's so dark. I'm scared. I asked them to do it. I'm a queen, must be noble for my people." She fought unseen demons, pleading in a raspy voice. "No, I don't want to do this anymore. Come get me."

She stopped moving and her mad eyes fixed on Lily. "They can't hear me. He betrayed me, you know. My king, he betrayed me. He wasn't dead in battle. He went to her, the demon woman." Keira looked away.

"Keira."

She turned her head sharply toward Lily like a small skittish bird. "Keira, who is Keira?"

"Keira, listen. It's me, Lily, your friend."

Keira screamed and fell back on the couch. "Be brave, must be royal Queen Clothilde." She whimpered now as tears welled in her eyes. "I am not queen anymore. I am dead. The Morrigan, why her, my love, why have you betrayed me?" Her voice sounded very different now, foreign somehow.

"I am dying. Death take me, death claim me, the earth shall swallow me, and I will join Renaud, *Renaud mon roi*." Had she spoken French? Keira's breath became labored.

She continued, sounding like herself again. "Lily, I

don't want to die." Her eyes suddenly went blank, fixed on the ceiling.

Lily looked around her, bewildered. What on earth could she do? With horror, she remembered Morag's warnings about Theuron, the sacrifice, the pyres, the quest for human feelings.

What had the evil mage done to Keira? He must have been sending her these visions for his pleasure.

Keira writhed on the couch, moaning to herself, her eyes closed.

Lily drew the quilt over her friend and felt for her pulse, found it a little fast but normal. She rested the back of her hand on Keira's cheek. She was feverish. Lily had to get her out of this trance.

Morag would know what to do.

But no, she could handle it by herself. Morag had taught her everything she needed. She'd had four full magical rituals so far, had used her power many times on children. She could certainly do it on a grown woman. The earlier panic left her and she felt strong.

Lily took a deep mindful breath and laid a hand on Keira's forehead. As her self-control rose, she focused on her task, pushing away all thoughts of Theuron's darkness.

Threads of powers rose in her and she reached for them, held them in her mind, in her body. As it built up, she felt the cold mist on her cheeks, dampening her hair. The now-familiar female voices whispered in her head.

Yes, it was working. She let out a slow breath, then sent out her quieting powers to Keira all at once. It tingled through her arm, into her fingers, then rushed to her friend.

Keira opened her eyes wide and turned to stare at Lily. "Help me. Get me out of that coffin. I'm trapped."

Tears welled up again as she tugged at her gown, baring her small breasts, exposing erect rosy nipples.

"Renaud, you betrayed me." Keira suddenly became very still and her eyes fixed on nothing.

"Keira, talk to me." Lily was stunned. It hadn't worked. Her powers had failed her, failed for the first time.

Keira was possessed by Theuron. Lily was suddenly really scared.

She again put the quilt over Keira as her friend moaned and rocked. Then she got up and paced the floor. She needed more. She needed a ritual, needed to invoke Cerrwiden's protection. She had nothing with her, no pentagram, no elements, nothing.

Candles—she had some black candles. Yes, they would help.

Keira whimpered again.

Lily found a pen and paper and quickly drew a full pentagram, first the five-pointed star, then the circle around it.

She set the paper on the floor in front of her and placed the candle in the middle, wishing she had a silver candle or at least a shell, to call on the goddess.

No, this would have to do.

She recalled Morag's instruction: cast the circle first, clockwise, call upon the elemental guardians—earth, air, fire, water—then invoke the goddess. She'd never done it, but had watched Morag enough to remember it all.

Lily bit her lips. What if she did something wrong? Morag had warned her of misusing magic. But no, she shouldn't worry. The goddess was good; she would help.

Lily knelt and lit the candle in front of her. Then she got up and slowly walked the circle.

She ambled on a bleak land. Thirteen stones surrounded her, tall thick standing shapes hovering over her.

The mist was heavy, but she could still see them. She looked everywhere, circling the stones, the moss-covered ground damp under her feet.

"Cerrwiden. Come to me, I summon you." Lily lay her hand on the rough stone surface, her fingers brushing the moss attached to it. It had a strange hue, like heather, light pink and dusty blues mixing with the various shades of gray, arranged like veins layering the rock.

She called Cerrwiden again. Why didn't the goddess answer?

Lily walked to the center of the circle and sat on a polished flat stone. Suddenly, she felt a presence next to her, a strong rotting smell making her jump in disgust. She turned to the newcomer.

This was not Cerrwiden.

An ancient and extremely ugly woman sat beside her. Her teeth were rotten, her gray hair matted and filthy. Her thin, lined skin had a grayish tone to it. She held a long staff in her skeletal fingers. Its length was carved in Celtic loops and at the top lay a beautiful lavender gem enclosed in vicious-looking claws. Who was this?

Lily recoiled in distaste.

The old woman laughed, a horrible cackle shattering through Lily's head. "Cerrwiden. I am Cerrwiden. Have you not called me, *chloinne*?" The woman smiled, a wicked grin stretching her thin, cracked lips.

"But you can't be."

"Why, because you have never seen this side of me? Foolish child. I take many forms. Last, you saw the crone. Now you see death. I am the whole circle."

Cerrwiden got up and rested her hand on the staff. "Do you know that when I finally found Taliesin, that fool who drank my potion, I ate him?"

The goddess's words made Lily's mind swirl in confusion. Was she trying to scare her?

Cerrwiden laughed again. "A year and a day, it took. All this time, to make my poor son Gwion handsome. All this work, gone."

She narrowed her eyes at Lily. "A year and a day in front of that cauldron. Now would you have such patience?"

Lily lay speechless.

"Tell me, child, do you fear me?"

Scared to death, Lily didn't want to answer the question. She thought of Morag. The priestess had taught her to be brave. All this was already part of her.

"I need help."

"Oh, help. And what makes you think I'll help you?"

"I've studied with Morag. I summoned you. I'm a priestess."

"Morag, yes." Cerrwiden pursed her lips. "She is called Cailleach to me. Silly goddess to spend so much time meddling in human matters. Must be love, I guess."

Cerrwiden bend down to examine Lily closer. She narrowed her eyes as cold ran through Lily's blood. "So Morag thinks you're ready, does she?"

"No, she doesn't know about this ritual." Lily pulled back slightly. "I was in a hurry, my friend Keira—"

Another horrible laugh interrupted her.

"Impatient, are we? Presumptuous, I'd say." The ancient woman gave her an irritated look, and all of a sudden she was gone.

Then Lily heard Cerrwiden's haunting laughter again. It echoed everywhere, all around her, resonating deep into her brain. She covered her ears in pain and sank to the damp ground.

"Learn, child, that I do not share my powers with those who are not ready." A loud disembodied voice reverberated in the mist. "'In a hurry.' Really." The cackle resonated in the air.

"What a miserable soul you are, *chloinne*, my child. A few incantations you learned somewhere and just like that, you think I, Cerrwiden, will help you. What have you given of yourself? Not much," the creaky voice said. "Leave now, leave."

"But Keira . . . ?" Lily found some courage deep inside her. She wasn't prepared to accept failure yet.

"Ah yes, your little friend. Morag makes strange choices in her future priestesses. Well, I'll grant you that you are generous. Hope is not all lost." Cerrwiden let a deep sigh. "So, you want to save your friend?"

"Yes."

"Would you do anything to help her?"

"I would, yes." Her control had returned. She knew what she was doing.

"Very well, then. Let Keira be saved for now, and pay the price." A touch of sadness altered Cerrwiden's voice. "Farewell, little Lily."

All of a sudden Lily was torn out of her trance and found herself returned to reality.

She first noticed the candle, still burning at the center of the black pentagram, then Keira, who breathed peacefully.

Joy filled her, she had the power. She had succeeded. She couldn't wait to tell Morag.

All she had to do now was to give thanks and walk the circle again.

Lily started to get up.

A searing pain pierced the left side of her chest, forcing her to clutch at her heart.

"Lily, open up," Gabriel shouted through the door of Lily's apartment. "Lily." Where was her great-aunt?

Gabriel grabbed the handle and rattled the door as

hard as he could, his heart pounding fast. He knew she was in trouble. He had known it the minute he'd felt her invoke the elemental guardians. There was no time.

After taking a step back he slammed into the door, shoulder first, ignoring the pain shooting down his arm.

The door shook but held.

Tightening his stomach muscles, he braced himself. Then he rammed the door with his whole body again. It worked. The door swung open on its hinges, tearing part of the frame with it.

Gabriel quickly surveyed the scene in the living room. In shock, he saw Lily sprawled on the floor, her head beside a coarsely drawn pentagram, the flame of a black candle dangerously close to her hair.

A blonde woman seemed to be sleeping on the couch beside her.

Gabriel could feel the energy in the room—the circle was still cast. He reached under his fatigues and took out a long knife from the scabbard at his calf.

"*Geàrr fùdar, Geàrr.*" He cut through the shield and the power receded.

He made a cut in his hand and let blood fall on the black candle before swiping his bloody hand on the sleeve of his white thermal. An offering couldn't be too careful.

Kneeling beside Lily, he held her head. Her skin was pale, her breath faint. *Please*, mon amour, *hold on*. He could feel her life thread flowing through him. She was alive, but barely.

Protective feelings mixed with alarm for her over-whelmed his mind. He gave her a gentle kiss, then started to work. She was his to protect, and he wouldn't fail her.

He shut his eyes and he said the words, ancient words coming as easily to him as a mother tongue. As his hand rose high, he knew he had connected with her. His eyes opened and he reached inside his black coat for a vial.

He broke the beeswax seal and held the bottle above Lily.

Mumbling the incantations again, he shook the bottle over Lily, and tiny droplets of a crystal-clear liquid sprinkled all over her.

His whole mind focused on her, his concentration alert. His hand drew spirals above her and he was one with her, in her mind, in every cell of her body. He touched her soul.

Cerrwiden—he should have known. Why had Lily felt she was strong enough to summon the goddess on her own? Rage at Morag rose inside him.

Got to focus.

He reached for the inside pocket of his coat again and found the rose petals. He crushed them in his hand and scattered them over Lily.

His consciousness initiated the words to call her to him. *"Eirich Trobhad, Eirich."*

He found her heart, a faint beat. His mind started to work on the filaments, at the cell level. *Pump, come back to me.* He singled out the rhythm, pounding, in tune with his. *Synchronize, that's it. Faster, stronger.* His body filled with the throbbing of her heart pulsing through his veins.

Suddenly, Lily opened her eyes wide and took a big gulp of air, as if she'd emerged from the water. She sat in one swift motion.

"Gabriel."

He'd done it. Relief swept over him; she was safe. "God, you scared me." He embraced her, brushing the rose petals from her silky hair, then pulled back to take in her drawn expression. "What the hell were you doing?"

"I had to help Keira."

He cast a quick glance at the sleeping woman and shook his head. "Lily, you could have died." What would have happened if he hadn't rushed to her place? She'd be dead, he was sure of it. His love, his life, dead.

He tightened his grip on her. Never, that could never be. He let rage swallow him now, furious at the High Priestess who had encouraged Lily to perform such rituals. Her training was much too dangerous.

"I'm okay." Lily's voice filtered to him, faint but clear. "You can loosen your grip now, I'm okay."

He cupped her face with his hands and brushed her hair away. "Lily there's so much you don't know." His body trembled as he spoke. "You're my soul mate."

When she didn't respond, he added, "You're my lost Evangéline, my fiancée. Remember the poem you read? She's been reborn in you. You have to understand, you're her. You came back to me."

Ignoring her bewildered expression, he wrapped his arms around her, elated to have finally told her the truth.

Twenty-one

"She could have died." Still fuming, Gabriel paced the floor in the Callans' library while Morag sat calmly looking at him. He thought of Lily recovering under her great-aunt's care and his anger increased. He couldn't wait to return to her side, but first he wanted to let his fury be known.

"I've changed my mind about her." Morag's lips curled into a slow smile. "She's got spirit."

"She failed."

"Yes, but she tried. That shows a lot of courage. She traded her life for her friend's. She may not have realized the extent of her bargain with Cerrwiden, but she still showed loyalty."

Gabriel sat down across from Morag, then got up to pace the floor once more. "I don't want Evangéline to be taken away from me again."

He remembered standing in front of her tombstone in New Orleans. How his whole life had felt completely empty with her gone forever.

"Evangéline? We're talking about Lily here."

"We are, same thing." He examined Morag, now an old gray-haired lady, her light tartan around her shoulders. He couldn't be fooled, though. She was anything but fragile.

All her Priory stood for was control and selfishness. He'd learned that after he'd tried to escape and find Evangéline on his own. But they'd tracked him down to the icy lands of Labrador and dragged him back into their fold. Eventually, he'd realized they were his best hope. All he could do was bide his time and play along.

Now Morag wanted Lily too. She'd been searching for the thirteen priestesses of her Coven. And Lily was one of them. Why had he been so blind?

He gave Morag one last glance and, without a word, left the room.

Trapped again by Morag's scheming.

Nothing he could do now but go along and protect Lily, stay by her side.

"I'm glad you're feeling better." Morag busied herself wrapping spices in cheesecloth for the wassail she'd serve with the feast she was preparing.

Her kitchen was warm and cozy. Lily, still a little weak since her ordeal with Keira two weeks ago, enjoyed a cup of Morag's restoring herbal brew.

Tonight, they would be celebrating Yule, the day of winter solstice, or as Morag had explained, the day of the Sun's birth.

During her recovery, she'd realized just how much she needed Morag. Maybe it was the priestess's current elderly appearance, but Lily no longer feared her in the way she once had.

Morag had continued to mentor her, giving her more maternal guidance than Lily had ever gotten from her own mother. Gabriel didn't like it one bit, but Lily refused to stop now, when she'd already come so far.

"And how is your friend Keira?" Morag asked.

"Better too. She doesn't have the nightmares anymore." Keira had returned to work, put away all her glitzy clothes and no longer mentioned Theuron.

"Good, you may have saved her. Not bad for a first try."

"I nearly died." Lily winced, remembering the pain and the embarrassment of her encounter with Cerrwiden.

"Ah, yes, we want to avoid that next time." Morag gave her a mischievous grin.

"Will I ever be ready?"

"Of course you will, but a priestess is made in a year and a day. And even then she may not be quite ready to go about saving a friend possessed by Taranis." Morag dropped the spice bag in a large pot sitting on the stove. She whispered a few incomprehensible words over the fragrant mixture, then turned to Lily. "You shall be initiated when the time is right. I can still remember my initiation, how proud I was. My older sister Iona was the High Priestess then, the whole Coven present." Morag's gaze took on a dreamy look. "One hundred lashes I sustained, blindfolded, bound in leather cords. Ah, the price we pay."

Lily drew a hand to her throat in horror. A hundred lashes . . . she would die from it. "Lashes?"

Morag gave a mocking laugh. "What? Are you scared? Such a weakling you are. I'm afraid our ancient practices will have to be modified. You'd never recover from it. The scourge was used to put us in trance, but we'll find another way for you. I'm sure Iain has some elixir that will do the trick. But bound and blindfolded you shall be to be released into your new life, into the light."

Lily shuddered, not sure she liked the sound of it.

"But let's not worry just now. You still have a long time before you're ready for that."

Lily breathed a little easier. She'd have to deal with it when it came. Her mind shifted to more puzzling thoughts.

"Morag, what's this about me being Evangéline, reborn? Gabriel doesn't make much sense when he mentions her." After his first profession of Lily's connection to his dead fiancée at Keira's bedside, he'd been vague about it all, only insisting to her that she was his soul mate.

"Evangéline, yes. A long time ago, even before any of

the sorcerers were born, Theuron succeeded in cursing the souls of our people, forcing them to roam the earth, lost." Morag sat at the table across from Lily. "In fact, all the Priory sorcerers are reborn Callanish souls, and so was Evangéline. She and Gabriel were fated to be re-united, then to be torn apart. We couldn't prevent their separation. You see, Theuron's curse is tricky to break. We had to make Gabriel immortal, then wait until your birth. Evangéline's soul is in you."

Lily tried to absorb it all while Morag continued. "And now Gabriel and you have to reunite so that our tribe can be restored."

Lily ignored Morag's last words to focus on the one thing that really troubled her. "Are you sure I'm her? I don't recall anything. I don't even feel it."

Morag smiled. "You are she. I never would make such a mistake."

"What about Keira? She talked about seeing her past."

"Keira is like you, yes, a Callanish third-blood soul, but unfortunately Theuron got there before us. And we cannot help her any more than you did, not yet anyway. It is not her time." Her eyes turned dark and Lily knew she wouldn't get anything more from her.

Cursed souls, Lily thought. And if Evangéline was re-born, who had she been before? A Callan? One of Morag's lost priestesses?

Morag must have caught her thoughtful expression, because she smiled and her eyes turned bright.

"This is Yule, a time to be merry. Let's not discuss any more of these tragedies." She got up and gave her hand to Lily. "Come, Gabriel is waiting to take you to the village."

Lily held on to Gabriel's arm. Handsome in his usual black coat and boots, a navy watch cap was his only con-cession to the cold weather.

Snow fell on Langdon Village as they strolled its quaint main street. The thick and airy snowflakes brought Lily fond childhood memories of stepping into Angèle's backyard and making snowmen with her great-aunt.

Tonight's feast wouldn't be complete without the Yule log. Morag had rallied them to pick up the cake she'd ordered a few days before from the local bakery.

The lovely morning had prompted them to enjoy the holiday displays in the shop windows. The whole village had a festive air, with sparkling lights strung along its ancestral buildings, some dating from as far back as the seventeenth century.

Lily had always loved this season. She'd celebrated all her holidays with Angèle. No matter what would happen in her parents' lives, Lily would have a magical Christmas. Angèle would decorate a huge tree for her and she'd cook and bake for days. Friends would drop by for tea and for Angèle's special *sucre a la crème*, a fudge so addictive, everyone always begged for more.

Lily had loved sitting down and listening to the grown-ups, eating sweets while Christmas carols played in the background. The house had always been brightly lit and fragrant with the scent of pine and vanilla.

Now that Angèle had sold her house, they'd recreated the magic in Lily's small apartment, and some of Angèle's friends still visited them. But soon, Lily would buy the home of her dreams and all would be just as before. This year, Gabriel had promised to celebrate with them, and Lily couldn't be more content.

She gazed into his green eyes, wrapped her arm around his waist, and cuddled to him, her cheek on his shoulder, her memories making her feel snug despite the cold.

"Did you mind celebrating Yule instead of Christmas when you were a child? I mean, it must be difficult being different."

Gabriel smiled back at her as he picked a few snow-flakes off her hair. "I celebrated Christmas, just like you. I only met Iain when I was in my twenties."

"Oh yes, for a minute there I thought you were a normal boyfriend. I forget that when you were a child, it was what, seventeen hundred something?" She was still having a hard time trying to adjust to his immortality.

"I was born in 1733 and we did have Christmas, or *Noël*, as we called it. But now, I just drop by Morag and Iain's at Yule time if I'm around, but honestly, after so many years, the holidays just kind of blend into one another."

"Angèle calls it *Noël* too sometimes. I just love this time of year. I already set up a tree in the apartment—you have to see it. It's so big Angèle had to help me carry it up the stairs." Lily felt curious about his past again. She knew he must have been happy at some time during his childhood. "Did you have a tree when you were growing up?"

"No, there was no tree then. We'd go to midnight mass; then we'd have a big party, a *réveillon*. It was all about music and food, lots of food." Gabriel smiled and Lily was glad to hear him recall these happy moments. "My mother was famous in the village for her meat pies. My father would take my brothers and me hunting and we'd bring her the wild game she needed."

"Angèle told me about the *réveillon*. She celebrated it in her youth as well."

"Things don't change much."

Lily stopped him in front of the toy store. A model train ran around an adorable miniature village. At the back, a huge castle had been filled with knight and princess figurines. "I was so into damsels in distress and shiny knights in armor as a kid."

"Well, my damsel. May I pledge my allegiance to

you?" Gabriel had that twinkle in his eye again, making her laugh. He turned back to the display. "I love that train set. When we have a little boy, that will be his first Christmas present." Her heart beat faster at the mention of *we*.

"So you'll celebrate Christmas when you have kids?"

"When *we* have kids," he said, making her heart melt. "We'll celebrate both. It will be a great reason for me to have Christmas again." His eyes appeared full of hope and happiness.

They continued to an antique-shop display, where Christmas lights showcased the polished wood furniture. Lily pointed to a turned-wood chair carved with a flower motif.

"See that rocking chair in the corner? Angèle had one just like that and I loved to rock in it while I read my favorite books. That's my dream, you know, have a house just like hers and fill it with warmth and laughter."

Gabriel hugged her close and kissed the top of her hair, catching a melting snowflake on his lip. She was so warm and giving as she discussed her dreams that Gabriel couldn't stop watching and listening to her.

His heart burst full of love for her. He would never let her go. She was the one. His body had known it from the first time he'd seen her at the gas station that day. Now his heart was certain. Her presence reminded him a little of the day he'd proposed to Evangéline on the porch of the Bellefontaine's house in Grand Pré.

"Lily, there's something I want you to have. I thought of waiting, but I just can't." His hand shook as he reached into his pocket. He pulled out the ring, opened her hand and gently deposited it into her palm.

His heartbeat raced. How long had he waited for this moment? He breathed in slowly, his gaze fixed upon her.

Lily remained silent as she examined the pewter ring. Gabriel shifted his stance, overcome with worries. Maybe this was the wrong time.

But it was too late now.

He swallowed.

"It's for you. I was supposed to give it to Evangéline. I had it in my pocket when they took me away. I made it for her, for our wedding, and well, you are her, it belongs to you now." He spoke too fast as he took her hand. "See the engraved fleur-de-lis? Lilies, just like you."

He settled the ring on the third finger of her left hand. Perfect. The ring had finally found its rightful owner. Nothing would convince him otherwise.

Her luminous hazel gaze raised toward him. "Gabriel, it's beautiful."

"I'm not good at this." He frowned, searching and searching for the right way to say this. "Will you wear it? I mean, forever?"

What he really wanted to say was "marry me." Yet the words wouldn't come out. Could she refuse him? She wasn't thrilled at the idea of being Evangéline, reborn. Maybe this was too soon for her?

He waited, holding his breath. *Say something, anything.*

"Is this a proposal?" Lily gave him a warm smile. A twinkle shone at the corners of her eyes. Hope rushed to his heart.

"Yes, it is." He closed his eyes for a fraction of a second. Then, opening them to revel fully in her sweetness, he said more forcefully, "We're soul mates, you can't deny it. We belong together. Will you marry me?"

Her smile broadened.

"Gabriel." She seized his hand tighter. "Of course, I will."

"You will?"

"Yes." She nodded. "We belong together."

"I love you, babe." He clutched her hand, feeling the hard pewter encircling her finger.

"I love you." She appeared so calm and confident as she thrust her arms around him and laid her head on his chest.

His arm around her shoulders, he carefully stroked her hair. His breath slowed. He rested his cheek on the top of her head, his heart swept by a happiness he'd forgotten could exist.

Lily sat quietly in the car. Her hand rested on Gabriel's muscular thigh as he drove Iain's car back to the Callans' house. She did belong there, she belonged with him. Yet if all her body and soul knew that, why did she detect a shadow in her happiness?

She went over all he'd said when he proposed to her. He'd been so sweet and also so forceful in his assurance.

Lily bit her lower lip. He'd said they belonged to each other. But was it Lily he wanted, or was it still Evangéline? Lily could sense the darkness of his lost love between them.

Gabriel took her hand and kissed her fingers gently, one at a time. He smiled at her, the gleam in his eyes hinting at what he had in mind for later that evening.

Lily returned his smile, heat running through her body. They felt so good together. She was confused. Was she really Evangéline? It was possible, but she didn't remember, or feel any different. Yes, she was aware of her powers now and had joined a whole new world unknown to most.

But inside, she remained the old Lily, and she wanted Gabriel to love her as she was. She didn't want to be loved because he believed she was his old love, returned.

She shrugged off the uneasiness that hovered over her, then blew him a kiss as she gently took her hand away from him to examine Evangéline's ancient ring. He'd made this, centuries ago he'd made it for his fiancée, then saw his dream being taken away, forced to leave his homeland and his promise of happiness. How awful she was for doubting him. He'd suffered enough.

Twenty-two

"Tonight is the longest night." Morag seemed focused on her blessing. "The sun returns, born from the dark. The Lord of Death becomes the Lord of Rebirth, darkness becomes light. We are not afraid of darkness and death, for they bring back light."

Gabriel had always become impatient during these rituals, but tonight Morag's words seemed important to him.

Soon Lily would be his wife.

And the festive surroundings only increased his joy. He usually didn't prefer spending an entire evening with other Priory sorcerers, but tonight everything seemed perfect. He would soon have a family of his own with Lily.

The dining-room table was decorated in holly, pine boughs and gold candles. Tasty-looking dishes waited for them to start the feast: roasted vegetables and wild game, pots of cider, wassail and ginger tea. The log cake from Langdon lay on the sideboard table.

With Lily's fresh scent next to him filling him with contentment, Gabriel couldn't wish for more.

Morag paused, bending over her cauldron. "We are waking from the land of dreams. Tonight, the light of hope returns. A new life is born."

Gabriel smiled and took Lily's hand. A new life. How he wanted a new life with his new fiancée.

Morag continued her ritual, speaking the ancient tongue, invoking Cerrwiden and the oak lord, Cernunnos.

She lit the large golden candle floating in the middle of the cauldron.

"The light has returned. The Sun is reborn. Bright blessings." She smiled at everyone, then sat at the table.

"The food looks lovely," Iain said. "Can we eat now, Morag?"

Gabriel gave Lily's hand another squeeze while he took a deep breath. It was time to share his joy.

"Before we eat, I think this is a perfect time for an announcement." He gave Lily a quick look and she nodded at him. He stood up, filled with pride. "Lily has agreed to marry me." The words felt so right as he said them, so wonderful.

"Oh, that's fantastic." Morag beamed at them and got up to embrace Lily.

"Welcome to the family, Lily," Iain said, his stormy gray eyes suddenly sparkling. "Marvelous, really marvelous."

Gabriel didn't notice the others. He was entirely focused on Lily as Loïc lightly touched her back in approval. How pretty she looked, her dark hair shining in the candlelight.

"Congratulations," Phoebus said. "You did get her a nice ring I hope, Voyager."

As Lily extended her hand across the table to show the ring, flashes of the hours spent in his father's forge came back to Gabriel. That ring had been made for another, but now it could only belong to Lily.

"An antique," Tara said as she took Lily's hand. "It's beautiful."

"Isn't it?" Lily said. "It's very special."

Gabriel caught the dark warning in Tara's eyes but ignored it, lost in his delight at the sight of his fiancée, so beautiful in her red silk dress, happily showing her engagement ring.

"A toast." Iain's voice filled the room as he lifted his glass. "To Gabriel and Lily, for eternity."

"For eternity," Gabriel said, his eyes locked on his soul mate.

Lily lay in bed on her back, her body shattered from pleasure, as Gabriel explored every part of her, the sun pouring on them both.

"Evangéline, you're my Evangéline," he whispered to her.

Lily froze as she heard the words. No, not again.

"Gabriel, I'm Lily, just Lily." She gave him her darkest look, then turned to her side, away from him. She pulled the sheet over her.

"I know that, but you are also Evangéline, reborn." He reached for her hip.

She sat up in bed, then drew her knees to her body, feeling as if frost had descended upon her. "I don't remember anything besides my own life. I like who I am. I don't know that I want to be someone else."

"I'm not asking you to be." No, he hadn't, but he kept mentioning that she was his lost fiancée as if it should make her happy.

"Then would you love me even if I turned out not to be her?" She started to fear that his interest in her had nothing to do with who she was. Calling her by Evangéline's name just after they'd made love was just too hard to accept, no matter how much he'd suffered.

"But you are."

"We don't know that for sure. And maybe I don't want to be her. I don't see how we can make this work if you're in love with somebody else."

"But I am in love with you. You are Evangéline. I will always love her, just as I love you. You're the same in my mind."

She didn't want to be the same as someone else. She wanted to be the only one he loved. She quickly got out of bed and started to get dressed. "I don't know that I can accept that, Gabriel. I think you're forcing yourself to be in love with me to relive the feelings you had with her. Cherish her memory, but don't make me her."

"Come back to bed, babe. Where are you going?" Gabriel seemed completely lost, as if he had no idea what she was mad about.

She ignored him and put on her jeans. She knew it might be cruel, but there was no other way. She couldn't spend the rest of her life pretending to be someone else.

"We can help you remember. Morag can do it. It will take time, but it can be done."

Her blood froze. "You say that as if you want to fix me." She had tears in her eyes now. She felt as though she didn't even recognize him anymore. All this time she'd thought he cared about her, but all he really wanted was someone who no longer existed. Everything they'd shared was built on a lie. "You gave me her ring. You call me by her name. You need to sort out what it is you really want. But not while I'm here."

He started to get up and she raised her hand to stop him.

Her voice was dead calm, completely different from the fury and sadness she felt inside. "I have to go now, before I say anything I will regret. I need to go home. Until you sort out who you really love, Gabriel, I don't want to see you anymore. I can't marry you if you still love another."

"Lily, come back, let's talk about this."

She left the room, ignoring his pleas and stunned expression.

Crossing his living room, she noticed the familiar boots and jacket by the door. What was she doing? Big tears rolled down her cheeks, but she wouldn't let her determination fail. She grabbed her handbag and headed out.

She loved him more than anything, but she deserved to have the same in return.

Gabriel lay in bed, still stunned long after she'd left.

Had he done that? Had he used her to cure his obsession? The thought of losing Lily was too horrible to face. Yet Evangéline was the only love he'd ever known. He'd been fixated on her, with his first love, unable to let go of his anger over their fate.

He got up and walked to the window, taking in the view of the city still white with snow. Lily would have driven home though this, her car threatening to slip on the ice.

He'd carried his obsession over centuries, had thought of only one thing: finding her again. It'd been so simple when Lily had shown up in his life. Now confusing emotions buzzed through his mind and he couldn't think clearly.

What were his true feelings? Had he fallen in love with Lily to ease the pain in his heart, or did he really love her for who she was?

Agony seized him. His body ached for her. It was her lovely face he envisioned, her scent still lingering on his body. Evangéline's image had turned faint in his mind.

And it was Lily's smile he wanted now, her soft hair on his fingers, the warmth and tightness around him as he entered her, her sweet whispers as he pleased her. Her pleas when he'd use his spells to increase her ecstasy.

Gabriel sat back on the bed and held his forehead in his palms, completely defeated. Dread overtook him. To have been so close to happiness and have it taken it away from him. And this time, it had been entirely his fault.

He had wanted Lily to be Evangéline, to ease the

angst of the last centuries. He was guilty, he knew it. That's why he hadn't run after her this morning.

He missed her already, needed her. He could not give her up. But she'd been right. He couldn't go back to her when his heart was still full of Evangéline. He'd have to face his shadows.

Twenty-three

Today was his day to guard her. Gabriel worried as he sat in a nondescript sedan, parked a few buildings down from Lily's apartment.

After he'd finally roused himself from the bedroom, he'd taken a trek in the woods to try to clear his head. He still hadn't quite sorted out his feelings, but he needed to make sure Lily was safe. So he'd told Morag that he'd help the sorcerers watch her today.

He pushed his hair out of his eyes as he observed her building's entrance. He felt bad following her like this, like a stalker. He should just get out of the car, climb the steps to her apartment and talk to her. No, sweep her in his arms and kiss her, tell her how much he loved her. Here she was, the love of his life, and he was too stupid to just go talk to her and sort things out.

Patience, he told himself.

Lessons learned among the Abenaki natives returned to him. *Gabriel, take your time*, their leader had said. *Learn the truths lying within yourself.*

He would tell him the same thing now.

Yes, Gabriel had to take time for both their sakes. He wanted to love her the way she deserved to be loved, and right now he wasn't sure of anything. Trying to be noble killed him. The longing to be with her remained always present, deep inside him.

Sudden movement at the front of Lily's building made Gabriel's heart beat faster. There she was, with her great-aunt. She looked all business today, in a fitted skirt, black pumps and matching peacoat, a chic bag on her shoulder. He smiled at the sight of Angèle's energetic steps, her little red hat bobbing up and down.

His gaze returned to Lily and he couldn't help himself. He wanted to pick her up and carry her to his bed so he could feel her sweet body next to him. He sighed. Maybe Morag was right. He was too involved.

Patience. He probably needed to lose himself in the wilderness again to sort his head out, the only place where he could face his soul. It had always worked in the past, but this time the image of a lovely dark-haired woman had kept intruding into his thoughts. Lily or Evangéline—it was still too early to say.

Gabriel saw Lily and Angèle get into her small red car and drive out of the parking lot. He followed, leaving a few cars between them so she wouldn't notice him.

Tara had mentioned they'd seen some of Theuron's Keepers near Lily a few times. They'd been mostly in public places: the grocery store, the library and downtown. But no one had seen Theuron yet.

After crossing the city, Lily's car headed toward the suburbs. Traffic was light on Sunday morning and Gabriel had no trouble keeping up with her.

It was hard to know what the dark mage really wanted. He might not be directly after Lily, but hurting her would hurt the Priory. Which meant Theuron would enjoy the pain even more.

Lily parked in front of a small ranch-style house with a for-sale sign on the lawn. The home wasn't bad, with its white siding and green shutters, but Gabriel knew it wasn't Lily's dream. The real-estate agent greeted Angèle and Lily at the doorstep and the three women went in.

Gabriel parked a few houses down the street. He reached for his coffee and sat back to wait. She must be looking around the rooms now. *Please don't settle for this*, he thought. *You deserve much better.*

He'd managed a few sips of coffee when movements in his rearview mirror caught his eye. A black luxury car passed by and parked in front of the house Lily was visiting.

They were following her. His blood pressure started to rise, his protective instinct taking over. They had no right to be so close to his love.

He tightened his fists, got out and walked to the black car. He stood by the driver's window and waited, taking long, steady breaths to calm his building irritation.

The window lowered. The driver wore all black, his shaved head covered in an intricate tattoo. Definitely a Keeper.

"I want to talk to your boss." Gabriel's voice was calm but his muscles taut, ready to uncoil at any moment. The window went up. Nothing moved. Gabriel just stood there.

Then the back window lowered. "Gabriel Callan. How nice to see you again."

Theuron, finally. A young redheaded girl leaned beside him. Her hair hung below her breasts in complete disarray. She wore a short white fur coat over a rose satin slip.

The images he'd read in Theuron's mind came back to him—the girls, the sacrifices—haunting Gabriel as he now looked at the fathomless black eyes taunting him. Theuron's lips curled into a vicious hint of a smile. Malevolent energy exuded from him, an incredible force meant for destruction.

But Gabriel's fury had mounted to a level where he just didn't care. "What do you want with Lily?"

"I find her intriguing, don't you?" Theuron slowly

caressed the Kyrie's bare thigh, his hand burying itself between her legs as she faintly moaned.

"There's nothing for you here. Leave her alone." Gabriel kept his gaze steady.

"She's looking at a house, isn't she? Why aren't you with her? Aren't you two to be married?"

Before Theuron could react, Gabriel reached in the car and grabbed the mage by the collar of his suit. He yanked him halfway out the window.

"Leave her alone," he said, edgy from weeks of built-up frustration.

Theuron clasped Gabriel's wrists in his hands, his icy touch slicing through the bone, and started to recite forbidden words, his eyes a dead pool of black.

Gabriel yanked harder.

He punched Theuron in the face before he could complete his spell. The mage went back, blood pouring from his nose. His head fell on the girl's lap. Everything had happened so quickly, the Keeper at the wheel didn't have a chance to react.

Gabriel straightened up, readjusted his black coat and slowly walked to his car, ignoring the commotion behind him. That felt good. He opened the door and sat back, reaching for his cup of coffee.

Loïc was there, lazily studying Theuron's car. "What was all that about?"

"What are you doing here?"

"Just visiting. What happened?"

"Nothing."

"You punched him. The man can kill with one word, and you go out and break his nose?"

Gabriel shrugged.

"You're crazy, man. You know he'll get you back for this."

"Maybe."

"Let's get out of here before we find out."

"Can't. Lily's in there." Gabriel nodded toward the house.

They both watched the limo pull out and leave.

"Looks like you got away with it."

Gabriel ignored Loïc to keep his gaze fixed on Theuron's car. A tiny light flashed beside it as the car drove farther away.

The light turned brighter and bigger, coming straight at them. Damn. It seemed he was not getting away with it after all.

"Monk?"

"*Reizh crìoch.*" Loïc's spell caught the huge ball of fire just before it hit their car. A shattering of light surrounded them, blinding Gabriel for a moment, then all returned to normal.

It'd happened so fast, it had left Gabriel no time to react. Without Loïc's counterspell, their car would have blown up and roasted both sorcerers within.

"Man, you're good."

A slow smile curled on Loïc's lips as he turned to Gabriel. "Aren't you glad I came?"

"Hey, it's me."

Lily grasped the phone tighter and took a deliberate breath to settle herself.

"Gabriel, hi. How are you?" Trying to keep her voice steady, she slowed her steps in the darkening evening as she walked to her car.

"I'm good."

A few seconds of silence passed between them.

"Good. I'm glad to hear that." Her voice strained, she couldn't find anything to say. Why did this feel as though he were the one who'd left her?

"Yes. It's good, but . . ." He paused again. "I miss you."

"Oh?" She breathed slowly again, cautious, not wanting to push. Waiting to see what his intentions were in calling her.

"I'm sorry." He sounded hesitant. "Did I catch you at work?"

She fished her keys out of her handbag and fumbled with the car lock, half-relieved for the small talk but hoping for more. Had he realized he loved her fully?

"No. It's okay. I just finished my shift. I'm on my way home," she said, half-hoping he'd ask to see her.

"How's Angèle?"

"Good, she's good. She's been asking about you."

"Ah."

"Yes." Lily flung her bag on the passenger seat and settled into the car.

He paused again while she raked her mind, searching for the right thing to say, her breathing still very careful.

"What did you tell her?" he said.

Could she really tell him the truth? That she'd told Angèle that it was over, that she was moving on with her priestess training, but that he was no longer in her life? Could she tell him she caught Angèle's pained look each time she frantically checked her calls and e-mails? How well her aunt knew she was miserable without him, hoping for a sign.

Lily shifted in her seat. "I told her we were taking a break from each other."

"Ah."

"Well it's true, no?" She couldn't stand this conversation anymore. What did he want with her?

"Is it?"

She rested her shaking hand on the steering wheel. "Gabriel, why did you call?" *Please tell me the words I want to hear*, she begged silently. That he was ready to put the past behind.

"I called because . . ." He stopped himself. "Look, babe, you can't do this. You can't cut me out cold like this."

She closed her eyes tight. "Gabriel." She chose her words carefully. "Gabriel, you love another. You still live in the past."

"Maybe."

Her heart sank. He didn't deny it.

"But we can talk at least. I miss having you in my life. I miss you so much."

"Gabriel. I miss you too, but you need to sort out your feelings on your own."

"You can't do this to me, Lil. You can't just run away from me."

"I'm sorry." Tears were near. He needed her. She knew that. She was so close to letting go of her determination and agreeing to see him.

"Why can't you just accept that you're her?" he said. "When you say I love another, that's not true. You are her. I love you."

I love you. No, he didn't. She wanted to cry. Why did it hurt so much? Why did she have to love him? Why him?

Because he'd made her feel alive.

For the first time in her life, she'd felt joy. Happiness. His carefree spirit had brought a whole new meaning to living.

But she couldn't settle for less.

"I'm not her. I'm different." She didn't know what else to say. "Gabriel, you called me Evangéline when we had sex." The words tumbled out. Tears now fell freely on her cheeks.

"I know, babe. I'm so sorry. It won't happen again."

"It doesn't matter. It's what's on your mind that matters, in your heart. You are still thinking of her, all the time."

"But can we at least talk, be friends." Again he didn't deny her words. "Can we go for coffee or something?"

"No." She nearly shouted her refusal. She knew she was hurting him, but she needed to protect herself. How could she forget and heal while still seeing him?

"You have to understand," she said. "It hurts. It hurts knowing that you still love Evangéline. I'm trying to make it so that I hurt less. I can't do that if I talk to you, if I see you." She sunk in her seat, wrapping her wool coat around her with her free hand. "It will kill me every time I leave you."

"I understand, Lily. I understand."

Why wasn't he making it easy for her? Telling her he loved her now, loved only her? So that she could run into his arms and know that all would be fine again. But no, he couldn't say that. He was honest. And she loved him for it, but it didn't make her feel better.

"You're right," he added. "I need more time. I think I do still love her."

A deep pain surged in her. She rested her head back. She wanted to turn the phone off.

"You do." Her gaze settled on the dark winter sky.

"Yes. And I love you too. I love you so much. I can't breathe when you're not around."

She closed her eyes at his words. Her heart beat madly. She was a wreck. Why had he called?

"I know," she said. But she didn't know.

She wasn't sure if she was just a substitute for his lost fiancée. Having dreamed of Evangéline for so long, he might believe he loved Lily, so that his pain was less. But how much did he truly care about her?

He'd blurted out on their first day together that he'd marry her. A rush of mixed emotions swallowed her. How did she know that he didn't cling to her out of need alone?

"Can I call you at least?" he said. "Now and again?"

More determined now, she focused on the fact that he admitted to still loving Evangéline.

"No, Gabriel. I need my head clear. It hurts too much. You need to let go of the past."

"Tara said you'd say that."

"Tara? You talked to her about us?" Somehow this new image in her head really bothered her. She sighed and stared blankly as the car next to her pulled out of its parking space, leaving a trail of white smoke in the cold evening.

"Yes. She's good to talk to."

"Oh." Tara. They had known each other for centuries. Certainly they'd have a certain companionship.

"But we're fated, Lily. You're my soul mate. We are supposed to be together."

"Maybe." Lily shook away an image of Tara in the club where they first met, resting her hand on Gabriel's shoulder, leaning toward him to hear him better. Her fit body barely covered by the black tank top exposing her cleavage.

She willed the disturbing image away. "Morag has taught me much these days," she added. "One thing I know is that if we are meant to be together, then we will be." She paused wondering how to say this. "But I trust my instincts. Right now it is not good for me to be around you."

"Please. Just a few e-mails. Don't do this." The angst in his voice threatened to break her resolve. She both felt for him and wished he'd understand her pain.

How would it feel to receive an e-mail from him? She'd go right back to where she'd started when she flew from his house.

She touched the ring at her neck under her uniform. She had taken it off her finger as soon as she'd run from his apartment. But she hadn't been able to part with it completely.

She looped her finger inside it. "If you do love me, you have to understand. I can't be with you while you use me as a substitute for Evangéline." She let go of the ring suddenly. The dull ache in her chest wouldn't subside.

She needed to reach a point where the pain wasn't so fierce, when she could remove the ring from her neck and let go.

"I understand," he said. "It's just that I loved her for so long that I don't know how *not* to. But you appeared in my life and made everything so wonderful."

"Then there is hope." She steadied her breath. "Maybe you need time too. Time to think about it. But I can't help you with that." *For my own sake.*

"It's okay. I understand." His voice was hoarse. "I love you."

"I love you too." She inhaled deeply, reclined her head back and closed her eyes. "Good-bye, sweetheart."

"Good-bye."

She didn't wait for more, and quickly turned off the phone.

She stared at the number on the screen for a few minutes, then slowly shook her head. *So that's that.*

Twenty-four

Morag wrapped her tartan around her. "Come, dear, take that." She handed Lily the deer-hide pouch containing the sacred tools. "Let's walk. You have been a faithful follower. I think you shall soon be able to protect yourself."

"You've taught me so much, Morag. I'm starting to feel the goddess's powers in me." Lily curled her arm under the pouch and held Morag's cauldron in her free hand, wondering what Morag planned to do with it tonight.

As they walked to the clearing, she still felt uneasy about being in the woods in the middle of the night, but her emerging strength and the priestess's presence gave her courage.

Morag turned to her with a serious look. "The goddess yes, but what about the god?"

"What do you mean?"

Morag carried the Cathair Sword wrapped in a thick wool blanket. They had retrieved it earlier from its hiding place in Iain's lab.

"There is a duality all around us. Two poles—one cannot exist without the other. We need balance, just as this spring day of Ostara is the day of perfect balance between night and day." She sighed. "Maybe that's why Theuron has crossed to the dark side. He has pushed away from one of the poles." Lily detected a hint of frustration in her voice.

"But what about you? You follow Cerrwiden."

"Yes, but I have Iain. He is my consort, or husband, if you want. We form a unit. Each has his place. Together we are strong. If we ally our strength, we can stop a heart-beat or make it go forever."

"Like Gabriel. That's how he became immortal, isn't it? You did that."

"Yes."

"Even though I told him I couldn't talk to him until he sorts things out, I still keep hoping he'll try to get in touch. But it's been eight weeks now." Eight weeks, and Lily still checked her phone and e-mail constantly in the hope he would finally reach her.

"I know. And you have not contacted him either." With a quick word, the priestess lit the torches around the sacred clearing and Lily squirmed under her piercing gaze. Morag took the deer-hide pouch from Lily and opened it on the altar. "I'm an old fool. I brought you two together and I would do it again, but Gabriel won't let me."

"You brought us together?"

"Well, fate brought you here to Langdon, but once you were in my house, I pushed things along."

"A spell? Our first night together?"

"If you two were not meant to be, the spell would not have worked. But you are true soul mates. I had to do it."

"So you pushed me to his bed? Even when we were strangers?" She didn't like the idea of Morag interfering in her life so casually.

"Lily, it is what you wanted at the time. I just removed a few of your inhibitions."

"Does Gabriel know?"

"Yes, and he was furious with me when he found out. He wanted you to know him better."

Lily remembered how good she'd felt that first night, the passion she'd shared with him. The memory warmed her despite the cold of the night. He'd been so sensual, so assured in his lovemaking. He'd known all of her body's secrets. She'd come home to him.

Morag was right. Lily had wanted him since she'd first seen him striding toward his bike.

"Morag, I dream of him." Lily set the cauldron down and wrapped her arms tightly around her. "I think I dream of how he was centuries ago." It had been so strange to see him in her dream, happy and youthful, dressed in coarse breeches and a white shirt. The shore had been different from New England, bordered with reddish cliffs and deep-set beaches.

Morag smiled. "Of course you do."

"It's confusing, it feels so real. Do you have anything to do with that?"

"I've sent you only one dream, Lily. I panicked and I showed you Theuron's true form." She paused. "You probably dream of Gabriel in Acadia because you are Evangéline."

Lily sighed. *Here we go again.* She'd have to deal with this, face the fact she might indeed be Evangéline, reborn. It felt like an intrusion, the idea that she was more than who she'd thought she was all her life. "No, I can't be. I've read the poem. My brain is just putting images together."

"Can you really believe that, a purely clinical explanation? Have you ever been to Nova Scotia?"

Morag was right. It was impossible that the images of the foreign shore had come from something she'd seen previously.

"How long has it been since you saw Gabriel?"

"Since just before Imbolc, two months ago."

"And you always dream of him in Acadia. Forget about your brain. What does your heart say? You want to be Evangéline, Lily. You are she, and you long for him."

Lily sighed. "My great-aunt told me the same." Angèle had been gentle, trying to make her niece accept her fate. Still, it wouldn't change the fact that she wanted to be loved for herself.

Lily stared at the sacred tools Morag had arranged on the altar: the pristine white shell, the golden shiny rock, god and goddess, the two poles. There were no doubts that she was just a shadow these days. How incomplete she felt without him.

Morag picked up the cauldron in her wrinkled hand. "You are doing well with the shield spell. Let's find more about what lies in your heart tonight."

"You'll make me see Evangéline, my past life. Gabriel said you could do that." A chill went through her as she remembered how he'd wanted her to be his lost fiancée.

"I can't change the essence of who you are, Lily. But you can find out what you truly believe. Who knows what Cerrwiden will reveal now? We are in the midst of the days of Annwyn. Scrying will work well tonight. Let me get some water." Morag walked to the lake, filled the cauldron, then returned to face the altar.

She searched the small pouch at her waist and retrieved some sage, which she crushed over the water in the cauldron.

"Are you ready?" Morag unwrapped the sword from its wool covering and proceeded to cast the circle.

When she returned, they both knelt in front of the altar.

Morag reached for her pentagram. "Look at the water while I call her."

Lily focused on the water's surface, vaguely aware of Morag's voice, her clear whispers in the wind.

"Cerrwiden dihuniñ."

Light danced in Lily's eyes as the full moon reflected on the dark water that rippled in the gentle wind.

Lily noticed Morag in her peripheral vision, then all became blurred, the female voices chanting in her mind. She'd reached the stones.

A breeze caressed her naked skin, the gray mist clothed her, sky-clad. They were thirteen, the priestesses of the Callanish Coven. The High Priestess had drawn down the moon with the aid of her High Priest. They lay intertwined on the flat logan stone at the center of the circle, their naked limbs wrapped around each other in heated passion.

Iona of the Callanish people had channeled the goddess.

Morag chanted beside her, along with the other priestesses. It was a different Morag, young and pure. She turned to her and smiled with bliss. "Ael, Cerrwiden is with us."

A beautiful immaterial young woman appeared before her, fresh and sweet, just out of childhood. "Welcome back, chloinne. *Welcome back, Ael, my priestess."*

Lily came out of her trance blinking, then stood away from the cauldron.

Morag stood up now, scattering seeds on the ground in offering. "Ah you're back. You met the Maiden this time."

Lily recalled the angelic face and long fair hair of the vision. "Yes, she called me Ael." Lily became full of joy at what she'd just experienced. She'd been embraced by Cerrwiden, who'd welcomed her as one of her own. "And you were there. You stood next to me in the circle."

"So you are indeed Ael, my coven sister. Before you were born, before Evangéline, your soul was Ael's, the Angel. I suspected that much, but Cerrwiden had to tell you herself."

After these revelations by the goddess, Lily had no doubts. She was a Callanish soul, fated to be reunited with her mate in this century. She wasn't just Evangéline. She was Ael, she was Lily. All belonged to her.

Morag fished within the deer-hide pouch and came out with a white-handled knife similar to the one on the altar. The shiny blade was six inches long, the handle engraved with a Celtic triangular symbol and the triple moons. She handed the knife to Lily. "This is for you. It was Ael's *athame*. You are now worthy of carrying it. You may now cast your own circle to call Cerrwiden." Morag's face looked as if it was lit from inside. "Welcome home, Lily."

Twenty-five

"Come on. One more store." Angèle hurried down the street with small but perky steps.

"Just one. Then I'm taking you for coffee." Lily rushed behind her. "If all else fails, we'll find the present for Mrs. Desmarais at the mall."

Lily had agreed to help her great-aunt shop for her friend, thinking it might do herself some good to get some fresh air and think of something other than Gabriel's silence and the fact she still hadn't found a house.

"Wait." Angèle stopped dead in the middle of the sidewalk. "Isn't that Gabriel?" She pointed to a lone man leaning on his motorcycle, appearing to be waiting for someone.

Lily's heart did a fast skip. *No, it couldn't be.*

But it was. The black duster, the long legs and dark curls—even more enticing than she'd remembered.

Her body started shaking at the thought of going near him. She held on to Angèle and whispered, "Let's turn back. I don't want to talk to him."

"Come on, sweetheart. Just say hi. Let's not be impolite."

"Oh, Angèle, I can't." Lily had to get out of here, now, before she did something stupid—either yell at him, or fall into his arms.

"Relax, it will be fine." She took Lily by the arm and dragged her toward Gabriel. Lily was too stunned to protest.

"Hello, Gabriel," Angèle said as they got near.

Gabriel turned toward them, giving Lily the full effect of his smoky green eyes. Her knees gave up and she gripped Angèle's arm tighter, standing a step behind her.

"Mrs. Bellefontaine, how nice to see you." Gabriel nodded, a hint of surprise crossing his eyes. "Lily." He turned her way and smiled slowly.

The way he said her name brought a series of memories. She saw his face above her, whispering her name as he took her. Her body was a rush of emotion.

"Hi." It was all she could trust herself to say.

"How have you been?" Gabriel asked Lily while Angèle let go of her arm and stepped away to look at a nearby shop display.

Lily bit her lower lip. "Oh just fine, you know, the same routine."

"What, work, swimming, the library?" She thought she detected a hint of sarcasm in his voice.

"Yes, pretty much." She wrapped her coat around her.

"Are you happy?"

"Well, yes I guess I am. It's familiar. How about you?"

"You asked me to think, so I'm thinking."

"Good, that's good." She shifted a little and stared at her feet. "I still see Morag."

"I know."

"Well, it's safer that way, isn't it? I almost got that protection spell down."

"Yes. You need to learn to protect yourself." She was dying to talk about Evangéline, ask him if he'd sorted out his feelings, but she couldn't bring herself to discuss the subject that hung like a dark shadow between them.

"I like Morag. She makes me understand things about myself."

"Good." He nodded toward Angèle. "I'm glad you're enjoying yourself."

"Oh yes, Angèle wanted to go out." She gave him a small smile.

"It's good to have family nearby." Was that sadness she heard in his voice?

"I'm lucky to have her."

Still leaning on his bike, he lifted his hand toward her, but then a rich female voice stopped him.

"All right, Gabe, I'm all done here."

Gabriel's eyes darkened and he lowered his hand, still looking intensely at Lily as if he wanted to say something. Then his gaze left her to focus on his companion. "Good, then let's go."

Lily shifted and saw Tara striding toward them. She exuded sexiness in a short black fur coat over tight leather pants and high-heeled boots.

"Lily, I am so happy to see you." Tara smiled warmly at her.

Angèle rushed to Lily's side. "Gabriel, a friend of yours?" She narrowed her eyes at him.

"Yes, meet my cousin Tara."

"Oh, your cousin."

Gabriel put his hand on Tara's back. "Got to go."

Tara strode to a motorcycle parked next to Gabriel's and straddled it, not bothering with a helmet.

Gabriel paused to give Lily a brooding look, then rode away, closely followed by Tara.

"Cousin," Angèle said. "For a minute there I thought Gabriel had found another girlfriend."

"Actually"—Lily forced a smile—"they're not really cousins. They're friends, very good friends."

"Don't you have any diet soda in here?" Tara stared inside the fridge in Gabriel's apartment.

Gabriel ignored her.

"Oh, never mind."

Gabriel left her in the kitchen and headed for the bedroom as he heard her search through the cupboards. He closed his door, stripped and stepped into the shower.

He couldn't stop thinking about Lily. Damn. Why did he have to see her today?

She'd looked so small and vulnerable standing on the sidewalk. All he'd wanted to do was take her in his arms. Take her with him, make her safe and warm. He'd just wanted to show her how much he desired her, loved her.

Then why hadn't he?

Anger swelled though him, anger at his fate and anger at himself for not being strong enough to put his past behind him. The scorching water hammering over his body wouldn't relax his tense muscles.

Evangéline had looked just like that when he left the Acadian shore—small, vulnerable, trusting, standing beside her father. A rush of feelings for her came to him and again he didn't know whom he loved.

It'd been ten weeks since Lily had left him. But what was ten weeks when he had spent two hundred fifty years in agony, obsessed with another?

But how obsessed was he really now? Lily was flesh and blood, warm skin, soft hair, joyful laughter. She was gentle hands on his body. And Evangéline seemed so far away.

Lily had been right. She mustn't be changed. How would she react if she was made to feel the horrors of that fateful day in Acadie.

Gabriel turned his face toward the strong jet of water, trying to drown his dark thoughts.

He'd been told Evangéline's father had collapsed with grief the day of the deportation. She'd had to bury him on their ancestors' land before being forced onto the last boat.

Gabriel didn't want Lily to live through that. She had her own troubled past. She didn't need to suffer Evangéline's burden as well.

He groaned, still confused.

He stepped out of the shower, got dressed and walked to the living room.

Tara had finally found a can of soda. *Probably left by Lily*, he thought with misery.

"You know," Tara said, swallowing a mouthful of soda, "you should stop being so stubborn and just go to her. You've been completely miserable these last months without her."

"I can't."

"You have to," Tara insisted. "We've all been watching her, trying to protect her. But you know better than anyone Theuron will make a move soon. She's not safe."

"You don't need to lecture me about keeping her safe. Right now the safest thing for her is for me to not be around. I don't want her to get pulled into this."

"But she already is in this, Gabe." Tara put her can on the coffee table. "I think Theuron's ultimately after Morag. He'll destroy Lily to get to her."

Gabriel raked a hand through his wet hair.

"He's got Lily's friend again," Tara pressed.

Gabriel tightened his fists. He should be with her, watching her every minute. "What I decide about Lily is my business. Not yours. Not Morag's." He was sick of people trying to control him.

Tara jumped off the couch and got in his face with one fluid move. "Do not compare me to Morag. Ever." Her eyes were a pure black pool, filled with hatred.

"Tara, lay off. Geez."

Tara relaxed a little and pulled back. "You'll lose your soul if you don't return to her."

"I don't care. I don't have much of one anyway. I never asked for this kind of life."

"Yes, you did. You went through the ceremony, just as we all did. Don't blame it on Iain. You could have said no."

"This is not how it was supposed to be."

"You have to let Evangéline go, Gabe. Live now, in the present." She rested a hand on his shoulder while her voiced softened. "You can have Lily forever. If you take her, she'll be just like us."

Gabriel pushed her back. "Maybe I don't want her to be just like us."

Twenty-six

Gabriel drove down the winding path to the Callans' house. His bike slid a little on the dirt road, raising gravel, but he didn't notice in his hurry to see her again.

After he'd stormed out of his apartment and left Tara, he'd ridden, turning thoughts over and over in his head. Finally, he realized that the only thing that really mattered was being with Lily. Seeing her in the street today, being so close, had shown him the truth.

Tara was right. He belonged to Lily.

He knew that Lily went to Morag's every Saturday evening for her training.

She'll be there now.

He rode in the dark, his mind focused on a single aim, to see her.

It'd been five months since her ritual at Samhain. She would be more powerful by now. He remembered how frantic she'd been after the ritual, seeking comfort in his arms, then how she'd nearly died while trying to save Keira. Did she have anyone to comfort her now, or was she strong enough to handle the magical effects by herself?

The silhouette of the cedar-paneled cape and its lit porch emerged from the shadow. His heart picked up speed. Soon she'd be in his arms.

He'd been such a fool. He had to admit to himself that it was Lily he loved, flesh and blood Lily. He'd hung on to a dream all this time. A dream mixed with anger at the fate of the Acadians.

He'd loved Evangéline since he was a boy, cherishing her memory for centuries. He hated to admit it, but Tara had been right. It was time to move on, to let go of his obsession.

Lily had soothed his anguish, made him forget the past. He would have a future with her, a beautiful future. He felt the tension leave his muscles as he pictured her delicate yet strong body nestled in his arms. He revved his bike up a notch. He need to see her as soon as possible. To push all foolishness behind and redeem himself. He hated himself now for having put her through this.

Lily's small red car was at the front of the house and he sighed in relief. She was there.

He caught movement at the door and soon it opened to let Morag and Lily out. Nervousness crept inside him as he parked his bike, and he paused to look at them.

Morag's shoulders were covered in white plaid over her customary black clothes. Lily looked different than she had this afternoon, a priestess now, in a long black skirt and matching short-sleeve turtleneck. Her loose hair fell down to the gentle curve of her back.

A pewter pentagram hung from a leather cord at her neck. She radiated strength. This was nothing like the meek woman he remembered, desperate for protection and reassurance. Would she even want him anymore?

"Blessings, Ael, my child," he heard Morag say while the two women embraced.

Gabriel took his helmet off, his hands shaking. He slowly walked up the steps, and Lily stopped dead in her tracks as she saw him. He became painfully conscious of the picture he presented, haggard from his long ride and riddled with uncertainty.

Hesitant, he finished climbing the stairs, vaguely aware Morag had stepped back inside. "Lily. Listen to me." He stopped, looking at her, his words suddenly lost.

He felt like a bumbling oaf next to her. What a fool he was to come like this. He'd been so focused on seeing her, he'd forgotten how she'd cast him away. Her words still resonated in his mind. And now she was a priestess, full of power. She didn't need him in her life.

"Gabriel." Her eyes filled with tears as she said his name.

He shook his head, stared at the floor, and the words just tumbled out of him. "I've been such a jerk. I was so blind." As he spoke he realized how true that was. His life was no longer back in Acadie, in the past. It was now, right here with her.

Lily gazed at him without a word, calm and solid but with tears falling on her cheeks.

"I love you, Lily." He reached for her hands and she smiled through her tears. Her beautiful smile—how he'd missed its loveliness. "You, only you. The past is over."

"Gabriel, I love you." She was half crying and laughing. "I never stopped."

He wrapped his arms around her, pulling her as close as possible, stroking her soft hair.

His heart was a mix of relief, love and desire as he found her lips and tasted the sweetness of her. His tongue met hers as his hand fondled the luscious skin along her spine under the smooth fabric of her sweater.

She wrapped her arms around his waist and under his T-shirt, stroking the bare skin of his back and sending tremors of desire straight to his groin. Her fresh scent was intoxicating, its familiarity enveloping him, and his body hardened at the multitude of emotions and sensations her presence provoked. How lost he'd been without her, how doomed.

He heard the ring of her cell through her handbag and was happy that she ignored it, responding to his kisses with surrendering passion.

Their lips were tasting each other, hungrily, their bodies united, when Morag came back on the porch, a phone in her hand.

Her voice came from far away. "Lily, I'm sorry." Gabriel turned to the old priestess and his heart jumped at her stricken expression. "A Mrs. Desmarais just called. It's your aunt. She had a stroke."

Lily did a quick four-lane change as she took Exit 15 into Providence. She was numb, completely numb. How could she have been so selfish?

The doctor had warned her many times about Angèle's heart condition. Lily should have been there. With her emergency training, she could have helped, given her a better chance at survival.

It was a miracle that Angèle's friend had come over to drop off a coffee cake unexpectedly. Otherwise, her aunt could have been there, unconscious in the apartment, for hours. Longer even, if Lily had gone anywhere with Gabriel.

She shook her head. Gabriel. How could she even think of him at a time like this? She was so self-centered, ungrateful. These selfish pursuits would have to be put away. Playing at witchcraft . . . Really. Even her love life would have to be put on hold.

A small drizzle started and fog filled her car windows, lights from incoming cars blinding her. The rhythmic sound of her windshield wipers was eerily comforting.

Everything around her moved too slowly, her car, the traffic. She should be at Angèle's side, now.

Lily pulled into the parking lot of the hospital and circled around a few times, getting more and more anxious as she searched for an empty space.

She looked at an old man walking slowly toward his

Jeep, and her knuckles turned white from her tight grip on the steering wheel.

Come on buddy, get in, start your car. She drummed her fingers and mumbled to herself. Finally, the man pulled out and she zoomed in, seconds after he'd left his spot.

If only Angèle pulled through, Lily would have a second chance. She'd remain by her side, no longer neglecting her. Angèle had been there all her life, sacrificing herself for Lily's well-being. And now Lily had failed her.

Lily pushed open the thick glass doors and crossed the hospital lobby.

The night receptionist motioned her. "Lily, she's still in the ER."

"Thanks," Lily said. She walked past the reception counter and almost ran through the empty corridor leading to the emergency wing.

Twenty-seven

The apartment seemed bleak in the near dark of the early morning. Angèle's perfume lingered in the air. All the familiar had become strange. What if she never came back here? Lily felt heavy, so heavy she couldn't force herself up from the couch.

The hospital staff had sent her home. Angèle still lay in intensive care but remained stable. It had been less than twenty-four hours since her stroke; it was too early to predict if she would get better.

Why had she been with Morag when her aunt needed her?

She stared at her handbag gaping open on the floor. Ael's *athame*. It was there, looking shiny and pure, waiting for her. Ready for a solitary ritual, Morag had said.

Lily looked around her, at the flowers that Angèle had arranged the previous morning, her good shoes laying neatly beside the door. Everything was quiet, except for the comforting sound of the grandfather clock. As if Angèle would soon walk to the kitchen in her robe to make herself a cup of tea for breakfast.

Pain gripped her heart as she remembered her aunt's fragile body and pale lined face, many tubes and wires coming out of her, so small and hopeless in the midst of all of the health-care technology.

The *athame* called Lily again. As if it said, *Ael, take me, you have the power, the power to soothe, to protect, to heal.*

Lily stretched to her bag and picked up the knife. She stroked its white handle, traced the Celtic symbols engraved on the blade. She felt different, powerful. She thought of the sketch Morag had drawn her first night at the Callans'. Now she fit the image. She had become that woman, unfazed at anything. What if all was not lost? What if she could do it this time, heal her great-aunt?

A feeling of power surged through her.

In one swift move, she bolted up and ran to her bedroom. She fetched her box of sacred tools and returned to the living room.

She pushed plants and picture frames off the coffee table and covered it with a shimmering green cloth. Then she laid the altar: the gold candle on the right, silver on the left, the censer, bowls of water, salt and the red candle. She removed the pentagram from her neck and placed it in the center.

Her hand firm on her *athame*, she cast the circle, then proceeded with the rest of the ritual. She found herself not copying Morag's gestures exactly, but making them her own, something deep inside her providing guidance.

Soon she stood in the middle of the stones at the Callan house. With her hands raised high above her, she waited. The mist embraced her like a thick, heavy blanket. The wind blew softly around her, playing at her ankles, lifting the black skirt she wore. A strand of her hair caressed her cheek and a carpet of purple heather prickled her feet. Peace descended upon her. This was home.

When she saw the shadow coming toward her, she slowly lowered her arms. Cerrwiden lay before her, her belly heavy with child under a pristine white dress.

"Your compassion does you justice, Ael."

"Can you do anything for my aunt, my lady?" Her voice was composed, both respectful and assured.

"You wish for me to heal her?"

"Yes."

"I do not have the power to raise the dead or return

the very ill back to life." Alarm settled in Lily's consciousness at the goddess's words. "But Angèle is strong and your concern for her makes her even stronger."

Lily's guilt returned at once. "I failed her. I was distracted and left her by herself in the last few months."

"And what of the last twenty-five years? You forget the joy you brought to her life. You honored her as a mother, never failed her." Cerrwiden gently caressed her distended belly and smiled. "Your love for her will bring her back."

Lily's gaze lowered. She had a hard time believing this. She should have sacrificed so much more to the woman in her care.

"Angèle does not require that you forget your own life for her comfort. You brought that responsibility upon yourself. Are you not enjoying the role of the dependable niece? A little too much, perhaps?"

She did enjoy it. It was the one thing Lily knew she'd always done right. She'd taken pride in it.

"There is no reason for guilt. You have the right to fall in love, Ael. There is enough space in your heart for more than one to love." Cerrwiden lowered her gaze to her pregnant belly. "And your life shall be filled with even more to love."

Lily noticed Cerrwiden's expression for the first time. Her half smile was kind and full of compassion. She swore she saw her belly move with the new life she carried under the thin muslin.

She pondered the goddess's words. Had she done that? Had she been so afraid to love, she'd wrapped herself in the role of a faithful caregiver, ignoring her own dreams and possibilities, focusing solely on the one person she knew wouldn't hurt her? Unease crept through her at these disturbing revelations. No, Angèle had to be first in her mind and heart, always.

As if Cerrwiden had read her mind, she said, "Loving

Gabriel should not fill you with remorse. Go now and rest. Your aunt has many years ahead of her. She will be singing to your little ones. I shall require nothing from you in return, priestess. You have given enough." Cerrwiden raised her hand to Lily's cheek in a soft touch, then turned away and disappeared into the mist.

Joy burst in her at the news that Angèle's health would improve.

Kneeling in her living room, she blew out the candles, dropped milk in the offering bowl, then released the circle. The full moon shone in the clear sky and Lily smiled at it, as if to say thank you.

She'd thought the success of her first ritual would have filled her with proud satisfaction, but instead it'd made her serene. She'd done it. She didn't need to call the hospital to check on her aunt's status. Angèle would live. She'd rock Lily's babies.

And Lily had her own life to look forward to. She wrapped her arms tight under her chest. Would that also include Gabriel?

Twenty-eight

Pounding music blasting away, Gabriel lay on his couch doing online searches for new distributors. He'd seen Lily often since they'd heard the news of her aunt. They'd avoided further discussion of their future; at the time it had been enough just to be together. But now Lily was at work and Angèle was on the mend and resting peacefully, and the only thing that could keep Gabriel occupied was this mind-numbing work. Yet even now his thoughts kept returning to Lily, wondering when he could see her again.

His cell phone rang and he checked the number. Phoebus. Quickly, he answered the call. "What's up?"

Phoebus's voice was faint, a wild wind roaring in the background. "Gabe, Theuron has Iain."

"What?"

"No time to explain. Get your butt over here ASAP." Phoebus told him where he was.

"I'm on it." Damn. How could Iain be caught by Theuron? That made no sense.

All emotion and feeling left him as the sorcerer in him replaced the man, all his energy directed toward Iain's safety. He mechanically pulled on his boots, grabbed his coat, then went through all the inside pockets. He might need it all tonight.

Fifteen minutes later, he stood on the side of a rural road, next to Phoebus. A chapel was perched on top of a small hill before them.

"What's going on?" Mentally Gabriel tried to pick up any sign of Theuron from within the church.

"I don't know." Phoebus's voice was dead calm. "Theuron called me. Told me he has Iain. And he said to meet him here, inside the chapel."

"Have you tried Iain's phone?"

"I did. No answer, but it doesn't mean anything. He could be in a trance in his lab. You know what he's like."

"What's your plan?"

"I'm working on that at the moment." Phoebus opened his coat, checked a few inside pockets, then closed it back over his black jeans.

"You'll need a bit more brain if you want to lead this thing, Falconer," a deep voice said in the dark.

"Loïc, man, why do you always come out of nowhere?" Phoebus asked.

"I move in mysterious ways." Loïc gave them a half smile.

"Come on, Monk," Phoebus said. "What's your big, smart plan?"

"Are they in the chapel?" Loïc said.

"That's what Theuron told Phoebus." Gabriel narrowed his eyes toward the church. "But I can't pick up anything."

"Well, then, let's go in," Loïc said.

"That's your plan?" Phoebus shook his head.

"Sure." Loïc started to walk up the hill.

Phoebus and Gabriel looked at each other, then followed.

"Why the church?" Gabriel asked Phoebus.

"Theuron likes to be dramatic."

They reached the front step and Gabriel opened the heavy wooden doors.

"Come on, Theuron." Gabriel's voice roared as he

walked in the dark and deserted church, a faint scent of decay reaching him. "What do you want? Where's Iain?"

Silence met his words.

Loïc took a flashlight from his coat and turned it on.

"Flashlight?" Phoebus said.

"Very practical." Loïc walked along the center aisle, a faint light illuminating his way. Gabriel and Phoebus followed right behind him.

"*Solas.*" Phoebus made a small sweep of his hand and all the candles of the church lit.

"Show-off," Loïc said, then turned off his flashlight.

Phoebus shrugged.

"Theuron," Gabriel shouted again. "What the hell are you playing at?"

"Shit," Phoebus muttered.

The altar. The sorcerers stared down at the dead body of an old man stretched on the white marble. He was naked under a linen tunic, blood smeared over his chest. His wrists, bound in twine, were covered in ugly red and yellowish welts.

Taranis's death symbols had been sliced along the fleshy parts of his thighs and on his arms. The expression on the man's face was jarringly peaceful, as if he were still asleep, in disturbing contrast to the mutilation of his body.

"Who is he?" Gabriel had never seen him in his life.

"I've got no idea," Phoebus said.

"It's my colleague, Dr. Jackson." A loud disembodied voice echoed in the church, and then Iain appeared from the shadows.

"You're free," Gabriel said with relief.

"Of course, I'm free." Iain walked toward them. He had traded his rumpled tweed jacket for his long black overcoat. Not a sign of feebleness was apparent in his fierce expression. Gabriel wouldn't want to be the man at the other end of his spells.

"Blood sacrifice." Iain examined the body. "One stab through the heart. With the Taranis dagger, of course. He usually sets the bodies on fire." There was no compassion in his voice, just pure clinical assessment.

"We thought he had you," Phoebus said.

Iain raised his eyebrows. "Had me? No, this is a warning."

Gabriel looked at the body of the old scientist. His ankles had also been bound, the twine disappearing through the bloody flesh. He hadn't had much of a chance against the dark mage.

"He wasn't really that smart, but no one deserves to go like this." Iain gave one look at his dead colleague, then turned away from the body. "Boys," he said, "do your thing. I want his widow to think he had a heart attack at the office. No point in upsetting her more than she would be. She's a nice woman." He started to walk away, then turned around. "You'll need these." He threw something at Phoebus. "Office keys."

Iain vanished in the dark and they all looked at one another.

"Why do we always do the dirty work?" Phoebus asked.

A few hours later, Gabriel rode into the night. They'd all been so casual about it, but the death of Dr. Jackson had gotten to him.

Lily. The thought shattered his self-control. Could Theuron get to her as a warning? Gabriel's fists tightened with the urge to see her safe.

If Theuron was playing with them, he could easily take Lily and kill her too. This was no time to give her space—he had to warn her. And more, the aftershock of their discovery hit him hard now, and he was desperate for her presence.

It hadn't been a pleasant job. Loïc had labored at the cell level to remove all signs of stabbing. The body now showed the man had died of a heart attack. Loïc knew more magic than any of them could dream of, having been reborn almost a thousand years ago.

The sorcerers had worked quickly, and with the help of Phoebus's driver, the chemist's body now slumped over his desk, with all the appearance of having died of a heart attack.

But Gabriel burst with adrenaline, first from the scare of losing Iain, then from the thought of Lily at risk. He had to see her, needed to convince himself that she was safe.

His yearning for normality was also stronger than ever, and he wanted to feel her serenity. Thinking of her calm, soothing presence, his heart rate returned to normal, but his soul still agonized for hers.

Lily was nestled in the couch with a book when she heard the bang at the door. She was still alone in the apartment, Angèle having had to stay at the hospital for another week.

Midnight . . . Who could this be? Her heart pounding, she looked through the peephole on the door and froze at the sight.

Gabriel.

She opened the door. He looked awful, his black coat and dark curls covered in mud, his eyes filled with anguish. A mix of joy and nervousness rushed through her.

"Lily, I need you. God I need you." He reached for her, slamming the door behind him with his foot while he wrapped his arms around her. He closed his eyes and rested his forehead on the top of her head.

"Gabriel, what's going on?"

He didn't answer and leaned on the wall, bringing her close. Then as the stubble on his chin scraped her cheek, he took possession of her mouth in hungry kisses, deep and full of despair. Without much thought, she found her tongue raking his with a desire for more of him.

He pressed his body against her and reached under the plaid pajama pants to grip her naked buttocks. "I need you to hold onto," he said between kisses. "Don't lock me out."

Pushing her pink tank top above her breasts, he took one nipple in his mouth. His tongue flicked it, startling her with the sudden intense sensation that radiated all the way down to between her legs.

He held her, one arm firmly around her back. His free hand cupped her other breast and he rolled her nipple between his thumb and forefinger.

She was lost in sensation, yet concerned for his obvious agony. Everything happened so fast, her mind didn't have time to react. Her body burned eagerly at his touch, completely out of control. His heat and the feel of his hard shaft on her navel commanded a strong need for him in her very core.

The little part of her brain that remained in control wondered whether she should stop him, talk to him. She didn't know yet where their relationship was heading.

But she wouldn't stop him, her body betraying her. And it was more than from mere pleasure at his touch. Under his demanding passion, she sensed a deep emotional need. What was going on in his tortured soul?

"Gabriel, what happened?"

"Shush." His voice was all tenderness while he lowered his zipper, his lips brushing hot caresses on the sensitive skin of her neck. He kicked off his boots, then slid off his pants as she helped him along.

He was hard for her, large and superb. Still wearing his coat, he pushed her pajama bottoms to the floor. Then, scooping both hands under her buttocks, he lifted her up.

She wrapped her legs around him and held on to his neck. Wanting to merge with him forever, she tightened the grip of her thighs on his hips.

He turned around and pinned her against the wall, then rubbed himself where she was dripping wet, not penetrating her yet. He held her up in one arm, his powerful muscles flexing under her buttocks.

"Gabriel, slow down. Tell me what's going on."

He cut off her protest with another kiss and reached between her legs. His thumb started an enticing circling motion at the tender nub calling for his touch.

She moaned in pleasure. He knew her body well, but she'd never seen him so desperate to possess her. This wasn't a time for playful spells. She wished he'd tell her what was wrong, but she was soon overcome. She capitulated to his lead.

He pushed himself firmly inside her. He was so big that he filled her entirely, almost splitting her open with delight. It had been so long.

She had to admit it: she'd been waiting for him all this time. Tears welled in her eyes at the love she felt for him.

They looked at each other, Gabriel's gaze full of warmth, while he rocked into her slowly, each thrust filling her even more.

"Lily, I missed you," he whispered in her ear while his thrusts became fiercer and faster, his thumb still stroking her tight little bundle of nerves insistently. He seemed possessed with her.

With the hard wall at her back, she held onto him, his head nestled in her chest. His torment burned through her heart.

"I can't let you go, baby." His voice was raspy with desire.

Her pleasure grew. She was near agony, caught between the wall and Gabriel's powerful chest. She could only think of him, his smoky green eyes reading her very soul, his dark curls brushing her shoulders. He took her almost furiously, his claim sending tremors of escalating pleasure through her entire body. She would come soon from this.

Surrendering to him and wanting it to last forever, she said, "I'm here, Gabriel." She breathed in the male scent emanating from him. "I'm here for you."

Her body exploded, tides of pleasure washing over her, and she cried his name again.

When he came, his head was buried in her neck, his arms tight around her as if he would never let her go.

"I love you, sweetheart. I'll never let you leave me again." He held her close until the last quiver of their passion subsided.

After carrying her to her bedroom, he gently laid her on the lacy white bedspread. He took off his coat and T-shirt, joined her, then helped remove her tank top.

They were together, finally. She had no intention of ever letting him go, her sorcerer, her lover, her soul mate.

They cuddled under the blankets, skin to skin. Soon Gabriel felt his need rising again. This was no time for explanations. She'd have to wait until his passion was fully quenched.

Her core aching from the previous night, Lily woke up and suddenly grew cold as she realized Gabriel wasn't beside her.

She got up shivering and surveyed her room, noticing her discarded tank top on the floor. But his clothes were gone, and there wasn't a sound in the apartment. She felt numb. He couldn't have just left her after last night.

She wrapped herself in her white terry robe and headed for the kitchen. No sign of Gabriel; he had definitely gone. She sighed, not knowing what to think.

Walking through the apartment, she searched for a note or a hint that he was coming back, but found nothing. Weariness overtook her. What was going on with him?

She went to the kitchen and made some coffee. Then she took it to the living room, where a few hours ago Gabriel had desperately made love to her. After picking up her pajama pants from the floor, she folded them and sat down on the couch.

Memories of their lovemaking flashed in her mind. Between kisses, he'd sworn he wanted no one but her. It was Lily he'd wanted last night, not Evangéline. She'd truly believed he'd come back to her and had put the past behind. Now she was left confused. Why didn't he say good-bye? But he hadn't lied to her last night. She knew it in her heart.

She reached for her cell phone. Who knows, maybe he'd sent her a message.

A feeling of relief swept over her. *Gabriel*—there it was.

"Six A.M. Be back," the text message read. "Had to go. See you soon. Love."

Lily glared at her phone. She didn't know if she could take this. He had spent a whole night with her, emotionally closer than ever. And now she faced eleven short words.

Twenty-nine

"You haven't told her yet?" Morag paced the floor of the living room as the morning sun permeated the lacy curtains of the French windows. "You fool. This could ruin everything."

Gabriel sat fuming on the couch where months ago he'd deposited an unconscious Lily after finding her in the woods. "I don't want her to take me just for my salvation."

"You'll become Taranis's puppet if you don't mate with her before the day is over, Gabriel." Morag stopped walking to rearrange her tartan closer around her.

"Stop messing with my life, Morag. It's my choice." When the Priory mark had burned his arm in the early morning, he'd been loath to leave Lily. But Morag was not to be denied. And after the latest scare with Iain, he felt compelled to make sure she was okay.

He felt his frustration mounting at how the priestess manipulated him. He'd really thought Morag was in danger. But all she wanted was to make decisions for him, again.

"You and Lily are our only chance at restoring our people."

"But what about the others?" Gabriel forced himself to stay calm. Morag really knew how to make his blood boil.

"Who knows when they'll find their mates?"

"I can't take her without telling her what she's getting into. She has a right to make this decision for herself."

He should've told her everything last night, but he hadn't wanted to be the bearer of any more bad news.

"This isn't just about you."

"I can't do it. And I won't let you force her."

Morag shook her head. "I could not force her, even if I wanted to. At Beltane, you are the only one who has power over her."

Gabriel wanted to tell Lily about the curse. A part of him even wanted to force her to perform the rites—not to save his soul, but because he knew he couldn't live without her. But he wasn't sure it was best for her, to become one of them.

"I'll lose my soul and that's that. I've lived too long anyway." He looked at the priestess and felt sorry for her a little. "Your intentions are good. I know what you and Iain have sacrificed for your people. But this is my life, my choice. I can't force myself on a woman, not even if she loves me."

Morag suddenly sat down, her eyes focused on the empty wall behind Gabriel.

"It was horrible." She gave a long sigh, appearing oddly defeated. "The day the barbarians came for us. Theuron had joined them. After we'd banished him for performing Taranis's magic, he resolved to help them destroy us. First, they captured a few maidens of the village, wanting slaves."

A strange impulse forced Gabriel to put a gentle hand on Morag's shoulder. Gone was her aura, her usual might around him. The woman looked suddenly very old. This was the first time she'd ever mentioned her past.

"My niece was among the captives. She was so pretty, so pure. Theuron had always been obsessed with her." Morag set her palms flat on her lap. "When he found her in the barbarian camp, he offered to save her. He wanted her to stay with him, as his consort."

Gabriel wanted to say something but stopped himself, fascinated by Morag's confessions.

Morag seemed to huddle in her seat as she continued her story. "But my niece refused him, the traitor to her people." Morag gave Gabriel a small smile. "You see, she was in love too, promised to Lachlan."

Her voice became stronger. "Theuron became so enraged at her refusal that he led the barbarians in our destruction, helping them with his newfound dark magic. Iain and I managed to escape the slaughter, but the others perished.

"After the battle, he took my niece back to our village to see the massacre. She saw her family, her lover, all dead." Morag voice choked on the last words. "Trying to be gracious to her, Theuron let her build a pyre for Lachlan. She stayed by his body until there were only ashes left. Then she managed to steal a horse from one of the barbarian warriors and rode to the shore. She threw herself off a cliff.

"When they all left, I ran through our village with Iain. The horror was everywhere. The mutilated bodies, our kin, the children, they were all dead. The High Priestess, my sister Iona, lay slain in the middle of the circle of stones. She'd fought them with all she had.

"Then I felt the goddess in me. I was the leader now. She told me where to find my niece. Her body was broken, but there was still life in her. We learned about Theuron's obsession. How he was looking for Iain and me now, seeking our destruction. How, with a ritual within our own Callanish stones, he had cursed all of his people's souls and made me barren."

Morag pushed a strand of gray hair out of her eye. "Theuron will always be after us. This is bigger than you, Gabriel. I need you and Lily to join for life. She'll be immortal, just like you. We need our people back and strong. Theuron will take his time, but if he ever gets what he wants and destroys us, then there will be nothing left between him and the other realms. He'll be unstoppable."

"And what of the other sorcerers? Can't they fight him? Find their soul mates." Gabriel didn't see how the evil mage alone could be a danger to the whole Priory.

"Oh, some are much stronger than you are. Tris and Renaud, Loïc too, they are the oldest. But they are no match for Theuron. And with each soul Taranis possesses, Theuron only becomes stronger. You have to convince Lily to save your soul. It's not just about me. We are all together in this." Morag stood up to look at him with piercing eyes. "Lily already chose her fate. She is one of us now."

"She needs to fully understand what this means."

"You have until tonight, Gabriel—tonight."

"I'll go to her." Gabriel resigned himself. This was a decision they would have to make together, he and Lily. "I'll explain everything. She'll choose. I trust her. I trust her to the depths of my soul."

The heat of the Blue Circle club hit her as soon as she stepped in. The place was not busy, but Lily still hated the loud and dark atmosphere. Her phone rang and she answered it with relief as she recognized the number. Finally, the call she'd be waiting for all day.

"Gabriel, where are you?" Lily drew a hand to the ring on a silver chain at her neck.

"At your house. You said you didn't work tonight. But where are you?"

"I'm at the Blue Circle. Keira asked me to meet her here. She needs to talk to me." Lily had been visiting Angèle at the hospital with Mrs. Desmarais when she'd gotten Keira's frantic call. Without a thought, she'd asked

Mrs. Desmarais to drop her off at the club. But now where was Keira?

Lily heard a pause on the phone and knew Gabriel wanted to castigate her for going near Keira without him. She heard him taking a deep breath. Then he said, "Lily, you should've called me."

"Well, you just took off on me this morning."

"I told you I'd call back."

"You texted me, just eleven little words." Her voice was more exasperated than truly angry.

"Eleven? Really, that's a lot."

"Oh, never mind. Just come over. I'll need a ride home."

"On my way. Did you miss me?" Miss him? She smiled, remembering how she'd been looking at her phone every time she'd had a chance between her rounds at the hospital.

They talked a little longer while Lily glanced around nervously for a sign of Keira; then she hung up.

She considered getting a drink when a soft voice filled with sadness whispered behind her. "Lily, a priestess of the Callanish Coven." The familiar expensive scent enveloped her. "And me, one of Theuron's Kyries."

Keira. Lily looked back at her friend.

"What has happened to us?" Keira glided beside Lily and put a gentle hand on her arm.

Lily's heart sank to see her so weary, with her heavily black-rimmed eyes and her white-blonde hair pulled high in a messy ponytail that made her look like a fragile little girl. A bright fuchsia fur coat topped her tiny black slip.

"Keira, why are you still with him? He's dangerous."

Tears welled Keira's big blue eyes.

"There's nothing you can do for me, Lily. It's too late. I know you did try. Theuron is the only one who can soothe my nights." She gave a small smirk. "In fact, that's what sustains him these days. The intensity of my nightmares makes him closer to being human."

"But that's not a life, Keira. Let Morag help. You'll find your soul mate. Your nightmares will go away." Keira seemed so small and lost in the shadowy club.

"My soul mate? Didn't Morag tell you about my past life? In the thirteenth century, my husband and king went away to another while I grieved for him, thinking he'd died in battle." Her face twisted with pain. "I'd just given birth to his heir, and he betrayed me. I didn't know. In grief, I gave our son to his mother to raise, then forced my subjects to bury me alive, so I could join Renaud in the next life. I died, while he remained with another. Why would I go back to him now? No, leave me with Theuron. At least he doesn't lie to me."

Lily was filled with remorse as Keira told her story. She'd had no idea. Morag did tell her it was not time for Keira, that they could not save her yet. But surely there must be something they could do.

Keira stared at her insistently. "Lily, there's something you must know." Keira looked around the club, then continued, "I only have a few minutes before Theuron wonders where I am. It's about Gabriel. If you two don't mate before this day ends, he will lose his soul for eternity. He will be doomed forever, forced to serve Taranis in another realm as an undead." Keira's words infused Lily with anguish. Taranis—that was the dark god Theuron served.

"I'm not sure I understand."

"Today is Beltane. Gabriel must claim you, his true soul mate. Theuron cast some powerful magic on the day the Callanish people were destroyed, and this is their curse. On the night you two first slept together, you were both lost. Find him tonight, Lil, or you'll lose him. Theuron told me all about it." Coldness descended upon Lily's heart. She was horrified. So Morag had orchestrated it all, forcing them so they would have no choice. Why hadn't Gabriel told her? Why be so secretive?

Then she remembered his call and relief swept over her. He'd be here soon. She would save him. It was still early. They had time.

She reached for her phone to call him when a flat voice spoke above them. "Lady Keira, you have to come with us."

Lily looked up. Keepers, two of them. Her heart pounded in fear at the sight of their tattooed skulls and thick muscles under tight black T-shirts.

Without a word, Keira drew her gaze away from Lily and got up to follow them.

"You're to come as well. Our master wants to talk to you for a moment. If you please." One of the Keepers gripped her forearm tightly and Lily recoiled at the frigid touch forcing her to stand.

She couldn't let them take her. There was no time for this. She had to save Gabriel.

"Lily, I don't think he'll hurt you." Keira's voice had changed to that of a little girl. Keira continued, in a sing-song voice again, "Don't worry. He's after Morag, not you."

"Morag?"

"Yes, he wants to destroy her." Keira gave her a sunny smile. "He'll probably just ask you a few questions, then let you go. Right, Bear?" She edged over, rubbing her bare leg over the leather pants of the Keeper holding Lily.

"Not for me to say, lady." Bear didn't budge, apparently unaffected by Keira's attentions.

"Come with us, Lil, and then you can go back to Gabriel."

Lily checked around the bar. Then her gaze came

back to Keira and the two muscular giants. She felt for her friend, but she had to get away from them all, fast.

She was about to bolt when a tall dark figure appeared in front of her.

Theuron. Her knees buckled under her and she would have fallen into Bear's arms if the mage hadn't jumped forward to hold her free arm. Panic seized her and she forgot all of Morag's teachings.

"Just a few seconds of your time, love." Theuron's magnetism enveloped her and she had eyes only for him, enticing in a long gray cashmere coat over an immaculate dark suit, his perfectly manicured fingers stroking her bare arm.

She couldn't answer. With hesitation she glanced back to the bar. Gabriel was nowhere to be seen. She was all alone, and Theuron was dangerously attractive.

Keira and the Keepers vanished from her side as Theuron's sensual voice called to her. "Come. Have a drink with me." His eyes were pure black, strangely alluring. She was unable to tear herself from him. What was happening?

Her legs were weak and she leaned toward him. He caught her, wrapping an arm around her waist. She was enfolded in his scent of pine leaves and musk, the faintly detectable decay emanating from him oddly inviting.

He led her to the back of the club, then exited to the loading area. The cold air reminded her that she was clad in a small dress. She cuddled to him, following like a willing child.

Theuron's limousine waited, and after his driver opened the door, they both settled in the back. She crossed her legs, feeling the leather of the seat under her bare thighs as her dress hiked up.

"Let's get you something to drink." He reached in front of him to an ice bucket. "Champagne? Veuve Clicquot, the best. Not that I would know, of course, but your friend Keira enjoys it."

"Please," she said, strangely comfortable sitting there next to Theuron. He was so calm and commanding. Things would always go smooth with him, no surprise, ever.

"Here, love, enjoy." He presented her with a glass, then gazed at her while she took a sip. The bubbles bit her tongue and her body started tingling at the possibilities his presence offered.

She was beginning to be very attracted to him, even though she detected a speck of something ugly in his eyes.

"Now, how is Gabriel?" His dark voice went right through her. She felt vulnerable and self-conscious, all her doubts gone now, wanting more of him.

"Fine. I haven't seen him much lately." She smiled as she set her glass on a low table at her feet. What was wrong with her? Why didn't she just open the door and run away?

"I'm sorry to hear that." He leaned closer and settled a hand on her thigh.

Its sensuality shattered right through her, making her feel both revolted and needy for more. It was as if he drew her to do the most unspeakable things. She could bury herself in him, lose her soul, and she wouldn't be able to stop.

"How nice it is to be in love. I've been in love too, you know." His expert fingertips stroked the inside of her thigh, sending shudders of desire through her entire body. "But she didn't love me and I was utterly devastated."

"I'm so sorry. That's really sad." Lily meant it, her heart drawn to him.

"It was indeed. She killed herself."

Lily blinked, her mind in a fog. "How horrible."

Theuron's touch hiked higher up on her thigh. His

fingers still stroked her gently, his caress getting perilously close to becoming very intimate.

"Yes, isn't it? I had killed her lover," he whispered in her ear.

Lily's heart stopped for a second. She should leave—now.

But she couldn't extract herself from him. He was dangerous, yet steeped with longing for his darkness, she wanted him to continue touching her.

"You're very pretty, Lily. Maybe you would like to stay with me for a while?"

"Stay?"

"Yes, be with me. I've lived a long time. I can show you things even Gabriel knows nothing about."

Lily had become a mass of confusion. Her body ached for more of the mage's touch, his fingertips burning her skin. His voice was smooth, his lips sensual, and she was getting lost in him. Theuron's hand moved under her skirt as if he owned her. The pad of his thumb made a soft brush over the cotton fabric just where her nerves were most sensitive.

She gasped.

"Come, make love to me." His lips were inches from hers.

Her body was no longer hers to command and she leaned to kiss him, her lips begging for his.

He remained totally still, waiting for her to come to him.

As their lips nearly touched, she was jolted by a vivid image.

Watch his true form, Morag had said.

Lily shrank back in horror as she saw the cursed creature, all decaying skin and skeletal bones, replace the suave mage.

His spell broken, she hurled herself as far away as she

could. She rattled the handle, but found she couldn't open the door, even though it wasn't locked. He must have put a spell on it.

"What do you want from me?" Her knees huddled to her chest, her arms wrapped around them.

"Of you? Oh, just a little entertainment. I thought you liked me." The horrific image had gone from her mind and he looked at her, almost pouting.

"Leave me alone. Let me go." She started to slow her breath, trying to reach for her powers.

"Let you go? No, I need you. And your love for Gabriel is pure, Lily. I want to feel that again. I could force you to be with me as you are with him." He narrowed his eyes at her. "What do you think? Will I do that? It could be painful."

"I won't let you come near me." She fought hard to keep calm, her training with Morag starting to come back to her. She'd protect herself.

"Well, maybe another time, although it would be fun to take all feelings from you and leave what's left for Gabriel. I wonder if he would notice. I'm not sure he appreciates what he has in you."

"You're really crazy aren't you?" Lily visualized a shield encircling her. The familiar female voices were near, but not quite loud enough.

"Crazy? No, I don't think so. I have desires, like everyone else. Do you know what it's like not to feel anything? Everything is bland—the taste of an apple, a woman's skin under my fingers, her quivering emotions. I crave life." He sighed. "Taranis is not a kind god. He asks a lot of his followers. Oh well, at least I get to have control over everyone."

Lily hadn't yet raised her shield when she felt a foreign presence in her mind.

Theuron, he was trying to read her. He searched her

memory. She fought the surge of panic slamming into her and reached further for her powers, fighting him with all her strength.

Theuron forced her to remember the Callans' house, but she blocked him, focusing on the present, on the inside of the car where she crouched. As she felt his mind invading her further, she shifted on to simpler thoughts: shopping with Angèle, the wing where she worked, her favorite home-improvement show.

He let out a cutting laugh. "Is this all the power you have? Really. Is this all Morag has against me? We are far from the days of the fierce Iona."

Lily ignored him and focused on the mist she started to feel around her. She was close.

Theuron leaped at her and yanked her hair. She winced at the pain in her skull, his frigid presence seeping through her.

His face got really close as he tightened his grip.

She howled in pain. She had to focus, couldn't let the pain alter her concentration.

But soon he became too strong for her. He took over her consciousness, forced her to think of the path leading to the Callans' house.

She stood with Morag in Iain's lab, retrieving a bundle wrapped in a wool blanket. Morag carried the bundle to the sacred clearing. The moon shone full and high, the night warm. The vision was very clear, a gentle wind caressing her skin.

After placing the bundle on the altar, Morag unwrapped it. Lily felt Theuron's presence next to her. He was watching too. Morag took the object that so fascinated the mage.

Theuron's laughter of triumph erupted in her head.

The Cathair Sword. Theuron sought the sword, the only thing that could kill Morag.

Soon he was gone from her mind and let go of her hair. She stared at the man facing her, shaking, and her hand lifted to her skull, still hurting from his brutality.

"I do want to thank you for your help." He smiled at her pleasantly. "Very sorry to leave you, but I have some business to attend to."

She said nothing.

"A rain check perhaps? My offer still stands. You would make a wonderful little plaything." He tapped the window, and the door opened, a breeze of fresh air blowing over her flushed face.

Lily stumbled out of the limo, stunned. Theuron was after Morag's sword, and he knew exactly where it was hidden.

What had she done? He'd seen the path to the house, the cavity in the stone wall where Morag kept it. He'd witnessed the spell.

The spell—no! Theuron had seen Morag breaking the protection spell. He would be able to use it to free the sword.

Dread overtook her as she realized Keira had been right. Theuron wanted to kill Morag.

Lily felt awful. She hadn't been strong enough. Morag had trusted her and now Lily had betrayed her mentor. Because she was too weak.

Thirty

Lily ran back into the club, still in shock. Looking for Gabriel and not finding him, she checked her phone. He'd texted her.

"Looked for you at the club. Had to run back to the Callans' with Iain. Emergency. Sorry about the ride."

She texted him back, furious.

"Gabriel, Beltane?"

No answer.

She called Morag. She had to get to the Callans' house as well. Tell Morag what had happened with Theuron.

Morag didn't pick up her phone. Worry soon overwhelmed her and she tried to reason with herself.

How much danger could be threatening Morag? The priestess was so powerful. And with Iain and Gabriel with her, she'd be quite safe. But still, no one knew Theuron was after the sword.

Lily looked at her watch. Three hours until midnight.

If she got on the road soon, she'd be there before ten. Enough time to talk some sense into him, join in the Beltane ritual.

Yes, she could take a taxi home, then jump in her car. She would still make it before midnight.

Lily punched in the taxi company's phone number. But something familiar caught her eye.

Gabriel's bike. The big black machine stood right there by the entrance. What was it doing there?

He must have left with Iain. Knowing the extent of

the alchemist's powers, she wouldn't be surprised if they didn't need a car to reach the Callans' house.

She walked to the bike and examined it for a few seconds. It had a powerful engine. She'd driven it a few times on a dirt road, once on the highway. But Gabriel had been right there behind her, giving her advice.

Could she do it? I-95 would practically be deserted on a week night. She'd get there much quicker.

She drew herself tall as a surge of assurance seeped through her. Sure, she could do it.

She retrieved the spare key from the saddlebag. An old leather jacket lay at the bottom. She put it on.

It reached her midthigh. The sleeves were long, but with them rolled up, she'd be well protected against the wind on the highway. Her shoes were another problem, but she'd have to make do with them.

She straddled the bike and started the engine. How did she do it again? She adjusted the side mirrors. Gas, clutch, brakes and gear shift—she was all set.

Soon she drove off. Her bare legs were getting numb from the cool air, but she focused on controlling the beast between her thighs. Once she got going, it felt strangely easy. Thankfully the dock area was clear of traffic at night. She headed for the highway.

She couldn't stop thinking about what had happened in the limo. She shuddered in revulsion. How could she have reacted that way to Theuron, almost kissing him? She obviously wasn't as strong as she'd thought.

Discouragement swept over her as she yearned for Gabriel's strength. Why hadn't they waited for her? Here she was, freezing cold, driving his bike on the highway, when she should be with him, discussing the terrible curse holding him. She cranked up the throttle, anxious to see him.

Half an hour later, she rode on the deserted country road a short distance from the Callans' house. Almost there, finally.

All she wanted now was to run into Gabriel's arms. Together they could face what threatened them. Together they were strong.

She accelerated at a sharp turn on the gravel. The bike started sliding.

No. She tightened her grip on the handlebars in panic and turned the wheel the wrong way.

Her heart seized, then the ground slammed into her. She screamed as a huge weight landed on top of her body, her right leg sliced by an agonizing pain.

"Two against eight doesn't seem fair, does it?" Standing on the porch next to Iain, Gabriel observed Theuron and his four thugs. Three Kyries accompanied them, wearing lingerie, fur and leather boots and holding each other's hands. His heart sank as he recognized Keira among them.

"Well, it's actually three against eight. Morag is getting prepared." Iain stood completely erect and still. His dead stare focused on Theuron.

"It really isn't fair, then." Gabriel was as motionless as his mentor, his muscles ready to uncoil at any minute.

"Are those real?" Iain gave a quick nod at the four Keepers.

"Theuron, are your friends real? Or did you just dream them up to try to scare us?" Gabriel slowly studied his opponents.

Damn. All magic-users this time, it seemed. And with Theuron there, he didn't know how lethal the fight could get.

"Iain." Theuron stood straight, with his feet wide. Gone was his usual business suit. A bloodred cloak, runes adorning its black trim, covered his black robe. "I came to get what's mine."

"That's a very dramatic stance, Theuron," Gabriel shouted in the dark. "Did you need to practice?"

"Iain, get rid of the kid. Let's settle this together. I want my sword."

"You are not worthy of it, Theuron." Iain spoke calmly, his long gray hair flowing wildly around him.

"My father forged the Cathair Sword. My mother enchanted it. It belongs to me." Theuron's expression was full of rage.

"Not anymore, it doesn't." Almost gliding, Iain descended the steps toward the dark mage. "You lost it the minute you made a bargain with Taranis. You're his puppet, now."

Ready to move at any instant, Gabriel kept his eye on the Keepers, wondering what sort of magic they actually practiced. The four creatures stood a few feet behind their master, utterly still.

"You banished me!" Theuron nearly screamed the words, his voice wretched.

"No, Iona banished you. But I did agree with her." Iain's demeanor was stern, unforgiving.

"Iona." Theuron's upper lip curled up. "I destroyed her easily, didn't I? Just as I will destroy her little sister, Morag. You shouldn't have allied yourself with them, Iain. You should have stayed with me."

Theuron smiled, then continued. "I will take the Cathair Sword back. I know a lot more than you think. I met your pretty new friend tonight. She told me a lot of interesting things."

Horror seized Gabriel's heart. "Lily." He couldn't stop himself from saying her name out loud.

"I see I have you attention now, kid. She's yours isn't she? Or she was . . ." Theuron let out a small laugh.

"What have you done to her?" Gabriel's eyes narrowed.

"It shouldn't be any of your concern. She is done with you." Gabriel's throat constricted, his control seeping away. What if Lily was dead—or worse?

"Well, enough small talk now. Let's get what we came for. Kyries, Keepers proceed."

Almost as an afterthought, Theuron pointed to Gabriel, speaking one single forbidden word.

Flashes of light burst in the night and agony sliced Gabriel's skull. As he fell to the porch, he saw Theuron and his followers disappear in a blur.

No. Have to get up.

A last image of Iain swallowed by a swirl of wind reached him. Then all went black.

Thirty-one

Lily lay on the grassy side of the road, the giant bike on top of her. She groaned in the silent night. Her body hurt all over, but nothing seemed broken. The inside of her leg throbbed with pain.

What had she been thinking? Sharp focus soon replaced her initial panic as she assessed her situation.

She found that she could slide herself from under the bike. She'd skidded mostly on the grass, so she'd escaped having her skin scraped by the deadly gravel.

Touching the inside of her leg, she found no blood but a nasty burn from the exhaust pipe. She could move all her limbs.

Slowly, she got up on wobbly legs. Light radiating from a lone lamppost showed her the grim picture of the monster machine on the ground.

Her hope rose as she noticed that except for the completely smashed side mirror, the bike seemed unharmed. She grabbed the handlebars and braced herself. With all her strength, she managed to push the bike up. She wondered if it would still work. No need to call 911—her legs were solid again.

First though, she should attend to her leg. She opened the saddlebag where Gabriel usually left the first-aid kit and shook her head.

Gabriel's new computer had smashed to pieces. The bag had taken the brunt of the fall, and the computer had received most of the impact. She cringed at the mess, then turned her attention back to her task and proceeded to bandage her leg.

With a quick prayer to the goddess, she straddled the bike and turned the key in the ignition. To her surprise, the engine roared to life. Newfound hope flooded over her. Great, only a few miles to drive and she'd be there. Her leg hurt and her body was stiff from the fall, but she'd make it.

A few minutes later, Lily arrived at the Callans' property. She parked, then removed her jacket, an uneasy feeling creeping over her. The door to the house stood wide-open, and all was suspiciously quiet.

Her heart sped up as she noticed the shadow of someone sprawled on the porch.

Gabriel.

Oh my love, please be okay. She rushed up the stairs and knelt beside him.

She grabbed his shoulder. "Gabriel, wake up. It's Lily." Her voice shook with angst. "Gabriel."

He finally opened his eyes and relief sank in at his familiar charming smile.

"Baby."

"Are you okay?"

"Yes. Damn, Theuron." Gabriel sat up, frowned and raised a hand to his forehead. "He's after the Cathair Sword."

"I know. I came to tell Morag."

"Did Theuron hurt you?" He gave her an anxious look as he grabbed her upper arms with both hands.

"No, I'm fine, but I ruined your computer."

The tender expression in his green eyes melted her heart. Then he kissed her gently.

She barely had time to react before he was on his feet. "I have to go to the clearing. Morag and Iain are there.

You have to stay here, Lil. Stay in the house, in Morag's library near her altar. You'll be safe."

"But Beltane . . . there's not much time left." She was torn between her duty to Morag and her yearning to see him safe from Taranis's clutches.

"Oh, you know about that." He gave her a sheepish look.

"Keira told me." Lily raised her eyes. "You should have said something."

He shrugged as if to dismiss his own troubles, then seemed pained. "Keira was just here with Theuron. Sorry, Lil, but I can't do anything for your friend. They're out fighting Iain and Morag. I owe them too much. I have to go."

She knew he was right, but her heart had a hard time accepting this. She gave him a small smile. "Be quick. And know that I'll be here waiting for you to come back."

"Don't worry. I'll be back right before midnight. Watch this." He winked at her, then crouched down on the floor. She heard him chant an incantation, and he disappeared before her eyes.

She gasped at the sight of a magnificent bald eagle perched on the banister.

"Gabriel." She shook her head. Despite her fear for him, she couldn't help but smile. "You did it."

The eagle gave her one more look as if to say goodbye, then took flight.

Gabriel soared in the air and circled the sacred clearing. This was not his first flight. But despite the danger he would soon face, the feeling of being airborne was still new enough to thrill him.

He lowered as he saw Iain in a fierce stance, both palms in front of him, holding the Keepers at a distance with the force of his will. The old sorcerer was protecting Morag, who knelt behind him by her altar, apparently in a deep trance.

She had reverted to Brighid, her flaming hair wild around her strong body. Tightly gripping the hilt of the Cathair Sword, she had started to draw a protection shield. Iain just had to hold on while she finished the ritual, and Theuron's magic would be useless.

But the fight had only started.

Theuron stood behind his Keepers, looking at Iain as if bored by the whole thing. At his side, Keira and the two other Kyries held hands, completely still, mumbling bizarre words, their silk dresses whirling around their bare thighs. Strong psychic energy radiated from them.

Beltane. Gabriel knew he would not make it in time to save himself, but he would defeat Theuron, and Lily would be safe. It was a small price to pay for her sake, and even for Morag, the cunning priestess.

His heart twinged as he remembered Lily's trusting expression before he flew away from her. It may be the last image he'd ever have of her. He had to do this, for her.

After one more sweep, he landed right next to Iain. As soon as he hit the ground, he reverted to human form and stood in his long black coat, facing his enemies. A supreme power filled him. He was ready.

"Hey, old man, thought of leaving me behind?" He winked at Iain, then raised his hands toward the four Keepers.

Lily wouldn't stay at the house, no way. She couldn't just leave Gabriel alone. Besides, Morag could probably use her help.

She ran into the house to get a flashlight, then back to the bike to get her *athame* from her purse. She anchored the knife under her bra strap, the sharp tip digging slightly under her arm, and circled the house to take the path leading to the sacred clearing.

The moon was a small crescent in the black sky, barely big enough to be seen. Lily had never been there alone since the night when Gabriel had found her near death. She walked carefully. No, she wasn't scared. In fact, the forest lived around her, giving her the strength she needed.

She gave a quick prayer to Cerrwiden. "Lady, give me courage." It was as if the forest responded, *You're one of us now.*

Lily discarded her high heels and started to run, each step pounding the moss and the thick coat of spongy leaves. She sensed bats nearby, small crawling insects scurrying around, owls hunting for mice.

The forest brimmed with night life, and she'd become just another wild creature.

Soon she reached the edge of the sacred clearing. She didn't want to test her still-emerging power against Theuron, but she could aid Gabriel by sending a protection spell from the shelter of the forest. She wouldn't be a target. She could also get within the safety of Morag's ritual circle and help her High Priestess.

She heard muffled voices as she edged toward the altar. The usual lit torches shone through the trees, but she couldn't see anyone.

She turned off her flashlight and, instead of rushing to the clear space, buried herself in the woods to observe the scene from a distance. She got as close as she dared and started to shield herself. She visualized stillness and started the trance sequence, seeing the colors yellow, red, blue and finally indigo. She was protected.

Morag knelt in complete trance in front of the altar, the sword in her hand pointing to the ground, her hair like fire around her.

Theuron and Iain faced each other outside the ritual

circle. Lily barely recognized the old professor. A thick band of steel at his forehead encircled his long white hair, battered leather armored his chest and his black coat floated around him.

Lily gasped to see Iain's whole body hover above the ground, his eyes looking mad as he intoned the same word over and over again, pointing at Theuron.

Her heart sank when she finally caught sight of Gabriel facing four Keepers, their tattooed skulls gleaming in the torchlight.

He held them at bay with a sweep of his hand, creating a small storm to corral them, but three of the thugs whirled vicious swords around while another pressed his hands together and chanted, his eyes shining silver in the shadows.

Filled with fear for Gabriel, Lily started to summon Cerrwiden to shelter him, but movement by the altar caught her eyes.

Morag had lifted the sword over her head and started chanting in the ancient language. Her eyes fixed on the waxing moon above her. Lily recognized the protection-sphere spell. Soon the whole area would be protected and their attackers' magic would be ineffective.

The Cathair Sword started to glow. All should soon be over and they'd be safe. But a lightning bolt sparked in the dark and before Morag had time to complete the spell, it hit her straight in the middle of her back. Theuron had pried himself from Iain long enough to send her a lethal blast.

Lily repressed a shriek. Morag had fallen in a sweep of black dress, the sword lying beside her. It was too late now. The priestess had been the only one who could save them.

Thirty-two

Lily retrieved her *athame*, quickly cut a doorway through the ritual circle, then ran to the fallen woman.

"Morag, talk to me." She shook her mentor gently.

"Lily, child, you are here." Morag opened her eyes, her expression relieved at the sight of Lily bending over her. "Help me." Morag tried to get up. "Give me the sword, quick."

Still shaking, Lily reached for the Cathair Sword and dragged it to Morag.

But Morag couldn't stand. She lay on her hands and knees trying to get some air in her lungs. "You have to do it. I can't. Raise the sphere." Morag could barely speak. "Take the sword. Point to the sky. Create the protection sphere around the house, the lake. Cerrwiden will guide you."

At the corner of her eye, Lily saw that Iain was straining against Theuron. How could she succeed when Morag had failed?

"Do not question me, Ael. There is no time." Morag's voice brimmed with force.

The sound of her ancient name shook Lily out of her paralysis. Doing as she was told, she gripped the sword by the hilt and stood. The steel was so heavy that she wondered how she'd manage to point it to the sky.

Gathering her strength, she shot a glance in Gabriel's direction. He faced four menacing Keepers but seemed to have the upper hand.

Then Lily saw the spell-casting Keeper swirl his fingers as he mouthed an incantation. She tried to warn Gabriel, but Morag's command stopped her. "The sphere."

Lily forced the sword high above her head while her legs buckled under her. She fell on her knees, still keeping the sword straight and high toward the sliver of moon.

The sword came alive in her hand. Its power radiated through her entire body, giving her the energy to go on. She told herself to focus, to breathe, as she visualized the triple-moon symbol, kept it branded in her mind.

Then she mentally started to draw a sphere, high above them. She traced circles on top of circles, which became larger as she drew them all around the house, the lake and the battle scene. Time stood still as she created the circles, around and around, clear in her mind. She sent safety to those she had grown to respect, to the one she loved more than anything.

Lily was no longer on the battlefield. She floated, surrounded by stillness. The scent of heather, permeated with the maritime mist, welcomed her. And the stones, the thirteen solid Callanish stones, waited for her. She was home. The female voices, the many faces of the goddess, echoed in her mind. *You are almost there, Priestess of the Callanish. Stay with us.*

Still restraining the three sword-wielding Keepers, Gabriel had sensed the magical energy rising in the fourth one. He released his hold on the others, then focused his mind on heating the body temperature of the spell-casting Keeper until it became so hot, the creature combusted spontaneously. It screamed in pain, then disappeared.

Gabriel froze at the sight of Lily in the midst of it all, Morag defeated beside her. She hadn't listened to him but had chosen to fight along with them. An immense respect for her rose in his heart.

She looked small and fragile in her short white dress, but he knew otherwise. Her legs bare, she knelt on the ground, holding tremendous power in her hands. She was beyond normal beauty with her head thrown back, her eyes closed, thick dark curls cascading down.

She was their only chance now.

He sent her a silent prayer. Lily, his love . . . she could do it. She exuded power. He had faith in her; she wouldn't fail them.

The remaining Keepers also had noticed Lily and rushed toward the altar.

"*Flamm.*" He raised one hand and shot fire straight at one of the Keepers.

The giant burst in flame, then disappeared into the dark. The last two Keepers lunged at Gabriel, their lethal swords raised high.

With one flick of Gabriel's hand, the wind swirled tighter and tighter around his two opponents. A cyclone hauled them up, high above the trees. Gabriel spoke one word and the wind stopped.

The thugs fell in a fifty-foot drop. As soon as they hit the ground, they vanished in a blur of smoke.

A surge of adrenaline welled in Gabriel as he saw Iain collapse beside Theuron. The evil mage ignored the fallen alchemist to run to the altar, then stood at the edge of the priestesses' sacred circle.

Theuron raised his hand to blast Lily with a spell.

No! Gabriel hurled himself on top of the mage, and they both rolled onto the ground.

Theuron screamed, then cursed.

"It's over, Theuron." Gabriel smashed him to the ground.

"Your girlfriend was mine, sorcerer." Theuron became motionless as he spit out the words. "When you were still thinking of your old fiancée, little Lily flew right into my arms. Not very faithful, is she? Show her a bit of magic, and she's all yours."

Gabriel said nothing. The mage's lies would not alter his faith in his love.

"She's a hot little tart. But I'm done with her. Do you want her back?"

Gabriel reached for the mage's throat. "Now I have to kill you."

Theuron shouted one word and Gabriel was catapulted into the air. As he landed, he saw the mage roll toward Iain, grab the old man by his hair and press the Taranis dagger to his throat.

"You touch me and Iain dies."

Lily had been calm and focused, feeling Gabriel's spirit near her. At first, he'd been in control. But now she sensed turmoil from him.

Something was going wrong. He needed help. Fear for him suddenly overwhelmed her and she nearly dropped the sword to run to his aid.

Stay with us. The female voices stopped her. Whispers invaded her consciousness. *Your inner strength will save him. The sphere, draw it down.*

She forced her mind to return to the circles. She focused on them, blue rays of light swishing rapidly around her. The sphere was nearly completed.

Her legs cramped from the kneeling position and her bare knees burned on the gritty dirt. As her arms ached from the heavy steel in her hands, terror for Gabriel's sake challenged her concentration. She wanted to stop this, run to him and make the nightmare go away.

But she found strength deep inside and ignored the incredible pain in her body, forced her muscles to tighten. She kept the sword raised.

She glanced at Morag, who labored for breath, and wished with all her heart her mentor would be all right.

Lily could feel Gabriel nearby, as if he were there with her, helping with her burden. *I love him. I have to do this for him.*

Tears welled in her eyes. She no longer cared whether she was or was not Evangéline, reborn. She was his true soul mate, history or not.

Feeling the ancient powers surging through her, Lily knew she was no longer a regular woman. She'd become a Cerrwiden priestess. She'd been blessed. She was now worthy of her gift.

I feel you. She addressed the ancient goddess in a silent prayer. *Stay with me*, she begged silently. *Save us.*

An intense light suddenly came through the tip of the sword, shooting out to the sky. The light traced the exact path that Lily had drawn in her mind, around and around, leaving a glowing trace behind. Soon a huge dome of blue light appeared around the entire area, reaching through the forest and across the dark water of the lake.

She was now as still as a marble statue, the sword raised above her. Strength possessed her. Lily had become invincible.

She'd done it. She had drawn down the moon to protect them. She had channeled Cerrwiden.

She caught Morag smiling at her, looking at her young disciple with pride in her eyes, and then she heard Morag scream in horror as the High Priestess turned toward the battle scene.

Gabriel jumped to his feet and strode toward Theuron as Morag's shriek pierced the night.

"Theuron, you can't kill your own brother." Morag's voice swelled with panic.

Gabriel looked at his mentor in shock. Theuron, Iain's brother? That explained why Iain had never been scared of him.

"Why not?" Theuron smirked, his hand steady on the dagger at Iain's throat.

The old sorcerer lay still, not an ounce of panic in his eyes. "Theuron, let me go. You had your fun. It's over now."

Theuron shook his head. "Iain, my dear big brother. We were set to do great magic together, but you chose her instead." Theuron tightened his grip on Iain's chest. "You're next, Morag Callan. I'll kill you just as I killed the last High Priestess of the Callanish Coven." He kissed his brother's temple dramatically. "Then Iain will be returned to me. Dead or alive, he'll be mine again, as we were always meant to be. We brothers shall rise again."

Gabriel stood at arm's length from Theuron. He assessed the two brothers, his mind running swiftly as he caught Iain's thoughts.

Lily will save you.

At his mentor's silent plea, Gabriel's voice echoed in the night. "Lily, the sword."

Theuron settled his gaze on Gabriel and snorted. "You're a fool. No man alive can hold that sword—only a Callanish priestess, or the undead, like me."

Lily drew the blade behind her, then with surprising strength, threw the sword high in the air.

The Cathair Sword made a few loops as it flew.

Gabriel grabbed the mage by the front of his robe as the sword landed right in his free hand.

As he seized the sword in a powerful hold, he claimed, "You're wrong, Theuron. I'm the priestess's Warrior King."

He gave one last glance into the black eyes of the undead mage and without hesitation, plunged the Cathair Sword in his chest, the steel piercing his thorax.

Without a word, Theuron collapsed to the ground in a heap of red and black robes, letting go of Iain, who fell along with him.

Gabriel had accepted the sword. There was no turning back. He was the first Warrior King, the chosen one. He could no longer deny his fate.

He helped Iain to his feet, then heard a faint voice beside him. "Gabriel."

In a flash, he turned toward Lily, and his heart sank as he saw her starting to crumple. He jumped to her, Iain at his side, both leaving Theuron slumped on the ground.

"Keira." Lily fell into his arms. "Make sure she's okay."

The Kyries had stayed behind, praying to Taranis through the whole fight, and all he saw was a dark presence, a flash of white-blonde hair, then nothing.

His glanced at the ground where seconds before, Theuron had collapsed. The mage had vanished and with him, Keira and the Cathair Sword.

Thirty-three

Tara, Phoebus and Loïc strode out of the dark forest as Lily caught her breath, leaning on Gabriel.

"Where the hell have you guys been?" Gabriel held Lily tight in his arms as he hollered at them.

Loïc rushed to Morag, who still knelt on the ground, while the two other sorcerers looked around, puzzled.

"What happened?" Phoebus asked.

Tara neared Iain and patted him gently on his black coat. "How are you doing, old friend?"

"I am fine, dear. As tough as an old oak tree. I'll survive."

"I can assure you, the disappearing spell he used will be his last for quite a while," Morag said.

"Indeed, Morag. Didn't I feel you cast the sphere?"

"It wasn't Morag. Lily did it."

Lily smiled to hear the pride in Gabriel's voice.

"Yes," Morag added. "Lily is a full priestess now." With Loïc's help, she got to her feet. "There is no need now for that initiation you dreaded."

Lily sighed in relief at Morag's words. Then something caught the corner of her eye, something bright, flashing in the woods.

Her heart filled with hope. Keira. Lily could see her puffy fur coat glowing orange in the light of the flaming torch at the edge of the clearing. Apparently worn out, her friend leaned against the trunk of a birch tree.

Without a thought, Lily left Gabriel's embrace, ignoring his shouts for her. She dashed to the woods. This time Keira would listen and come with them. She was safe from Theuron.

Lily frowned with anxiety as she ran closer and realized her friend was in a trance, her head cast down.

Keira slowly lifted her eyes to stare at Lily. With her eyes full of horror, she mouthed the word *no*.

Lily barely registered a powerful-looking dark figure appearing behind Keira. A flash of lightning sparkled. No!—she'd walked beyond the edge of the protection sphere.

Extreme pain blasted through her chest. Was this dying?

She was airborne, the solid ground disappearing from sight. The wind whizzed around her. Her own weight dragged her down, blood rushed to her head. And a loud splash pierced her brain.

Gabriel heard Morag's scream, a howling shriek piercing the night. He saw Lily hurled through the air and into the lake.

He ran to the shore, stared at the small waves now disturbing the quiet dark waters. Where had she disappeared to?

He strode into the icy water, his mind numb with shock.

Morag rushed to his side. "Right there." She frantically pointed to the lake. "I sense her, but the image is blurred. Swim this way, Voyager. Bring her back." Her face was smeared with tears. "Bring my child back."

Gabriel then started to swim through the frigid water. He'd die drowning before coming back without her.

Lily slowly sank in a gentle, swaying motion. The throbbing pain and the blasting cold had left her body.

Kick your feet, a little voice said in her head. *Breast stroke, just get to the surface.*

But this time her body didn't respond. Oh, it was so pleasant here, drifting away. *Just sleep.* She didn't want to move.

Blackness welcomed her. Gabriel was there; they'd be together. The deerskin coat, the fur hat on his dark curls. She could see him now. They were in Acadia, happy together, an eternal life.

Death, welcoming.

Gabriel opened his eyes in the water, and even with his acute sight, all he could see was darkness.

Where could she be? Despair deadened him as he swam underwater and examined each rock, hoping he would eventually find her. How long could she survive in the icy water?

He'd rescued many in his days as a voyager, in rivers colder than this, but never in the middle of the night.

A faint radiance caught his eyes, there, just below him. He dived deeper to examine the glow and couldn't believe his luck.

The ring. Evangéline's ring, Lily had been wearing it. The ring he'd enchanted, it had protected Lily. It called him to her in its brightness. He could see it but also felt it in his consciousness.

A sliver of hope rose in his mind. Hope that it was still on her and had not been ripped off during her plunge into the lake.

He reached for the ring and long strands wrapped themselves around his fingers, Lily's hair. It was her. Without even touching her, he could feel her heartbeat pulsing through him.

He quickly scooped up her body and, with a powerful kick at the bottom of the lake, propelled them both to the surface.

Voices shouted at him as he emerged. They were all

gathered on the beach. A few more strokes and he reached the shore.

Morag stood knee-deep in the water. Her dress clinging to her, she tore at her hair.

Phoebus was the first to his side. He tried to help carry Lily, but Gabriel ignored him and pulled her small body tight to his chest as if he could restore her with his own heat alone.

She was unconscious, her pulse very faint. Despair ripped though him.

Where were they all, with their powerful magic? Someone had to bring her back to him.

"Morag!" he screamed into the still of the night, water dripping from him, his hair plastered in his eyes. "Morag!" His shriek was more a howl of pain that a word. "Bring her back."

He laid Lily on the sand and looked frantically into her face. He searched his mind for a spell. She was so far gone. Where was his coat?

Iain knelt beside him.

"Hold her hand, Gabriel. Stay close. Call her back with all your heart." Iain started to intone an incantation and the wind whirled around them both.

Gabriel was barely conscious of his Priory mark slithering into metal form as he heard a loud female voice joining Iain's chant.

Morag. She knelt beside her consort and voiced a matching chant in the ancient tongue.

Everyone remained silent except for the two ancient sorcerers.

Lily, come back. Restless with torment, Gabriel's fingers clutched hers. He could only think of her spirit, her soul. *Come back from darkness*, mon amour.

Iain and Morag were perfectly in tune, chanting as one. Gabriel had never before thought of them as a couple. A tremendous power rose from their bond as they altered the thread of life itself.

An eerie glow had appeared around the two still figures. They were not human, not even immortal, as were Gabriel and the other sorcerers. They were something completely different.

Iain took his vial of red mercury and an herb stone from the inside of his overcoat. He quickly crushed the stone and mixed it with the bloodred liquid.

He placed the mixture over Lily's heart. Then Morag laid her hand on top of his and they both stopped chanting.

All was still. Lily's body suddenly became illuminated by a single beam from the sliver of moon above them.

Gabriel invoked the Warrior King, the male essence itself, embracing his teaching as a Priory sorcerer and consort to the Priestess of the Callanish.

His heart swelled with hope. Was this her body moving? Her chest started to rise, up and down, first in a jerking motion, then more naturally.

Gabriel touched Lily's forehead and her mouth parted to take in a slow breath. Her eyes opened.

She looked around, coughing water, frowning. When her gaze settled on Gabriel, she smiled and tightened her grip on his hand.

Then a look of horror froze on her face. "Gabriel . . . Beltane, what time is it?"

Thirty-four

"Tell me there's still time, Gabriel. Please." Lily clutched at him hard, sitting on the sand. There was nothing that would separate her from him, ever.

"There is, sweetheart. Don't worry, there is," he whispered in her ear. She could feel his heart pulse against her chest and his muscles tense around her.

She looked behind him and became aware of the sorcerers beside Morag's altar. Theuron and his disciples seemed to have disappeared, but Lily didn't care. Nothing mattered right now but Gabriel.

"Are you sure you want to do this?" Gabriel pulled away slightly to gaze at her, his green eyes darker than usual as he searched for answers. "We will merge our souls. You can't change your mind after the ritual. We will be bonded forever. You'll be immortal as well. You'll be like us."

She smiled at him and her heart burst with love. Immortal, to be with him forever. How could he even ask her if she wanted to change her mind?

"There is nothing I want more. My future is with you."

"And mine with you." His expression became full of anguish as he pushed her hair back, then cupped her face in his hands. "Lily, the past is behind me. I love you." His lips hovered close to hers, his forehead resting on hers. "Will you join me, for eternity? Take this covenant?"

Her love for him welled within her and everything

faded away except for his presence. "I will, my love, of course I will."

She brushed his lips softly and he responded by taking possession of her mouth as if he worried he would lose her to some dark forces. Then he released his hold and his gaze rested on the silver chain with his ring attached to it.

"The ring I gave you, there's a special protection spell on it." He took the ring delicately in his hand. "It saved you."

"Gabriel, I've been wearing it every day since you gave it to me. I couldn't get rid of it."

He gently reached behind her neck and unfastened the chain. Sliding the ring into his hand he said, "I'll have another ring made only for you. This one is from another life."

He drew his arm back and started to throw it into the lake when Lily caught him.

"No, give it to me." She took the ring from him. "I want all of you, Gabriel. I can no longer deny who I am. I want you to love all of me, past and present."

She slid the ring onto her finger, convinced now that this was where it belonged. "We have been destined to be together for a long time. This ring is our past life."

She stared at him. "I felt her, Gabriel. When I was hovering between life and death, I felt her inside me, her essence. I felt your love. I saw Acadia, our home."

His lips curled into a smile. "You're an incredible woman, you know."

Her head slightly downcast, she glanced at him through her eyelashes. "So what is the Beltane ritual about?"

Lily sat alone on the large stone altar, which had been covered in thick fur pelts. The forest was dark and silent around her. A sliver of moon shone, casting a faint radiance on the clearing where she waited. A cool breeze played with her hair, upon which, just minutes before, Morag had placed a crown of tiny wild flowers.

Warm in the heavy velvet cloak tied over her maiden gown, a floor-length white silk laced at the bust, she felt conscious of the sheer fabric brushing her naked skin. Her bare feet touched the cool stone of the altar and she could smell the fragrance of violet, still clinging on her after the ritual purifying bath, mixing with the strong scent of the pine trees that surrounded her.

She hugged herself in anticipation of what was to come. The hold Taranis had on Gabriel would soon end, their sacred ritual setting him free.

Morag had told her to be vigilant. That Taranis may not give away a soul he had been so close to possessing.

But confident, she took a deep breath. Their future looked wide-open and full of hope and joy.

A mix of anticipation and reverence overtook her, knowing that out of darkness would come the Horned One, her Warrior King. The deer his symbol, he came for her at Beltane. A few sacred words from him as they made love and their union would be eternal. She would become immortal.

Morag had explained that if either Lily or Gabriel decided to be unfaithful, they would both die, falling into the shadows. And this rite would likely produce a child, to be born at Yule.

Lily smiled at the thought of a baby with dark curls and smoky green eyes. She'd chosen her king and now it was time for him to claim her.

Gabriel was coming.

The wind shifted. An owl hooted in the distance. The dry leaves rustled in the woods in front of her. Straining to look, all she could see was darkness. The sound grew louder, with a distinctive rhythm to it, powerful steps. Lily's heart pounded in her chest. Finally a shadow emerged from the wilderness.

Gabriel strode out of the dark, solemn and mystical.

Never before had she been so aware of his force. He'd taken the power of the wild. Imposing, a god rising to take possession of her, his animal essence merged with the prowess of the hunter.

"*Solas.*" As he made a sweeping gesture, flames burst to light the sacred bonfire that Morag had built by the altar. The comforting heat seeped through Lily's body.

Gabriel stood in front of her, silent. Her heart pumped louder and echoed in her blood, her lips parted.

Clad in deer-hide pants, nothing else, the thin animal casing revealed his need for her. His muscular torso was bare, his skin golden in the light of the dancing flames.

The Celtic-knot tattoo at his left bicep had transformed itself into a lacy silver band that embraced his arm. Part of his shoulder-length curls had been tied back in tiny braids around his head, some adorned with shells and eagle feathers.

The sight of him was mesmerizing, and he belonged to her.

Brushing her hair back from her face, he caressed the long strands before letting them fall on her shoulders. With care, he pulled on the ties holding her cloak, then parted the thick velvet to reveal her body, barely covered by the sheer fabric of her dress.

Seeing the wilderness in his eyes, she sensed the blood of the animal rushing through his veins. She didn't fear his intensity but welcomed it. While she longed to touch him, pull him close, she recalled Morag's warning that she would have to be patient during the ritual, let him come and claim her.

As he took the cloak away from her and laid it on the ground, she shivered, her nipples tender and needy under the flimsy dress, and she forced herself to stay still for him.

He whispered an incantation, and as his voice caressed her consciousness, she gasped. She knew the words, knew the power of his spells.

When he gave her an amused look, the familiar charming smile on his lips reminded her how much he enjoyed teasing her body into submission. As always, she was more than happy to let him indulge, overtake her with the delicious ancient words.

She'd been ready for him, but as the magic took over, her craving increased tenfold. Her nipples hardened to an almost painful state. Her senses grew keener as she buried her hands in the animal fur under her and pressed her knees together, moisture spreading between her thighs.

He'd pushed her over the edge, making her weak and willing, prey for his eternal possession. Now her soul was hungry to submit to his.

Her tender breasts spilled free when he untied the laces restraining the bodice of her dress and, her breath labored, she pleaded.

"Gabriel."

He smiled at her again, a beautiful smile filled with delight and joy. His powerful hands cupped her breasts, lifted and fondled them, lightly pinching the tips between his fingers. Her sensitive skin tingled with a pleasure resonating deep inside her.

At the intensity of her yearning, she realized he hadn't restrained the power he held on her and had cast the full potency of his spell.

Delight filled her as she reveled in every second of his commanding enchantment, every rush of enthralling need rising through her.

He played leisurely with her nipples, flicking and tugging at them, as if enjoying the hold he had over her, sending blazing waves of pleasure that made her painfully conscious of the void at her very core.

Wanting to cry her emptiness as he besieged her mind and soul, she ached for completion. But she forced herself to remain patient, to let him take the lead.

When Gabriel slowly lifted his hands away, she arched her chest toward him, whimpering faintly.

"Wait," he said in a soft voice like a caress on her soul. He put a finger on his lips.

He slowly lifted her gown, brushing her skin with the silk, up her calves, along her thighs and hips, then above her navel. He pushed her feet up on the altar.

She lowered herself, and her hands dug into the fur skins behind her, both soft and coarse on her fingers. Bliss descended upon her, and dying to trace the contour of his powerful chest, she waited for his lead, her body trembling with expectation.

Gabriel parted her legs wide, his hands firm on her knees, hunger in his eyes at her display. He whispered again, ancient words about a fertility god long gone. There she was, offered and waiting to be claimed by her Chosen One. The spring wind blew over her bare intimate parts as the wait for him killed her softly. Even if she'd wished to urge him on, she couldn't.

How delicious to be under his complete control, his words restraining her as surely as silk bonds would her wrists.

Gabriel undid the front of his pants, revealing his erection. He was stunning. Enticed by his rigid flesh, she longed to touch him, pleasure him, see the effect of her fingers trailing along the hard and smooth shaft. Contentment eased her frustration at the certainty that he fully belonged to her.

His expression full of tenderness, he parted her legs wider, then brushed her damp curls slowly, very slowly, while she pushed her core toward his touch. Would he ever give her what she needed?

He cupped her buttocks with both hands, pulled her gently closer and, taking her by surprise, thrust into her deeply.

Finally complete. She moaned at his thick warmth at her center, large and hard. How he filled her, always at the edge of being too much for her to take.

His arms a tight embrace, he found her mouth, his tongue claiming hers, his lips hungry and demanding. As he explored and nibbled, her tongue raked his, yearning for more of his masculine taste.

He was all over and inside her, so strong, so big, overpowering and loving her. She clamped her arms around him, pressing her hands on his smooth back, tracing each of his well-defined muscles and trailing down to the rough deerskin to cup his backside.

Gabriel was lost in the claim of his mate as he slid in and out of her, surrounded by her tight warmth. The spell he'd used had amplified his own desire for her and he took her with ancient primal need. Her scent intoxicated the animal in him. He needed to make her his.

He couldn't remember ever desiring Lily more. She looked so vulnerable and tempting in the flimsy gown, her breast bare to the elements, her skin soft under his palms.

He wanted to enfold himself inside her, lie in her essence. He was the Warrior King, claiming his Maiden.

All he wanted was to pleasure her, forever. She belonged to him, so sweet in his arms, so beautiful, her black hair falling on the silky skin of her shoulders, her catlike hazel eyes shining with lust.

The power of the woods merged with him as he drove in and out of her, each thrust sending an intense rush of pleasure along his spine and a searing heat radiating through his whole pelvis. He sensed their lovemaking affecting the elements, altering matter, as the wind blew harder and swirled around them.

Restraining himself so as not to hurt her, he penetrated her farther, then edged to reach between her legs, his finger stroking her. He found her tender nub pulsing with need, was elated by her cry at his touch. His lips left hers and he cradled her to his chest.

"Surrender, Lily. Give yourself to me," he pleaded, his voice almost commanding. How lovely she looked, lost in contentment. How precious she was. He gripped her closer, looking up at the sky where dark clouds rolled in.

So close, Voyager, so close, but this is not meant to be.

A chill seeped along his back. The voice in his head echoed from all around him. From the woods, the sky, his heart.

From Lily even.

Taranis.

Your soul is no longer yours, the disembodied voice added. *I need your sacrifice. Starting with her.*

No!

Lily. Confusion, deep despair rushed through him. He would not be allowed happiness in her arms.

Dread settled at the base of his spine, seeping through his whole body. He would lose her. Dark forces suddenly conquered him and he lost his control.

An uncontrollable rage and incredible power surged in his soul. His muscles tensed. If he possessed her fully and savagely, they wouldn't take her away.

Lily gasped under him.

No, he didn't want to harm her.

But the dark energy took over his consciousness. His sanity slipped.

Taranis ruled now.

"Didrouz peoc'h." Magical words were calling him back. "Gabriel, return to me." The voice sang clear and musical, yet so far away. *"Sàmhach, sàmhach.* Return, my love."

Lily called him. He suddenly felt great peace washing over him, soothing, comforting. Darkness receded. She was with him, his love, his life.

Stunned, he realized what had just happened. She'd used the ancient tongue to soothe his anguish. She was strong enough to tame him, to push the shadows away.

Love for her overwhelmed him.

"Mon ange, I love you so much." Embracing her, he stilled his thrust for a moment, as he continued to pleasure her, his thumb working at the apex of her slit to bring her to climax. "You're my angel, *mon ange venu du ciel,"* he whispered in her ear.

Still buried deep inside her, he rocked them both, tightly embracing her as she moaned her pleasure. He'd surrendered to her strength.

They were in perfect balance.

Lily pushed back a black curl falling into Gabriel's eye. He thrust into her again. She was so close to the edge of release.

She looked up at him with deep love as light from the bonfire played over his golden skin, and brushed his dark curls.

She hardly noticed when bright flashes of lightning suddenly sparked around them. Gabriel possessed her completely, sliding into her, one hand spread wide at her back. Her pleasure escalated with each flick of his finger.

Half-conscious of the soft raindrops falling on her, she nestled to Gabriel as he drew her closer to his chest to shield her from the rain while he continued to build her ecstasy.

Complete trust in him led her to surrender to the

scorching tides building in her, her wet dress plastered to her back. Her legs wrapped tight around Gabriel's hips, she tasted the crook of his neck, gathering raindrops mixed with his musky essence on her tongue. Never would she tire of his male presence.

And they loved each other as the storm raged around them, their passion sometimes hard and fierce, sometimes gentle and sweet. They whispered their mutual love over and over, tender confessions of eternal devotion. While the wind howled, the rain pounding them, they were lost in their love for what seemed like an eternity, riding each other, wanting it to last forever, always at the edge of release.

With wonder, Lily heard Gabriel recite the magic words. *"Ceangail unanadur."* Ancient words from the lost Callanish people, as old as the earth itself. *"Ceangail unanadur, Ceangail,"* he whispered, chanting the incantation that would bind them for eternity. He repeated the words again and again, his voice cutting through the sounds of the beating storm.

Unending pleasure suddenly burst though her, darting to the ends of her limbs, and while he whispered her name, Lily felt his own release.

All became clear. They were the One. Lost and separated for so long and now reunited in the ultimate balance, as the sun and moon reunited from darkness.

She was now as he was, immortal, invincible.

The rain stopped and Lily leaned on Gabriel's chest, now glistening with water.

Gabriel shouted a roar of victory, his voice shaking the still of the night.

Lily had freed him.

In a mix of love and triumph, he tenderly pulled away from her and tied the deer hide at his groin. After folding her wet dress back over her breasts, he slid her skirt down along her legs. In a swift motion, he lifted her into his arms and cradled her to his chest. His love eternal.

And they both disappeared in the dark wilderness.

"I pledge to you my living and my dying, each equally in your care. I shall be a shield for your back, and you for mine." Lily heard the reverence in his voice as she gazed into Gabriel's smoky green eyes, shivers descending through her body.

Lily's heart melted. They were already bonded from the Beltane ritual, but this was their wedding day, and all was perfect.

They stood in their garden under a large oak tree, beside a narrow creek. Flowers bloomed around them and along the shingled cape house, their house, where a cocktail reception had been arranged for their guests in the sunny dining room.

Lily looked at her family and friends, at Angèle in her small white hat covered with summer flowers. She now had her own little place at the back of the garden.

There were the Davenports, her friends from the hospital. And in the far row, Loïc, expressionless as usual; Tara in leather pants and a sheer black blouse; and Phoebus, trying to hold onto the leash of their new Labrador puppy.

Feeling pretty in a simple long white dress, Lily admired Gabriel, so handsome in linen slacks and pristine white shirt.

"Gabriel LaJeunesse Callan, with this ring I wed you." She slid a large plain platinum ring on Gabriel's finger.

"Lily Evangéline Bellefontaine, with this ring I wed you." Gabriel's expression was full of love as he took her hand. Her ring was a smaller version of his. He slid it on her finger, setting it next to the antique fleur-de-lis ring.

He'd chosen well, the platinum rings symbolizing their love for each other, pure and strong.

She smiled brightly at him and he returned her smile with a twinkle in his eye. Then he covered her hand with his and whispered one single ancient word.

When he lifted his palm, she admired the two rings. They were now fused together, the pewter engraved flowers next to the sleek platinum.

The rings fitted perfectly, just as her old and new selves were now parts of her.

Epilogue

Morag was grabbing two coffees from the counter when she saw Iain bumping Mrs. Freeman out of the way so he could be first to the most comfortable couch in the Langdon coffee shop.

She sighed. She'd never change him.

"You bumped her again." Setting their cups on the coffee table, Morag sat on the armchair beside him.

"What?" Iain barely glanced up from his grimoire.

"Mrs. Freeman . . . See, she is giving you the evil eye. Oh, never mind." Morag took a sip of coffee, cringed at finding it too weak. "She's pregnant, you know."

Iain flashed her a puzzled look. She'd finally caught his attention.

"Who, Mrs. Freeman?"

"No, silly old man. Lily. They wouldn't tell me, but I know she is."

"Lily and Gabriel, having a baby? Morag, I'm impressed. You succeeded."

"I guess you can say that, but there is still a lot of work to do." Morag smoothed her long black skirt and shook her head. Voyager was only one of the thirteen sorcerers.

"Have you located Theuron in Europe yet?" Iain sat back, a sharp expression in his stormy gray eyes.

She nodded. "As I suspected. France."

"Oh, interesting."

"Yes, I'm sending Falconer after him."

"Phoebus? One of your favorites, isn't he?"

"He will keep an eye on Theuron for me." She sighed.

"And ensure that Keira is safe." It wasn't Keira's time yet; it might never be, but Morag had promised Lily she'd try to save her anyway.

Iain raked his long white hair back. "I wonder if I was too hard on Theuron when I banished him."

"It is the law of the Callanish. Iona banished him, not you."

"But I could have appealed to her."

"You're too sentimental." Humans had such strange feelings sometimes. Morag gazed at the lined face of the fierce sorcerer before her and her heart burst with love.

All these years together, all these years when she could have just left him, returned to where she came from.

Iain still wasn't convinced. "He was so young. Look at him now."

"He brought it onto himself." She wouldn't waste her pity on her sister's murderer.

Iain sighed. "With the sword, he now has the power to kill you. You'll have to be very careful."

"He will need more than just the sword to kill me." A slow smile curled Morag's lips. "There is nothing to fear, nothing at all."

INTERACT WITH DORCHESTER ONLINE!

Want to learn more about your favorite books and authors?
Want to talk with other readers that like to read the same books as you?
Want to see up-to-the-minute Dorchester news?

VISIT DORCHESTER AT:
DorchesterPub.com
Twitter.com/DorchesterPub
Facebook.com (Search Pages)

DISCUSS DORCHESTER'S NOVELS AT:
Dorchester Forums at DorchesterPub.com
GoodReads.com
LibraryThing.com
Myspace.com/books
Shelfari.com
WeRead.com

Enter into the Otherworld with . . .

Erin Kellison

Shadow Bound

Death

Some people will do anything to avoid it. Even trade their immortal souls for endless existence.

Wraiths

Secretly, inexorably, they are infiltrating our world, sucking the essence out of unsuspecting victims with their hideous parody of a kiss.

Segue

Adam Thorne founded the Segue Institute to study and destroy his monster of a brother, but the key to its success is held in the pale, slender hand of a woman on the run. There is something hauntingly different about Talia O'Brien, her unknowing sensuality, her uncanny way of slipping into Shadow.

Twilight

This is the place between life and what comes after—a dark forest of fantasy, filled with beauty, peril, mystery. And Talia is about to open the door.

ISBN 13: 978-0-505-52829-2

Go deeper into the Otherworld with . . .

ERIN KELLISON

SHADOW FALL

SACRIFICE

Custo Santovari accepted pain, blood, even death, to save his best friend. But a man with all his sins just isn't cut out to be an angel.

MYSTERY

One moment he's fleeing Heaven; the next, he's waking up stark naked in Manhattan. In the middle of a war. Called there by a woman who's desperately afraid of the dark.

SHADOW

It gathers around Annabella as she performs, filled with fantastic images of another world, bringing both a golden hero and a nightmare lover.

WOLF

He pursues her relentlessly, twisting her desires even as she gives herself to the man she loves. Because each of us has a wild side, and Annabella is about to unleash the beast.

ISBN 13: 978-0-505-52830-8

✂ ☐ **YES!**

Sign me up for the Love Spell Book Club and send my
FREE BOOKS! If I choose to stay in the club, I will pay
only $8.50* each month, a savings of $6.48!

NAME: _____

ADDRESS: _____

TELEPHONE: _____

EMAIL: _____

☐ I want to pay by credit card.

☐ **VISA**   ☐ **MasterCard.**   ☐ **DISCOVER**

ACCOUNT #: _____

EXPIRATION DATE: _____

SIGNATURE: _____

Mail this page along with $2.00 shipping and handling to:
Love Spell Book Club
PO Box 6640
Wayne, PA 19087
Or fax (must include credit card information) to:
610-995-9274
You can also sign up online at **www.dorchesterpub.com**.
*Plus $2.00 for shipping. Offer open to residents of the U.S. and Canada only.
Canadian residents please call 1-800-481-9191 for pricing information.
If under 18, a parent or guardian must sign. Terms, prices and conditions subject to
change. Subscription subject to acceptance. Dorchester Publishing reserves the right
to reject any order or cancel any subscription.